THE BARTEND
TO MURDER

DEATH IN
TRANQUILITY

ALSO BY SHARON LINNÉA

FICTION

*Chasing Eden * Beyond Eden *Treasure of Eden * Plagues of Eden with B.K. Sherer*
These Violent Delights
Agent Colt Shore: Domino 29 with Axel Avian

NONFICTION

Princess Kaiulani: Hope of a Nation, Heart of a People
Raoul Wallenberg: The Man Who Stopped Death
Lost Civilizations
Chicken Soup from the Soul of Hawaii

THE BARTENDER'S GUIDE
TO MURDER

To Janet

DEATH IN
TRANQUILITY

Cheers!

Sharon Linnéa

Sharon Linnéa

Arundel
PUBLISHING

This is a work of fiction. All of the characters, organizations and events portrayed in this novel are either products of the author's imagination or are used fictitiously.

ISBN 978-933608-15-0 (paperback)

First Edition September 2020

Cover Art and Cover Design by Robert Venables
Formatting by Polgarus Studio

For William Diderichsen Webber, Dad.
Full of love and surprises

1

Death in the Afternoon

"Whenever you see the bartender, I'd like another drink," I said, lifting my empty martini glass and tipping it to Marta, the waitress with teal hair.

"Everyone wants another drink," she said, "but Joseph's missing. I can't find him. Anywhere."

"How long has he been gone?" I asked.

"About ten minutes. It's not like him. Joseph would never just go off without telling me."

That's when I should have done it. I should have put down forty bucks to cover my drink and my meal and left that magical, moody, dark-wood paneled Scottish bar and sauntered back across the street to the train station to continue on my way.

If I had, everything would be different.

Instead I nodded, grateful for a reason to stand up. A glance at my watch told me over half an hour remained until my connecting train chugged in across the street. I could do Marta a solid by finding the bartender and telling him drink orders were stacking up.

Travelling from Los Angeles to New York City by rail, I had taken the northern route, which required me to change trains in the storied village of Tranquility, New York. Once detrained, the posted schedule had informed me should I decide to bolt and head north for

Montreal, I could leave within the hour. The train heading south for New York City, however, would not be along until 4 p.m.

Sometimes in life you think it's about where you're going, but it turns out to be about where you change trains.

It was an April afternoon; the colors on the trees and bushes were still painting from the watery palate of spring. Here and there, forsythia unfurled in insistent bursts of golden glory.

I needed a drink.

Tranquility has been famous for a long time. Best known for hosting the Winter Olympics back in 19-whatever, it was an eclectic blend of small village, arts community, ski mecca, gigantic hotels and Olympic facilities. Certainly there was somewhere a person could get lunch.

Perched on a hill across the street from the station sat a shiny, modern hotel of the upscale chain variety. Just down the road, farther south, was a large, meandering, one-of-a-kind establishment called MacTavish's Seaside Cottage. It looked nothing like a cottage, and, as we were inland, there were no seas. I doubted the existence of a MacTavish.

I headed over at once.

The place evoked a lost inn in Brigadoon. A square main building of a single story sent wings jutting off at various angles into the rolling hills beyond. Floor-to-ceiling windows made the lobby bright and airy. A full suit of armor stood guard over the check-in counter, while a sculpture of two downhill skiers whooshed under a skylight in the middle of the room.

Behind the statue was the Breezy, a sleek restaurant overlooking Lake Serenity (Lake Tranquility was in the next town over, go figure). The restaurant's outdoor deck was packed with tourists on this balmy day, eating and holding tight to their napkins, lest they be lost to the murky depths.

Off to the right—huddled in the vast common area's only dark corner—was a small door with a carved, hand-painted wooden sign which featured a large seagoing vessel plowing through tumultuous waves. *That Ship Has Sailed*, it read. A tavern name if I ever heard one.

Beyond the heavy door, down a short dark-wood hallway, in a tall room lined with chestnut paneling, I paused to let my eyes adjust to the change in light, atmosphere, and, possibly, century.

The bar was at a right angle as you entered, running the length of the wall. It was hand-carved and matched the back bar, which held 200 bottles, easily.

A bartender's dream, or her undoing.

Two of the booths against the far wall were occupied, as were two of the center tables.

I sat at the bar.

Only one other person claimed a seat there during this low time between meal services. He was a tall gentleman with a square face, weathered skin, and dark hair pulled back into a ponytail. I felt his cold stare as I perused the menu trying to keep to myself. I finally gave up and stared back.

"Flying Crow," he said. "Mohawk Clan."

"Avalon," I said. "Train changer."

I went back to my menu, surprised to find oysters were a featured dish.

"Avalon?" he finally said. "That's—"

"An odd name," I answered. "I know. Flying Crow? You're in a Scottish pub."

"Ask him what Oswego means." This was from the bartender, a lanky man with salt-and-pepper hair. "Oh, but place your order first."

"Are the oysters good?" I asked.

"Oddly, yes. One of the best things on the menu. Us being seaside, and all."

3

"All right, then. Oysters it is. And a really dry vodka martini, olives."

"Pimento, jalapeño, or bleu cheese?"

"Ooh, bleu cheese, please." I turned to Flying Crow. "So what does Oswego mean?"

"It means, 'Nothing Here, Give It to the Crazy White Folks.' Owego, on the other hand means, 'Nothing Here Either.'"

"How about Otego? And Otsego and Otisco?"

His eyebrow raised. He was impressed by my knowledge of obscure town names in New York State. "They all mean, '*We're Just Messing with You Now.*'"

"Hey," I said, raising my newly delivered martini. "Thanks for coming clean."

He raised his own glass of firewater in return.

"Coming clean?" asked the bartender, and he chuckled, then dropped his voice. "If he's coming clean, his name is Lesley."

"And you are?" I asked. He wasn't wearing a name tag.

"Joseph."

"Skål," I said, raising my glass. "Glad I found That Ship Has Sailed."

"That's too much of a mouthful," he said, flipping over the menu. "Everyone calls it the Battened Hatch."

"But the Battened Hatch isn't shorter. Still four syllables."

"Troublemaker," muttered Lesley good-naturedly. "I warned you."

"Fewer words," said Joseph with a smile that included crinkles by his eyes. "Fewer capital letters over which to trip."

As he spoke, the leaded door banged open and two men in chinos and shirtsleeves arrived, talking loudly to each other. The door swung again, just behind them, admitting a stream of ten more folks—both women and men, all clad in business casual. Some were more casual than others. One man with silvering hair actually wore a suit and tie;

4

another, a white artist's shirt, his blonde hair shoulder-length. The women's garments, too, ran the gamut from tailored to flowing. One, of medium height, even wore a white blouse, navy blue skirt and jacket, finished with hose and pumps. And a priest's collar.

"Conventioneers?" I asked Joseph. Even as I asked, I knew it didn't make sense. No specific corporate culture was in evidence.

He laughed. "Nah. Conference people eat at the Blowy. Er, Breezy. Tranquility's Chamber of Commerce meeting just let out." His grey eyes danced. "They can never agree on anything, but their entertainment quotient is fairly high. And they drive each other to drink."

Flying Crow Lesley shook his head.

Most of the new arrivals found tables in the center of the room. Seven of them scooted smaller tables together, others continued their conversations or arguments in pairs.

"Marta!" Joseph called, leaning through a door in the back wall beside the bar.

The curvy girl with the teal hair, nose and eyebrow rings and mega eye shadow clumped through. Her eyes widened when she saw the influx of patrons.

Joseph slid the grilled oysters with fennel butter in front of me. "Want anything else before the rush?" He indicated the well-stocked back bar.

"I'd better hold off. Just in case there's a disaster and I end up having to drive the train."

He nodded knowingly. "Good luck with that."

I took out my phone, then re-pocketed it. I wanted a few more uncomplicated hours before re-entering the real world. Turning to my right, I found that Flying Crow had vanished. In his stead, several barstools down, sat a Scotsman in full regalia: kilt, Bonnie Prince Charlie jacket and a fly plaid. It was predominantly red with blue stripes.

Wow. Mohawk clan members, Scotsmen, and women priests in pantyhose. This was quite a town.

Joseph was looking at an order screen, and five drinks in different glasses were already lined up ready for Marta to deliver.

My phone buzzed. I checked caller i.d. Fought with myself. Answered.

Was grabbed by tentacles of the past.

When I looked up, filled with emotions I didn't care to have, I decided I did need another drink; forget driving the train.

The line of waiting drink glasses was gone, as were Marta and Joseph.

I checked the time. I'd been in Underland for fifteen minutes, twenty at the most. It was just past three. I had maybe forty-five minutes before I should move on.

That was when Marta swung through the kitchen door, her head down to stave off the multiple calls from the center tables. She stood in front of me, punching information into the point of sale station, employing the NECTM—No Eye Contact Tactical Maneuver.

That's when she told me Joseph was missing.

"Could he be in the restroom?"

"I asked Arthur when he came out, but he said there was nobody else."

I nodded at Marta and started by going out through the front hall, to see if perhaps he'd met someone in the lobby. As I did a lap, I overheard a man at check-in ask, "Is it true the inn is haunted?"

"Do you want it to be?" asked the clerk, nonplussed.

But no sign of the bartender.

I swung back through into the woodsy-smelling darkness of the Battened Hatch, shook my head at the troubled waitress, then walked to the circular window in the door. The industrial kitchen was white and well-lit, and as large as it was, I could see straight through the shared kitchen to the Breezy. No sign of Joseph. I turned my attention back to the bar.

Beyond the bar, there was a hallway to the restrooms, and another wooden door that led outside. I looked back at Marta and nodded to the door.

"It doesn't go anywhere," she said. "It's only a little smoker's deck."

I wondered if Joseph smoked, tobacco or otherwise. Certainly the arrival of most of a Chamber of Commerce would suggest it to me. I pushed on the wooden door. It seemed locked. I gave it one more try, and, though it didn't open, it did budge a little bit.

This time I went at it with my full shoulder. There was a thud, and it wedged open enough that I could slip through.

It could hardly be called a deck. You couldn't put a table—or even a lounge chair—out there.

Especially with the body taking up so much of the space.

It was Joseph. I knelt quickly and felt for a pulse at his neck, but it was clear he was inanimate. He was sitting up, although my pushing the door open had made him lean at an angle. I couldn't tell if the look on his face was one of pain or surprise. There was some vomit beside him on the deck, and a rivulet down his chin. I felt embarrassed to be seeing him this way.

Crap. He was always nice to me. Well, during the half an hour I'd known him, he had been nice to me.

What was it with me discovering corpses? It was certainly a habit of which I had to break myself.

Meanwhile, what to do? Should I call in the priest? But she was within a group, and it would certainly start a panic. Call 911?

Yes, that would be good. That way they could decide to call the hospital or the police or both.

My phone was back in my purse.

And, you know what? I didn't want the call to come from me. I was just passing through.

I pulled the door back open and walked to Marta behind the bar. "Call 911," I said softly. "I found Joseph."

It took the ambulance and the police five minutes to arrive. The paramedics went through first, then brought a gurney around outside so as to not freak out everyone in the hotel. They loaded Joseph on and sped off, in case there was anything to be done.

I knew there wasn't.

The police, on the other hand, worked at securing the place which might become a crime scene. They blocked all the doorways and announced no one could leave.

I was still behind the bar with Marta. She was shaking.

"Give me another Scotch," said the Scotsman seated there.

I looked at the bottles and was pleasantly surprised by the selection. "I think this calls for Black Maple Hill," I said, only mildly surprised at my reflexive tendency to upsell. The Hill was a rich pour but not the absolute priciest.

He nodded. I poured.

I'm not sure if it was Marta's tears, or the fact we weren't allowed to leave, but local bigwigs had realized something was amiss.

"Excuse me," the man in the suit came to the bar. "Someone said Joseph is dead."

"Yes," I said. "He does seem to be."

Marta swung out of the kitchen, her eyeliner half down her face. "Art, these are your oysters," she said to the man. He took them.

"So," he continued, and I wondered what meaningful words he'd have to utter. "You're pouring drinks?"

It took only a moment to realize that, were I the owner of this establishment, I'd find this a great opportunity.

"Seems so," I said.

"What goes with oysters?" he asked.

That was a no-brainer. I'd spied the green bottle of absinthe while having my own meal. I poured about three tablespoons into the glass. I then opened a bottle of Prosecco, poured it, and waited for the milky cloud to form.

He took a sip, looked at me, and raised the glass. "If I want another of these, what do I ask for?"

As he asked, I realized I'd dispensed one of Ernest Hemingway's favorite libations. "Death in the Afternoon," I replied.

He nodded and went back to his table.

It was then I realized I wasn't going to make my train.

Ernest Hemingway's **Death in the Afternoon**

Ingredients

3 tablespoons (1 1/2 ounces) absinthe
1/2 to 3/4 cup (4 to 6 ounces) cold Champagne or sparkling wine

Method

Hemmingway's advice, circa 1935: "Pour one jigger absinthe into a Champagne glass. Add iced Champagne until it attains the proper opalescent milkiness. Drink three to five of these slowly."

2

No Known Address

Since I found the body, I got to talk to the lead investigator.

He was in his mid-thirties, just under six feet, walnut skin, black hair cut short. He would have benefitted from a beard. He looked ripped; the king of ripped you got from taking out your frustrations in the gym. His demeanor was no-nonsense.

"Investigator Spaulding," he said, and he pulled out a notebook. "State Police."

"State Police? Isn't that the same as State Troopers? Don't you manage highways?"

He stopped writing in his small, leather-covered notebook and looked up.

"Common misconception. The local P.D. is small—only 9 on staff. When something big happens, they ask for assistance."

"They ask?"

"It's a dance."

I wasn't a suspect (yet), so he didn't need to write down my stats, but I could read upside down as he made notes. He asked my name, and began guessing at the rest. Nash, Avalon. Female. Caucasian. Blonde hair. 5'7 was his guess at my height. The next thing he wrote down could go seriously south, so I said, "healthy weight."

He looked up.

"5'7" and at a healthy weight," I supplied. "If I'm charged with something, we'll get more specific."

"Age?"

Did he really need to know all of this? "Twenties," I said, waiting to see if he'd have the gall to object. He didn't.

"Best way to reach you?"

I gave him my cell number.

"Permanent address?"

"I don't have one."

He looked up.

"I'm in the process of moving from California to New York. I'm only in town to change trains. I don't have a New York address yet."

"A relative's address?"

I held up my phone. "This is your golden ticket," I said. "If you want to reach me, this is it."

I saw him write 'no known address.' Yep, that pretty much summed it up. I glanced at my watch. Seven minutes until my train pulled into—and, soon after, departed from—the station.

"Um, Detective," I started.

"Investigator Spaulding," he corrected.

"Investigator Spaulding, my train is about to arrive. I don't know anything except what I've told you. I came in for a drink and helped Marta find the bartender, whom I hope died of a massive heart attack—well, of natural causes. You know what I mean."

At that point, his phone buzzed and he gave me a just-a-minute finger. He answered, listened for a while, and started to write. Then he hung up, flipped his notebook shut and said, "I can't let you leave. He was murdered."

"Great," I said, the tone somewhere between rueful and intrigued, as I headed back toward Marta, then I turned back toward Investigator Spaulding. "Can I continue to pour drinks?"

He considered less than a moment. "By all means, serve truth serum to anyone who will imbibe."

Then he turned and walked toward the other officers.

I went to stand with Marta behind the bar. In my imagination, I heard the train chug in across the street.

Investigator Spaulding cleared his throat, and the room went silent. "Ladies and gentlemen," he said. "This is now a homicide investigation." He had to pause as everyone shuffled or gasped, or cried out. "Please do not leave until we have taken your statement."

A woman in her fifties came and sat down in front of me at the bar. Her hair was in a no-fuss bob, she wore a free-flowing skirt with a linen jacket, both of which were in style twenty years ago, but they worked on her. "Got anything stronger than those Death things?" she asked. "I'm not big on Champagne."

"Sure." I said. I sized her up. "Layers in a martini glass work for you?"

"Honey, it's the strength, not the glass." She looked shaken and sad. I went for the rums and found Malibu Black, the stronger brother of the original. What a bartender Joseph must have been! I decided to try something new. Malibu Black, mango pineapple vodka, and pineapple juice. I mixed it over ice, shook, and poured. I sank some Chambord and topped it with Jägermeister Spice.

"See if this does it," I said.

Her hand shook slightly as she held up the glass, appreciated the layers, and then took a sip. The jury was out. She took another. She nodded and smiled.

It occurred to me that everyone in the room knew Joseph. They'd lost one of their own.

Another woman in skinny white pants and a white shell with a fancy pink sports jacket came and sat next to her. They were about the same age, if I had to guess, but the new woman was thin as a rail, muscular, and with her blonde hair in a ponytail. I was guessing she colored her hair not from a darker shade, but to cover the white. The two women embraced. "Suzanne," said the new arrival.

"Gillian," said no-fuss-bob Suzanne. Then, "Can't believe it."

"I can't, either," replied hard-bodied Gillian. She had the remains of an Eastern European accent. They sat a respectful moment. "What are you drinking?"

Suzanne looked at me. "No Known Address," I said.

"Okay," Gillian said. "I'll have one." She then turned and I was dismissed to my task.

"I can't believe it. One of the only straight, available guys between forty and crotchety, and he's gone!" said Suzanne.

"There's Mike," Gillian said, tilting her head toward the state police investigator. "And I'm not sure Joseph was available."

"First, really? Maybe if he worked out. Second, you or I crook our little fingers and get a guy away from Sophie." They both looked back, shooting daggers toward one of the three women in the center wall booth. I knew which must be Sophie, as one of them was crying copiously while the other two petted her solicitously.

"And do we have a suspect?" asked pink jacket Gillian.

This time, they looked at a younger woman who sat at a table with two newly arrived Chamber men. She was gorgeous—skin the color of chai latte and hair as dark as a sky at new moon. She was staring off into space.

I almost said, "*You know I can hear you.*" But maids, taxi drivers, and bartenders… well, we're invisible, which is partly how we get the good gossip.

They stopped talking abruptly as two men approached. "Can we get some food?" asked the first. He was in a polo and navy blue slacks.

I heard snuffling and saw that Marta was in the shadows, leaning back against the wall. "Hey," I said, "would you ask the chef if we can continue to order food?"

She nodded and swung through the kitchen door.

Arthur, the man in the suit who had ordered earlier, accompanied the newcomer in the polo. Arthur addressed his companion in an audible hiss. "I'm telling you... we can't let word of this get out. Tranquility has to be considered a safe haven. For everyone. For...the festival folks. It's part of what lures them here. Change of pace."

"How do we not let the word get out? It's a matter of record! And everyone in town knows about it—or will, within minutes."

From the furious pace of thumbs texting throughout the room, it was clear he was correct.

"I mean, don't print this as front-page news."

"It *is* front page news, Art. And, the film festival folks are already committed. They've submitted their films. They'll come."

Marta returned with a positive nod. I slapped down two menus. "Marta will be out to take your order," I said. As they turned, I added. "And if it's a film festival, you don't need to worry. Film people eat news like this for breakfast."

Arthur looked at me in surprise, but gave a raised-eyebrows look that inferred I could have a point.

They left with the menus and I turned back to Marta, trying to help get her mind on something other than her boss's death. "Can you help me add these drinks to people's tabs?" I nodded toward the POS.

For the record, I hate point of sale machines. Each one hates humans in its own unique way. I pointed at people and she pulled up their tabs and showed me how to input the drinks I'd served.

I only had the Scotsman's tab left undone when the man in the artist's shirt stopped right before me. He was likely late 40s and had a face that was long but not unattractive. His shoulders were unusually broad, and he exuded self-confidence and a self-trained impishness. His shirt had one too many buttons left undone.

"Okay," he said, "I wasn't going to drink, but Joe…"

"You weren't going to drink because it's late afternoon, or because you've been sober for seven months?" I had no interest in tipping someone off the wagon.

He laughed. "I haven't been drinking because this isn't my favorite crowd," he said. "And I don't usually drink. But murder seems an excuse, if there ever was one." He extended his hand. "Michael Michel," he said, and smiled, waggling his eyebrows as if this should mean something to me.

I took his hand and shook. It was apparent I didn't recognize him.

"The Painter Who Brings You Home," he said, and the trademark practically bled from the words.

"Right," I said, trying to sound impressed. "Nice to meet you. I'm Avalon. What'll ya have?"

"Vodka tonic lime."

"Care which vodka?"

He shook his head while saying, "Whatever you've got. Grey Goose."

Ah, a fellow who pretended not to drink, who knew exactly what he wanted.

I poured and went for the garnish tray. The limes were gone. I looked at the back bar and found lemons and oranges. No limes, though clearly there had been some. I walked along the front bar and found, below patron eye level, a small cutting board with a lime on it. The lime was half-cut, some of them in rounds, a few in quarters. Some juice was dripping down onto the floor.

I reached for a wedge, and then I stopped short.

Joseph never would have left this on purpose. It was obviously what he'd been doing when he was interrupted by death—or someone who led him to his death. Or by symptoms that eventually spelled death.

I leaned down and sniffed.

It was lime-y. But there was something else, also.

I backed away. I walked over to Marta and said, quietly, "Don't let anyone near that end of the bar."

Then I walked over to Investigator Spaulding, where he sat at a booth interviewing someone. "Investigator?" I said. "Sorry to interrupt, but this is important."

He looked at me, squinting, then seemed surprised, since I'd made such a point of being Ms. Just-Passing-Through.

He stood up and stepped away from the booth.

"I believe I've found the murder weapon," I said.

As we walked together, I realized that the door to the smoker's porch sat open. It was crawling with half a dozen or so more crime scene people.

Together we walked to the limes. I said, "Don't touch them. If this is what Joseph was doing when he died, if they are poisoned, my guess is that the poison can be absorbed through the skin."

Investigator Spaulding looked at me like, *Of course I knew that*, but he stepped back. As another officer and two crime scene investigators came over, I backed away, removing myself as far as possible from the action.

I returned to the Artist Shirt. "I think today we're going with a lemon and a cherry," I said. I smelled them before putting them in the drink.

It struck me then that perhaps Joseph hadn't been the intended target. Maybe there was someone who consistently ordered a drink garnished with lime, and the murderer had injected the poison into the lime, not realizing it could be absorbed as well as ingested.

Like, for instance, the man before me, Mr. Vodka Tonic Lime.

Still, this was a pretty non-specific way of poison delivery. The limes could have been served to half a dozen people before anyone realized they were toxic. Who would do something like that?

The police were letting people go once they had been interviewed. I asked Investigator Spaulding if I could go. He nodded, adding, "Please stay in town until tomorrow morning, in case we have any further questions."

As if I had a choice. All the trains had gone, except the 11 p.m. to Montreal.

The bar had been sealed off with crime-scene tape, a welcome relief as I didn't relish closing a dead man's station on the night of his murder. Why would I even think that? I didn't work here. But my need to leave a bar in pristine condition ran down to bone and marrow.

As I headed for my bag, which I'd left on my original stool, I saw I wouldn't even be allowed to access the POS machine.

The only patron whose drink I hadn't input was the man in the kilt. I looked around the emptying room to find he'd moved to a pub table over to the side. "Sorry, sir," I said. "I wasn't able to enter your drinks into the machine. I guess you're on the honor system to pay up another day."

He gave a small smile. "Lass," he said, "I'm Glenn MacTavish. Owner of this place. Seems I'm out a bartender and will be needing another. You have any interest?" he asked.

I stopped and stared. "There's really a MacTavish?" I asked.

"Aye, and you're looking at him."

"But… you don't know anything about me."

"You keep a clear head and you know what you're doin'. That's all I really need to know. Besides, you don't know anything about me, either."

"I, well—thank you for the offer. It's a beautiful bar. Can I think on it overnight? I've been told not to leave town."

"Aye," he said. "You can tell me in the mornin' if you might be stayin.' And while you're decidin', I could pay you for your services tonight with a room here at the hotel."

That seemed fair. The Hotel Tonight app was offering me a room at a local chain. Staying at MacTavish's Seaside Cottage for free seemed infinitely more attractive. "All right," I said. "I should probably let you know they're expecting me in New York City."

"All right," he said. "I should probably let you know Joseph isn't the first bartender to work here who's been murdered."

No Known Address

Ingredients

½ oz. Malibu black
2 dashes Chambord
½ oz. mango pineapple vodka
2 dashes Jägermeister Spice
1 oz. pineapple juice

Method

Shake pineapple vodka, Malibu Black and pineapple juice over ice and strain evenly into martini glasses.

Sink a dash of Chambord into each flute by running it down the side of the glass.

Layer a dash of Jägermeister Spice in each glass.

3

Wet Your Whistle

It stormed overnight. I'd left the window open, and the water tumbling in sheets from sky to lake laced my dreams with contentment. The night after I'd discovered a murder victim, I slept better than I had in months. People died. They died every day, without it being my fault.

I woke refreshed to find the foaming clouds had retreated, and the sun shone over Lake Serenity. I made a cup of coffee in the single-cup brewer in my room and stepped out onto the small balcony.

MacTavish's Seaside Cottage was truly one-of-a-kind. According to the information card on the desk, it opened in 1889 as a getaway for the wealthy. Wings and floors had been added as the MacTavishes prospered. They were built to fit into the landscape, and reached this way and that into the hills surrounding the lake. Most hallways had two or three stairs in several places as the hills rolled. I could see why the fellow at check-in had asked if the inn was haunted. If I was a ghost, I'd rate this my number one on Trip Advisor.

I, myself, was oddly at peace.

While the single-serve coffee with the fake cream had gotten me vertical, it was time to go in search of real food. I was fairly certain I was on the back side of my 24 hours in Tranquility, so I may as well take in the sights. Traveling with only one large suitcase and one tote limited my clothing selection and made it easy to choose a long black shirt with navy blue buttons, black leggings, and navy blue flats. I grabbed the key and headed out.

Fortunately, at every juncture arrows pointed the way to the lobby, as well as to various halls and room numbers. This only underscored the nonconformity of the layout. If there was a power-outage, likely half the guests would never be seen again.

I wasn't expecting the open can of mint-green paint sitting in the hallway as I rounded the penultimate corner toward the central building. In an effort to sidestep it and avert disaster, I instead crashed over a small dog sprawled in the middle of the carpet. Both dog and I yelped, and I went down.

The Pomeranian and I were now on the same level, and we regarded each other with surprise.

"Whistle!" a voice called, and a young man in painter's whites dashed from the room with the open door. I didn't really think he wanted me to whistle, but I sat up, flummoxed, and stared at him.

Mid-twenties, maybe, thin but muscular, skin the color of sweet tea.

"Whistle?" I asked.

"Sorry. So sorry. Thought I'd finished the room, but then saw where a touch-up was needed. Shouldn't have left the paint uncapped. Glad you didn't trip over it."

"Nope, didn't trip at all. Everyone tells me you can't miss sitting in the hall outside room 134. Thought I'd give it a go."

"Sorry, sorry," he said, coming forward to offer me a hand up. Then, to the dog: "Whistle, come over here."

"The dog is named Whistle?"

"I used to dog-sit her for a guest. Her full name is Wet Your Whistle, which is what the guest was famous for doing. She always talked about how much the pup loved her walks with me. Frankly, the poor thing just needed some attention. After one summer's stay, the guest took off, bill unpaid, in the middle of the night."

"Leaving Whistle."

"Leaving Whistle. Such a trauma that the poor thing shadows me everywhere. And who could blame her? Not that I'm implying guests don't pay—that you wouldn't pay—"

"You caught me. In fact, I have no intention of paying."

"Excuse me, what?" He had ducked back into the newly painted guest room to clean off the roller and return the unused paint to the can.

"Mr. MacTavish comped my room."

He stopped short and returned to the hallway.

"Excuse me, *what*?" He said again.

"Mr. MacTavish comped the room."

"That's what I thought you said. I've just never heard that group of words in the same sentence."

I laughed. "I filled in at the bar last night, after the..."

"Murder."

"Murder. And, in lieu of paying me, he offered me the job and comped the room while I thought about it."

"You must be one hell of a bartender," he said.

"Actually, yes, I am. But just about now, I need some food. Where do the locals go to grab breakfast? I'm assuming not the Breezy?"

"You're right. The Breezy breakfast is rolled into an expensive sleep-and-dine package. If I were you, I'd go down Main Street to the Cardamom Café for some coffee or masala chai."

"Masala chai?"

"Yes. And tell Avantika that Philip sent you."

"I will. Thank you, Philip."

The day was full-on spring, the air wound with sunbeams. My spirits were buoyant, as if I'd found Eden, or come home. Or, perhaps more concerning, found Willoughby.

There was an old *Twilight Zone* in which a man in the daily grind of his train commute passes a town called Willoughby. In it, children run and laugh, a band plays in the gazebo, families stroll and picnic, and everyone is happy. They wave to him. Finally, one day, filled with longing for this happier, simpler life, he gets off when the train stops at Willoughby.

The episode ends with the conductor and the police trying to figure out why the man committed suicide by jumping from the moving train in the middle of nowhere.

Perhaps Tranquility was my Willoughby.

But, on the other hand, in the *Twilight Zone*, you did get a glimpse of the man once he was in Willoughby. The boys invited him fishing, and a winsome woman in summer whites brought a wicker basket of food, while the oompah band played. For him, it seemed to end well.

Hadn't these local people shared their murder with me?

I knew if I thought about Joseph, or the trauma of discovering a murder victim, the magic would vanish. So I gave myself the length of Main Street to enjoy the intoxicating freedom of being neither in Los Angeles or New York. Being simply Avalon; no family, no friends, in this place, in this moment, with a sky of cornflower blue…a huge, endless sky, which I'd only seen in tiny puzzle pieces bleached by light pollution above the Hollywood landscape or in a rectangle slice above my grandparents' townhouse in Brooklyn.

MacTavish's, the Olympic complex and skating rink, and the upscale chain hotel were all on the west side of the street, overlooking Lake Serenity. Across the street was the train station and a large town park. Continuing north along Main Street you quickly reached Tranquility's downtown, which ran along the banks of another body of water across the road. According to a tourist map posted in a kiosk, this was Fretful Pond, and Main Street curved around it. It said the town founder named the lakes after his two daughters, Serenity and Tranquility; he also had a son. It was easy to assume the son was fretful, no matter his true given name.

A grand white clapboard old hotel welcomed strollers to the village. It was rectangular and stacked with floors, each of which had a balcony running its full length and overlooking the lake-sized "pond." Tourists who weren't breakfasting at the Breezy sat outside on a wooden deck extension under a sign reading "Bier Garten" advertising a Full American Breakfast.

Continuing on, I passed shops of every description, small, independently-owned establishments that catered to posh visiting guests. (Why else would you need a shop that sold a dozen flavors of popcorn, including one with "moose" in the name, involving chocolate and nuts, which I would need to buy on my way to the train?)

The Palace Theater, built in the heyday of the Hollywood studio system, sat across the street. It had apparently been carved into three auditoriums and was playing current films. I assumed it was impatiently awaiting the advertised First Annual Tranuality Film Festival, come August.

Less than ten minutes' walk from MacTavish's, next door to an intriguing shop called the Spice Trade, I found the Cardamom Café. I also found the locals.

Once the door was opened, I was embraced by the scent of coffee, cardamom, cinnamon, and ginger. People stood in line to order coffee, latte, English breakfast tea and chai. The menu was a surprising mix of American and Indian, including eggs, veggie wraps and pancakes. Large pieces of original art grace the walls, in bright colors.

"Brent, your order's up," said the Indian woman at the counter. She wore a sari and a graceful expression.

"Thanks, Avantika," said Brent, a man I recognized from the night before. Today he wore the same blue slacks, but instead of a polo, he wore a striped Oxford shirt, with one button open. As he headed out, the door opened and Arthur arrived. He was wearing another suit—this one was light grey—and carrying a newspaper under his arm.

"Mr. Mayor," Brent greeted him, with a nod.

Ah, so Arthur was the mayor.

The response from Arthur was a glare. As he shook the newspaper in Brent's direction, the front-page headline and photo were clear: *Local Resident Murdered*, along with a photo of Joseph.

Brent accepted the glare with a slight smile and held the door open for the mayor's companion; a teenage girl, slight, straight blondish brown hair, troubled eyes. Art had such a head of steam up that I stepped to the side and let him order. "We'll both have the usual," he said, only glancing at the girl I took to be his daughter. "You want the usual, right?" he asked.

She gave a shrug, and it occurred to me that she purposefully made herself as invisible as possible.

Avantika nodded and sent the order back to the cook. When I stepped up, she took a moment to smile at me. "You're new here," she said. "Visiting?"

"Kind of," I answered. "I'm Avalon. Philip steered me in this direction. He says hello."

"Oh, so you're one of us," she said. "What would you like?"

I ordered a curried banana wrap with coconut and almond, and a Masala chai.

As I waited, the bell rang, and Suzanne, the Bohemian woman in her fifties, floated in.

"Egg whites and veggies and black coffee," she announced.

Avantika nodded. "What time are you opening today?" she asked.

"I don't know, Avantika, sad day," she muttered. "Sad day. But probably as soon as I finish eating."

Suzanne went and sat at a table already occupied by the Painter Who Brings Us Home©. Couldn't remember his last name, but did remember his drink. Michael Grey Goose would have to do.

As she sat, Suzanne saw me. She registered recognition, but it took a moment for her to put the pieces together. "Oh," she said. "You were there last night. You're the bartender."

"Yes," I said.

"Sad, very sad," said Michael.

"Very sad," I agreed.

I saw a thought ignite. "How long are you here?" he asked.

"I'm not sure," I said. "Glenn MacTavish has offered me a job. I'm considering it."

"So you'll be around this evening?" he asked. "I hear the Battened Hatch is closed for at least another day. I'm having a reception at my gallery, and I could use someone to oversee the bar."

I didn't know what to say. I was still running on one cup of fake coffee.

"What time?" I asked.

"Six to eight p.m.," he said. "I would be happy to pay your going rate."

"It's $50 an hour," I said, hoping that would settle it one way or another. "What will you be serving?"

"Wine, mostly," he said. "So we're set, then?"

Fifty dollars an hour for pouring wine? What the heck. It wasn't like there was anything waiting for me in the city. Assuming Mr. MacTavish would let me stay another night as I considered his offer.

The mayor's order came, and he motor-boated his daughter quickly through the diners and out the door.

I grabbed an empty table under an evocative painting of what I took to be a forest path with birds—although it was more of a Rorschach test in greens, blues, and purples with orange/golden leaves. I stared at it longer than I meant to, but there was a feeling of longing—of being lured forward—that wouldn't let me go. The former inhabitant of the table had left the day's newspaper and when my order came, I ate slowly, reading carefully.

It didn't say much about Joseph. His last name was Emberg, and he'd come to Tranquility from Iowa fifteen years past. He was "a craft bartender and local fixture at the Battened Hatch where he was beloved by the local clientele, and where he ultimately met his demise."

Well, that kind of put things into a new light. I didn't want them to be able to write the same sentence about me.

It said the police were "following all leads, and ask that anyone with information contact them immediately. Investigator Michael Spaulding says he does not believe the public at large is in any danger; 'we will all sleep better once the perpetrator is off the street.'"

As I headed back to MacTavish's, I passed Suzanne opening up the Spice Trade next door. From the front window I saw it sold spices and olive oils flavored in interesting ways which you could pour into fancy containers yourself. Suzanne turned on the lights and hung her colorful shawl on a wall peg behind the counter. Then she rested her head against the wall. It looked like she was weeping.

My spirits were less buoyant on the way back.

I stopped at the train station and checked the schedule. There was a New York City-bound train at noon and one at 4 p.m. A train left for Montreal at 3 and another left at 11 p.m., and that was about it. It wasn't exactly Grand Central Station. Really, I didn't owe the Painter Who Brought Me Home© anything. He wasn't crafting cocktails at his reception. Anyone could pour wine. I could get his number and beg off.

The melancholy surrounding me after reading about Joseph's death was compounded by sadness at knowing I would be leaving Tranquility.

Back at the hotel, I followed the arrows past a large framed magazine cover of Pepper Porter—a golden era movie star who had likely stayed here—and continued up and down and around the hallways until I got back to my room.

The cleaning staff had visited. The bed was made.

On the center of the bedspread was a notecard.

I picked it up, wondering if it was from Mr. MacTavish, asking for my decision.

It wasn't.

Instead, there was spidery script, which looked like it had been purposely written by someone's non-dominant hand.

Leave this place. You aren't safe here. This was all it said.

Crap.

How could I possibly leave after a warning like that?

Wet Your Whistle

Ingredients

Dried apricots (2 per drink)
1.5 ounces apricot brandy
1.5 ounces gin
.75 ounces (1/2 jigger) grenadine
Seltzer

Method

Soak the apricots in enough brandy to cover for at least 15 minutes.

Shake the rest of the brandy, the gin and the grenadine over ice until cool; strain into martini glass.

Top with seltzer.

Cut the apricots into quarters; add to drink with remaining brandy. Enjoy!

4

Willoughby

The Welcome Home Gallery was two doors down from the Palace Theater. Michael needed me from six to eight, but the fact I was arriving at six meant the event was already starting. I hadn't mentioned my usual set up and breakdown fee, which might be just as well. That way I could hightail it out at 8.

A banner out front declared "Back Home Again. A Brilliant New Series Debuts."

Upscale vehicles were turning in to the parking lot in the back. The patrons arriving from the sidewalk were mostly thin, coiffed, and dressed in neutral colors. Not to mention very European American.

Basic bartender black fit right in. I was glad I'd decided on a skirt and flats instead of sticking with knit pants. It was my nod toward dressing up.

Michael Grey Goose had been correct about the Battened Hatch being closed. Crime- scene tape still crossed the door. That couldn't be good for future business. Or perhaps it would be—irony runs deep through the human psyche.

Golden light spilled from the Gallery onto the sidewalk in front. The soft light continued inside, and I saw that 'golden' light was right—all the ceiling lights were poseable and filtered in a soft gold or beige. The smell of fresh-baked chocolate chip cookies permeated the air, and old-fashioned platters of them dotted the landscape of comfy chairs and throw rugs. Three gas fireplaces blazed away, each topped by a huge painting that was either three feet by five feet or four feet by six. They depicted idealized houses, Main Streets, or town parks filled with families laughing and playing and hugging. There was no question—Michael Michel was good at what he did. The light and shadow, the depth and even the reflections in puddles, lured you into the vision of being welcomed home.

And then it hit me—these paintings weren't of Tranquility, though many of the buildings looked familiar. They were his versions of Willoughby—the home each of us wanted, thought was ours by right, but would never fully have. Apparently many collectors would pay tens of thousands of dollars to own the feeling, if nothing else.

I looked for Michael, and as patrons shifted, I saw him by one of the fireplaces, no fewer than three photographers snapping away. He stood by a pleasant-looking woman who must have been his wife. And four—no, five—no, *seven* children, all seemingly under the age of nine or ten.

"Look quickly," said a voice behind me. "You won't see the wife or kids again, at least till he trots them out at the next opening."

I turned to find Suzanne from the Spice Trade. "He told me to watch for you. Come on back this way."

As I followed her, I heard a child's voice say, "But I want a cookie!" It was followed by a toddler demanding, "Cookie! Cookie!" Soon the wail of an infant joined the chorus. Who could blame them? I wanted a cookie, too.

"And... they're gone," said Suzanne under her breath.

I turned back to find the Michel family had vanished, as if through a trap door. If you're selling idealized family life, no point in letting the real thing intrude.

Suzanne led me to the built-in service bar. Wine glasses were already set out on one half of the table, with bottles of Malbec and Chardonnay at the ready. The other half had Champagne flutes, with a bottle of Veuve Clicquot chilling, and others in the iced trough behind.

"Be stingy with the bubbly," she whispered, "without seeming so."

I was at first pleasantly surprised to see what I thought was a tip jar at the far side of the table, but it turned out to be a jar for checks. Beside it was a colorful sheet asking for contributions to the Drug-Free Tranquility campaign. The first check inside was folded enough so that it stood on end, but not enough that you couldn't read the amount ($10,000) or that it was made out to Drug-Free Tranquility, LLC and signed, with a flourish, by Michael Michel.

I'd seen tragedy through misuse of drugs, and was certainly all for keeping the citizens of Tranquility from the clutches of terrible addictions. But I also saw the irony of putting the jar on a table laden with alcohol. Since no one else apparently did, and more checks and large bills kept appearing, I said nothing, and tapped along to the strains of Tony Bennett, Nat King Cole, and the Carpenters.

"Feel like you're drowning in the Mayberry watering hole?" asked a male voice, about an hour into the fiesta.

I turned to find Brent Davis, the newspaper editor, standing on the other side of the table. He'd added a jacket to his chinos and shirt, with a contrasting tie.

"Chardonnay?" I asked. "Or Champagne?"

"No beer? Ah, well, I'll carry around a Malbec." He nodded and took a glass. Apparently his reporting was over, as he dug at the knot in and loosened his tie. "We have to cover these things, even though they're not really news," he said, leaning against the exposed brick wall. "But being the town immortalized by Michael Michel has brought much lucre to our streets."

"Golden light, too, apparently." Then I nodded to the jar. "Is there a big drug problem in Tranquility?"

Brent considered his answer. "There's a drug problem everywhere, we don't pretend there isn't," he said. "If you ask, they'll talk about the heroin problem in some poorer communities nearby. But the fact is, Drug-Free Tranquility is code for 'keep the artists out.'"

"Why on earth would you fundraise for something like that at an artist's show?"

"Oh, they're not looking to keep out artists like Michel. He's a 'good artist.' Has a wife and extensive family."

"Which artists, then?"

"The dangerous ones," he said, and laughed. "You know, non-representational. There's a movement to make the old Olympic villages into artist's colonies, and fund painters, writers, musicians, actors, and the like. Some people see it as a way to breathe new life into this old town. Not everyone agrees."

"So, the money collected by Drug-Free Tranquility goes to…?"

He smiled at me. It was a friendly smile. "Always read the fine print," he said, and raised his glass as he walked away.

I poured for two more patrons before picking up the sign by the jar. At the bottom, in tiny print, it said, "Drug-Free Tranquility supports the mayoral candidacy of Arthur Bristol."

Alrighty, then. Brent was right. The fine print was mighty crucial.

The shindig was billed to be over by 8 and indeed the doors were locked at 8:05.

It seemed successful. Most sales were smaller limited-run prints of these new huge paintings, but maybe ten out of the twenty mega-originals sported "sold" dots.

The last patrons gone, Natalie Cole abruptly stopped urging me to Straighten Up and Fly Right. The female gallery manager, along with Suzanne, the artist himself, and Mayor Arthur Bristol strolled back by the table. "Just cork the ones that are open," said the manager. "We'll pick up the bottles later."

"Where shall I wash the glasses?" I asked. I'd been impressed that they'd used glass over plastic.

"Oh, no need.. The rental company washes them."

"So," Mayor Bristol said, eyeing the donations jar. "Seems a profitable night, all around."

"It always is," said Grey Goose Michael.

He handed me two $100 bills, and said thanks.

As I did a final check of the "station," the gallery manager said, "You know, sad as it is, having Joseph gone will probably make things easier."

"Don't say that," said Michael Michel. "Never say that."

"But Joseph listened to... everyone. And everyone talked to him. He was a repository of listening."

"We regret his loss," said Mayor Bristol slowly. "And we move forward."

I looked up briefly to see the mayor gauging my reaction. When I smiled, he smiled back.

Of the four people remaining, Suzanne alone looked away. I wondered if her reaction flagged an opinion of Joseph that the others didn't share.

Out on Main Street, it was a Tuesday night between tourist seasons, and almost everywhere was closed. Lights were still on next door at the Palace Theater, as the 7 p.m. showings were halfway through.

Glowing streetlights dotted the way back through town to MacTavish's. Lights bathed the train station, awaiting the 11 p.m. to Montreal. This led me to realize I was more uncertain than ever about whether to go or stay.

Inside MacTavish's lobby, the police tape had been removed and a doorstop held the bar door open a couple of inches. I headed over and slipped in.

Overhead lights I'd never seen used added harsh shadows to the wooden furniture. The room was empty, but loud voices emerged from the kitchen area.

I quietly walked behind the bar and ran my hand along the expensive carved wood, then looked at the back bar and saw the well-chosen array of bottles. Joseph was more than a repository of listening. The man had taste—and I suspected we had another affinity with each other as well. I suspected he was a Collector.

I've always been fascinated by people and their lives. Then, in a middle school English class, we read the Spoon River Anthology, which is set in a graveyard. The narration goes from headstone to headstone, telling the story of each person's life. It stuck with me. Lodged deep. I realized that was what I wanted to do: hear people's stories. Wonder at the meanings of their lives. Collect them, like a real-life, walking Spoon River anthologizer. Doing so resonated and satisfied me in a place nothing else reached.

In high school, I found it easy to listen as my friends talked, to prompt them with simple questions. At first it was shocking how much one could learn by simply being interested. Indeed, being interested is the key. People are intuitive. They can tell when someone is nosy, as opposed to when someone actually cares.

Unfortunately, "story collector" isn't a paid position, and I struggled as well-meaning adults asked what career path I wanted to choose. I didn't want to become a psychologist or a sociologist or a counselor: I didn't want to have to do something with the information, didn't want to be responsible for fixing people or documenting a cultural trend.

My mother collected stories, in her own way, but twisted them to use as material.

And my father, as I'd recently discovered, used people's stories to control them and ruin their lives.

I went to New York University for two years. Home on winter break during my sophomore year, I was offered temporary work as a bar back. I never returned to school. Instead, I started filling in as a bartender. I never looked back.

Stories. Every day, every night. In my back pocket.

And the thing I heard time and again about Joseph? He was a good listener. To people, that meant he paid attention. Asked questions.

Not a doubt in my mind that he was a Collector, whether he'd put it into words, even to himself, or not.

God rest his soul.

I surveyed his kingdom; the beauty of the hand-carved dark wood, the specific placement of the bottles, colorful and upright, like soldiers in uniform for ceremonial display. Even the lighting beneath the bottles showed an artistic eye.

A Collector could do worse.

"What were you thinking? What the hell were you thinking?" came the yelling voice. "Leaving me without alcohol for a whole evening?"

"The bar was closed. It was a crime scene," came the second voice, calmer, but insistent.

"The Breezy isn't a crime scene! Think of what we lost!"

"You had wine. I can't think you lost that many orders for mixed drinks."

"That's it—you don't think! This place is run by morons!"

The door swung open, and the man whose photo I'd seen posted as chef of the Breezy, Paul Miller, came stomping through. He was a short man, compactly built, black hair with male pattern baldness, who could have been a day player on The Sopranos.

Glenn MacTavish followed him out.

"There's also the matter of respect," he said. "Joseph is dead. The bar can close for one day out of respect."

"Respect? How does being closed help Joseph? How does losing money honor his memory?"

"It's done now, Paul. The evening's done. You had wine."

The chef turned and took two angry steps back toward the kitchen before another point occurred to him. He turned, dudgeon high. Before he could speak, Glenn extended an arm, his second finger raised, a look of steel in his eyes.

Chef Paul stood for a moment, reconsidered, and stomped on back through to the kitchen.

Mr. MacTavish stood where he was, slowly turned around and looked over the room. His reverie lasted two or three minutes. His shoulders sagged. When he snapped back to himself, he saw me standing there.

"Ay, lassie," he said. "The chef wasna fond o'Joseph."

His Scottish accent had thickened noticeably since the argument.

"Let's talk in the morrow," he finished.

Fine with me.

Mr. MacTavish headed toward the lobby door. He pointed to the light switch, and I nodded. He shut off the intrusive lights. There were two night lights behind the bar, and two lighted exit signs elsewhere in the room, which served well, once my eyes adjusted.

The crime scene people had cleaned up the poisoned fruit, and the knives, and the cutting board. The hum of the ice machine was reassuring. And I noticed a breeze.

All the windows were closed.

I walked over and found the door to the smoker's porch was cracked open. Through the gap I saw two people outside. They had tall glass votives containing candles, both of which were lit. As my eyes adjusted farther, I could make out that one was Marta, the waitress, and the other was the teenage girl with troubled eyes—the mayor's daughter?—whom I'd seen at the coffee place. They were solemn, looking past the flickering flames, out over the lake.

"Thank you, Joseph," Marta finally said, and she blew out her candle.

"Yes, thank you," whispered the other girl.

As they spoke, I felt someone there next to me. I assumed Glenn had returned and was also watching the young women, quiet and touched by their impromptu memorial. But when I turned, I found myself alone in the small hallway.

No wonder people ask if the inn is haunted, I thought, and I hurried back toward the lobby as the other girl extinguished her candle as well.

I crossed the lobby thinking about what I'd just witnessed. The girls' heartfelt gratitude confirmed my own first impression that Joseph was a good man.

It made me want to know more about him.

It made me want to do whatever I could to help discover who'd killed him.

But was it enough to make me stay?

Willoughby Lemonade

Ingredients

1-1/2 cup water
1-1/2 cups sugar
1 ¼ cups fresh lemon juice (from about 6 lemons)
3 cups strawberries, hulled and sliced
3 cups cold water
3/4 cup lemon vodka
1/3 cup Malibu coconut rum
Ice

Method

Bring the sugar and water to a simmer in a small saucepot. Stir so that sugar melts completely then remove from the heat and let cool to room temperature.

Place the strawberries in a blender and process until smooth. Pour pureed strawberries in the sugar water and stir well. Add the lemon juice.

Combine the strawberry lemon syrup, vodka, rum and cold water in a large pitcher. Stir well and add lots of ice.

Serve lemonade with thin slices of lemons and strawberries.

5

Jekyll and Hyde

Magnificent clouds of white and grey tumbled across Lake Serenity in a mirror of those above as I sipped morning coffee on my room's small balcony. Both evergreen and deciduous trees ringed the shores. How I wanted to be able to inhabit, or at least grasp, the peace that came with nature.

I went inside and packed my bag. One way or another, this was my last morning in this room, on this balcony.

Philip the [other kind of] painter was working two rooms down from the room he was touching up the day before, as I made that penultimate turn towards the lobby. I heard Whistle yipping, so I walked past the framed color cover of Screen Book featuring the platinum blonde, Pepper Porter—who seemed saucier than I'd noticed before—and stuck my head into the room with the open door, emanating paint fumes.

"What's up?" I said.

"Oh, hello," he answered.

"I heard Whistle yipping, so I thought I'd say hi."

"You could hear her? Not good. She needs to go outside, but I have to finish this coat before I can take her. I'm falling behind schedule, which isn't allowed at MacTavish's."

"Yeah? So what is it like to work here? Is Mr. MacTavish a hard taskmaster? Would I regret signing on?"

He turned his full attention to me. He had a small patch of green on his hair. "Are you seriously considering it?"

"Well, I'm semi-seriously considering it. Nothing's knocked me one way or the other, so I'll probably be on the afternoon train."

"MacTavish isn't bad to work for. Especially bartending. I think he pretty much let Joseph do his own thing. Now, painting, on the other hand—" He gestured down the hall, "Then you've got the head of Housekeeping and Grounds on your tail, too."

"It seems like the painting job's already taken, anyway."

Phillip sighed. "Yep, guess so. For a while, anyway. Anything else you'd like to know, to help you make your decision?"

"Is the inn haunted?"

He grinned. "Why? What have you heard?"

"Overheard some folks asking as they checked in. And, I don't normally put too much stock in stuff like this, but last night when I was in the bar by myself, I sort of felt like... I wasn't by myself."

"Hmm," he said. "I haven't heard anything about the bar before. Usually when people ask, they're talking about Suite Seven."

"Suite Seven?"

Philip put his brush down and joined me in the hall, Whistle doing a little dance at his feet.

We walked together to the painting of the Screen Book cover. "Have you heard of Pepper Porter?" he asked.

"Seriously? Who hasn't?"

"These days? Lots of people."

"I guess people don't watch those old movie musicals much anymore, but I love them. She was a crazy good dancer."

Philip laughed. "Yeah. Apparently she was really something. One of the biggest stars in the studio system, for over a decade. Worked in Hollywood, but preferred the East Coast. She often took time off to come East and do Broadway shows."

"I'm assuming from the large framed photo that she stayed here?"

"MacTavish's was a favorite place of hers. She used to come up and bring her Hollywood and Broadway cronies. They'd rent the whole north wing, and party till the cows came home. Literally. According to stories, Old Man Lester's cows coming home for breakfast and milking was their cue to go to bed—or get back in their limos for the ride back to Manhattan."

"Must have been quite the time!"

"Oh, yes. Although Pepper herself was a celebrated prude. Sexually, that is. And alcohol-wise. Never drank. Was both bon vivant and scold, go figure."

"No wonder they put up a picture of her."

"The story doesn't end there. After a decade or so back in Hollywood, she moved in here to help run the place. Glenn MacTavish's mother had just died. The place was in need of a 'hostess,' and Pepper was apparently ready to retire."

"Really? So did she become hostess of Glenn MacTavish's father as well as of the inn?"

"Hmm. Not that I ever heard. Prude, don't forget. Think mega-prude."

"I think I'll stick with talented and sophisticated."

"And well-connected. When the town was in need, she almost single-handedly wrangled having the Winter Olympics here. Virtually saved the place."

"Wow. But I thought the competition for the Olympics was a very political thing. How... single-handedly did she do it?"

"Single-handedly knew which palms to grease and where to get the dough to grease them, most likely. In any case, we're all indebted."

"She lived here after she retired?"

"In Suite Seven."

"Aha."

"There have been stories that she died, but never really checked out."

"Yeah? So she's still in Suite Seven?"

"Frankly, I find it a little suspicious. Kind of like when folks do past life regression. Somehow, everyone was King Tut, no one was ever third slave to the left. Seems like the same principle. The rooms where normal people stay never seem to be haunted. But Pepper is allegedly still hanging around."

"So why bring it up if you think it strains credulity?"

"Because you asked if the inn is haunted, and that's the scuttlebutt."

"What is supposed to happen in Suite Seven?"

"People have reported waking up to see a woman in a dressing gown looking at them. Some guests have reported hearing voices or music when no one's there. My favorite is how people have heard footsteps, not walking, but dancing."

I smiled, imagining being awakened to a ghostly tap routine. "Wow. Have you ever been in there?"

"I've painted every room in this place."

"And?"

"Well, okay, what you said about feeling like you weren't alone in the bar last night? I would go that far. Never felt anything threatening, though. Not at all… Okay. Sometimes things weren't always where I thought I'd left them."

"Interesting."

Whistle's whining had become high-pitched yips we could no longer ignore, and her dance had become more insistent.

"I'm going out for coffee. I'd be happy to take Whistle."

"Really?" The relief in his voice was palpable. He returned with leash and doggy-doo bag faster than I could follow to the room where he was working. "Thanks a lot. I'll be here."

"Got it."

Whistle dragged me with the force of a Siberian husky to the nearest exit door, which we pushed through without setting off an alarm. She ran for a patch of grass, and made a sound more like a satisfied sigh than I'd ever heard from a non-human. Then we set off up the road.

Grey clouds had rolled in, and a chilly April wind teased at the treetops. It was good to see Tranquility in all its incarnations, if I was at all thinking of staying. Although, as the Pomeranian and I stopped at the train station to double check the schedule, I decided that, when I returned, I'd get my packed bag out of the room and ask the bellman to keep it until the afternoon. The next New York train was still posted for 4 p.m.

Many of the inhabitants of Tranquility greeted me—and as many again greeted Whistle—as we headed for the Cardamom Café. I wasn't sure what to do with the dog when I arrived, but I settled on carrying her in with me. That worked out fine. I ordered a breakfast sandwich I could eat one-handed, which I did, sitting on a bench outside. Then I picked up my chai latte and crossed the street to head back.

Whistle had done her business and was now happy to be sniffing and marking. She found something interesting on a lawn that sloped down to the sidewalk and went after the smell with vigor. She even squatted to leave her own mark, but as it had been a long walk, it was ceremonial at this point.

"Hello there!" The voice was booming, self-assured, male.

I looked up at a well-dressed gentleman who was standing in the driveway of the house. "Are you new in town?"

"Perhaps," I said.

"From down at MacTavish's?" The man was tall and broad-shouldered. He had grey-blonde hair with a careful part. A slight tan gave his white skin an orange cast. His navy slacks and open-collar shirt fit almost perfectly. He exuded an air of authority meant to be intimidating.

"Yes."

"You were the one who found Joseph?" He'd come down closer to me but was standing on the incline, which transformed his height from tall into towering.

"Yes."

"And your name?"

"Avalon."

That threw him, but only slightly. He stepped forward and offered his hand, forcing me to swap the coffee cup into my leash hand.

"Well, Avalon, welcome to Tranquility! Welcome! We're glad you're here!"

"And you are?"

"I'm Tim. Tim Layton. Welcome to the neighborhood."

He stood for a moment. Then his wide smile faded and fast as a lightning strike, and his hands tightened around mine. "And if I ever *ever* see you letting that little dog up onto my lawn again, there will be consequences. Do you understand?"

His voice had gone from cordial to nearly demonic with the flip of a switch. So fast, in fact, that I assumed he was kidding.

"Oh, she's just marking. She's out of pee."

"I saw her. More than that, I saw you. Letting her up onto my lawn—my lawn—not even trying to jerk her away. Not even trying!"

"What?" I asked. "I am picking up anything solid she leaves behind."

"This lawn…I pay thousands of dollars to put chemicals on this lawn to make it look this way. I love dogs, yes, and I love children. But keep them away… from… this… lawn."

I looked him steadily in the eye. He wasn't kidding.

As quickly as the threat had materialized, it was gone. He was back to his original self. "But welcome! Welcome! We're glad to have you here."

My eyes must have been as large as Frisbees. I'd never seen someone go Jekyll-and-Hyde quite so convincingly.

"I will avoid this lawn at all costs," I said. I turned back around, wanting to depart as quickly as possible. I re-crossed the street.

"Okay," he said. "Oh, and Wednesday night services start at 7, if you can come. We'd love to have you."

I glanced up and noticed that his large stone house at the top of the rise was connected to an enormous stone church.

Holy crap. I was shaking.

We continued on, in the opposite direction of MacTavish's, past the Cardamom, past another old hotel on Fretful Pond, and around the corner, out of sight of Tim Layton as fast as my—and Whistle's— legs would take us.

Whistle, who thought she was heading back to Philip, was confused, but she obediently trotted on next to me. I wanted to walk far enough and long enough that the crazy person would go inside.

We continued for a while, barely noticing as the businesses turned to residences, and then to long stretches of land.

Finally, Whistle dug in her paws and came to a stop.

I took several deep breaths, and looked around. In doing so, I inadvertently tangled Whistle's leash on a metal "for rent" sign planted in the ground directly in front of me.

Behind the sign stood a stone house, painted red, with old-style wooden shingles on the top. The house was tall but not wide, and practically growing out into the sidewalk. A dirt road ran right past it, and when I say "right past", I mean someone in the house could reach out and hand you flowers. Or you could turn it into a drive-through. The thin, tall house had personality and charm, but who in her right mind would rent it?

"I just put the sign out," it was another male voice, this one quiet, low, and rumbling. Slight Newport yachting accent.

"Caught the leash, sorry," I said, hoping not to launch into another dog-related neighbor incident.

"So you're not interested in renting?"

I turned to look at him and nearly jumped out of my skin. The speaker stood at my shoulder—as close to me as his house was to the dirt road. He was tall with a long face, pointed chin, brows that canopied blue eyes. Silver hair combed back emphasized his tall forehead. He was perhaps eighty, and wore an open collared shirt and navy blazer beneath a half-zipped designer windbreaker—as if he'd actually disembarked from a yacht.

"This house here?" I asked, pointing to the skinny house.

He raised an eyebrow and studied me. "Not from around here, are we?" he asked, employing the royal we. When I shook my head, he said, "Not that one. That's my place."

"Oh," I said, clueless, "there's another?"

"Seems so. Not my idea. I've been out of town since Saturday, and upon my return, I got the message from Mrs. Chander." He waved a piece of paper in my direction. "It's back beyond. If you'd like to see it, I suppose there's nothing I can do."

Without further ado, he turned and stalked up the dirt road past his house.

There seemed nothing to do but follow.

The road had a small sign, the kind that wasn't official but you could order, naming it Cherry Lane. It curved around under hundred-year-old oak trees. Main Street—or Elm Street, as it was called at this point—vanished behind us as we walked on. It was shocking to feel so isolated from town—from the rest of the universe—this near the beaten path. I wondered if it was wise to be following this odd gentleman out of sight of humanity. Could I take him, if I had to? He seemed fit. I did, however, have youth on my side. And, should worst come to worst, I would send Whistle out yipping, so at least Phillip could find my body.

We came to a wooden bridge, wide enough for one car. Beneath us ran an enthusiastic stream. Then the trees parted. Ahead was a wide clearing, the center of which was a round body of water. A waterfall leapt from a smaller pond above. Village noises had vanished. All I could hear was the tumbling of the water and the chirping and calling of myriads of larks and chickadees.

We continued up a hill. To the right sat a log cabin—more a lodge, really, the kind that starred in many Old Hollywood films, whenever people went to visit "the country." A room-sized screened porch ran the length of the front of the house. The whole place was overwhelmingly charming.

"Is that it?" I asked. Even Whistle seemed amazed.

"No," said my guide, sounding offended. "Over here."

We passed the cabin and ascended flagstone steps up a hill that brought us to the upper level of the pond. "Does this stream lead down into Fretful Pond?" I asked.

"It flows down from Lake Tranquility, into Fretful, on to Lake Serenity," as if his manners forced him to be polite in spite of his distaste for the task at hand.

"It's lovely back here," I said.

"It's the Mill Pond," he said. "There used to be a wheel for grinding."

I nodded thoughtfully.

"This will be it," he said.

A white footbridge arched over the water. Yacht man set off across it. He had a slightly odd gait, as if he'd been injured at some point.

Before we reached the other side, I saw a white picket fence surrounding a classic white cottage. Purple and blue wisteria framed the house, and pink morning glories climbed the porch posts.

This place couldn't be real. Someone had art directed it. It was the country lodge and cottage version of Neuschwanstein—the castle King Ludwig paid an opera scene designer to create.

"Let's move along," urged the property manager.

I closed my mouth and trotted up the walk behind him.

Inside, the cottage was small, furnished in blue and yellow chintz and china. Not normally my style, but it felt airy and cheerful. There was a sunny kitchen, a large bedroom, a living room/dining room, and a small second bedroom or office. "That's a pull-out couch," was the first thing my guide offered.

Behind the kitchen was a flagstone patio, with a mixture of wicker and wrought iron furniture.

"There are cushions."

A salesman he wasn't.

He didn't have to be.

I thought of my friends in Los Angeles with their functional Ikea-furnished apartments and blackout curtains—which, until very recently, had been my style as well.

"When is it available?"

"It's available."

"How much is it, to rent?" I asked.

"Oh." He looked at the note. "Seven-fifty."

"I'll take it."

We stood for a moment, each equally surprised.

But I'd meant it. My inner self had made this decision.

I was staying.

I was apparently living in a hidden cottage behind the home of an arrogant yachter.

Life is full of risks, right?

"We will need references," he intoned.

I nodded.

"As well as first and last month, and deposit."

I nodded again.

A sigh. "Very well, then. I'll have the rental agreement drawn up. Come back at two." As an afterthought: "Have you steady employment?"

"Yes," I said. "I'm the new bartender at MacTavish's."

A look of horror floated behind his eyes.

He turned abruptly and stalked away.

What had I gotten myself into?

Jekyll and Hyde

Ingredients

2 ounce preferred Rye/Whiskey
Dash of bitters
Dash of sweet vermouth
1/2 ounce habanero simple syrup
Fresh cut pineapple (about 2 chunks)

Method

In a rocks glass, muddle fresh pineapple. Add ice, habanero simple syrup, rye/whiskey, bitters and sweet vermouth. Stir ingredients together. Do not shake these ingredients as you may bruise your rye/whisky.

Habanero Simple Syrup
Bring equal parts of sugar and water to a boil. After simple syrup has reached its boil turn down heat on stove top and add fresh or dried habaneros. Simmer ingredients together for about 10-15 minutes so the oils from the peppers have time to release their heat into the simple syrup. Let habanero simple syrup sit until cool and then poor into desired container. Leave peppers in sugar water as they will make this spicier. Make sure to label and wear kitchen gloves as needed while making this as the oils from these peppers will get into your skin and leave a burning sensation.

6

The Late Train

Glenn MacTavish was in conversation in the lobby on my return. I took Whistle to Philip and hurried back. Waiting to the side, I noticed a framed black and white photo of Pepper Porter mounted prominently on the wall. In this one, she wore a swirling dancing gown. She was in the midst of a slide step, a joyous Hollywood smile on her face. It was signed, "To Everyone at MacTavish's. Love, Pepper Porter." Beneath it was a black button, which, of course, I pushed. It was if Pepper stood beside me. "MacTavish's is an enchanting place. Welcome! We're glad you're here," came her cheerful voice.

In my mind, I heard a Gershwin melody and (also in my mind) I began to choreograph a buoyant production number throughout the lobby. A hotel could have a worse "hostess."

Mr. MacTavish finished his conversation and turned to me. He was once again in full Scottish formal regalia. His work uniform. "Ms. Nash," he said.

"Mr. MacTavish. I'd be happy to accept your job offer." I smiled. He did not.

Instead, he said, "Very well. Let's do a month's try-out on both sides, shall we?"

I nodded. "I suppose I should also find out the hours and the pay."

"This way," he said, and led me back a narrow hallway to Mrs. Rumple, who, according to the sign on her desk, was their head of human resources. Glenn gave a curt nod and said, "New bartender."

Then he vanished.

I'd hoped for a little more enthusiasm. I thought MacTavish and I had hit it off, and he would be relieved and pleased I'd decided to stay on. Instead, Mrs. Rumple gave a sigh. "I wish he'd *tell* me when he's going to do these things!"

The salary and benefits were on the good side of acceptable. "Who else works the bar?" I asked.

She looked at me, confused.

"On my days off?"

"Oh, hmm. Joseph didn't take regular days off."

"He worked seven days a week?"

"He took off now and again, depending on his schedule. Used to take off Mondays, but then the Chamber started meeting on Mondays. There's Sam Hiller; he's an older fellow who does fill in sometimes. I don't believe he'd want to go regular, though," Rumple said.

"I would like two days off each week," I said. "Or at least one day."

I could possibly get by with one day off. Might as well work a sixth day and save the extra cash.

"I'll talk to Mr. MacTavish. In the meantime, when can you start?"

I checked my watch. "Four o'clock?"

I met my new property manager at the cottage at 2 p.m. For the official transaction, he wore a black suit, red vest with black paisley swirls, and a red pocket square and matching tie. His black and white walking stick gave the me impression he went for "dapper" and overreached. I paid cash for the deposit and rent. I'd emptied my bank accounts before leaving California, and was travelling with good amount of currency. I was happy to have some of it safely put to use.

When we signed the papers, his signature was illegible, and I broke down and asked his name. "Fenton," was all I got.

I lugged my worldly belongings into the cottage from the front step and unpacked, which took all of twenty minutes. Then I looked through the cabinets. There was a matching set of china plates, glasses and cups with an old fashioned floral pattern, but no food. My guess was this had been used as a guest cottage, adjunct to the Lodge, and was supplied with perishables only when inhabited. The floors were clean, though, and the linens were crisp, so someone had been keeping up the place.

There was also a heavy, 1950s style telephone on an honest-to-god telephone table, which included an attached seat covered by a small rounded floral cushion on which to sit and talk. The phone itself was white with a square base. It tapered up to the raised handset. I'd never seen one like it. All the rage in mid-century Beverly Hills, if I had my guess. It was plugged in with a heavy brown cord, but there was no dial tone. A ghost phone to another era, one I was sorry to miss.

I was moving into the neighborhood of a time gone by.

The kitchen featured a tea kettle—the British kind you plug in—and some tea bags, so I made a cuppa, found the plump outdoor cushions, and went to sit on my patio. It was enchanting. I couldn't believe my luck.

Apparently I had jumped off, knowingly and willingly, at Willoughby.

I arrived at the Battened Hatch, as its new barkeep, at 4 p.m.

I was still experimenting with light switches, trying to find the ones that gave acceptable illumination without searing eyeballs, when the door opened.

"Hello?" I said. "We'll be open in half an hour. I'm setting up."

"Here. It's these two switches," said Marta.

"Oh. Thanks."

She continued to stand. Hair still teal, nails a new violet/blue color. They were masterfully done.

"Umm," she finally said after a long moment.

"Umm?"

"Are you going to be the bartender?"

"Yes. Mr. MacTavish and I are trying each other out for a month."

She continued to stand. "Umm," she said again. "Do you still need me?"

I turned around. "How would I not need you?"

The tension released from her shoulders. "So I can still waitress?"

"I'd appreciate it if you would."

"And you need me on Wednesdays, right?"

Today was Wednesday.

"How else am I going to figure out how this place works?"

She almost smiled. "I mean every Wednesday. The deal needs to be I can keep my job if I work every Wednesday."

We both stood by the bar. I wasn't extra tall, but I did stand half a head above her. "There's a subtext I'm not picking up," I said. "Although I have figured out you need somewhere to be on Wednesdays."

"Otherwise, I have to go to church."

Ah, it came flooding back to me. "At seven p.m.? At Reverend Layton's church?"

She nodded.

"Well, I can see how that could be considered a terrible fate. Who would make you go?"

"Umm, Reverend Layton. My dad."

"Tim Layton is your father?"

She nodded.

"I met him today. I can't begin to tell you how much we count on you here on Wednesdays."

Marta went behind the bar and picked up a cloth with which to wipe down the tables. "On one condition," I added. Hesitantly, she looked at me. "A partial smile, perhaps?"

She did give me a tentative smile. Then I remembered Marta and her friend lighting candles for Joseph, and I felt like a jerk. "I'm sorry about Joseph," I said. "He seemed like a good man. I'd like you to tell me about him as time goes by."

She nodded. I got out my bar mat and began my opening routine. Marta finished the tables and came over. She showed me where to get ice, as well as where the extra glasses and clean bar cloths were kept. Then she pushed through to the kitchen to get the fruit for garnishes.

"So, the bar's open?" boomed Paul the Chef. "About damn time."

I swung into the kitchen through the door.

"Hi," I said, planting myself between Marta and Tony Soprano. "Avalon. New bartender." I extended my hand, and shook his firmly. "Any specials today?"

"We don't send the specials into the bar," he growled.

"Let me know if you rethink that," I said. "I'm great at pushing specials."

I gave him a searing smile and followed Marta back into our darkened but expansive hobbit-hole.

"Nice guy," I said.

She snorted.

"Hey, how old are you?" I asked her as she put the fresh limes, lemons, and cherries into a bin. "And let me smell those," I said.

They smelled fine.

"I'm eighteen," she said. "Would you like me to prep the garnishes?"

"You know how?"

"Sure."

"Are you still in high school?"

"Senior. About to graduate."

"Exciting. Let's see if I remember correctly. The law in New York State is that you have to be eighteen to serve alcohol or bartend, but you can't drink until twenty-one."

"Yes," she said. "That's right."

"Okay, here's a question. Did Joseph ever have you fix drinks?"

She looked at me, startled. "No."

"Would you like to learn how?"

"You mean, how to bartend?"

"You're eighteen. It would be legal."

"I'm not sure my dad would..."

"You'd have a saleable skill. The tips are better."

She grabbed a couple of lemons and a paring knife. Her hair hid her face when she looked down. "Sure," she said.

"All right, then."

I left her cutting fruit and did a careful inventory of the bottles on the bar, and of the juices and mixes in the fridge and checked the levels of the liquor bottles on the speed rack. I followed Marta's directions to the stock of wines used by both the restaurant and bar. I'd need to find out who did the ordering.

Then I went back into the Battened Hatch. There, I stood, simply stood, and took a moment to run my hands over the carved dark wood of the bar. It was magnificent. I closed my eyes and took a breath.

When I opened them again, I took a small jump back. Investigator Spaulding stood directly opposite me. He wore a brown leather jacket, unzipped, a fitted tan sweater underneath. It made me suspect he was undercover. Or incognito. Or something.

"Hello, Ms. Nash," he said.

"Hello, Investigator," I said.

"I seem to remember something about you just passing through."

"Yes. That was the original plan."

"You're staying?"

"I'm giving it a month, to see if it works out. If I'm still alive."

His raised eyebrows asked the question for him.

"It's been pointed out to me that Joseph was not the first of MacTavish's bartenders to die under mysterious circumstances," I explained.

That got him. He brought out his notebook and rifled through the pages.

"By whom was he predeceased?"

"I... don't know. I will find out."

"So you're staying in town."

"For a month." Was he not paying attention?

"You were never here before?"

"Never. Never heard of the place. Definitely didn't get off the train to create a job opening for myself." *Stop talking, Avalon. You're wading into dangerous waters.*

Investigator Spaulding leaned into the bar. "Out of curiosity—a very minor curiosity—do you still have your unused ticket for the completion of your New York trip?"

I thought for a moment, trying not to appear at all ill-at-ease. I grabbed my purse from under the bar, fished out the wallet, and triumphantly handed over the ticket.

He read it and handed it back.

"Thank you," he said. "Now. I stopped by to talk to you—or whomever had been hired as the new bartender—to ask a favor."

This time, I let my eyebrows do the heavy lifting.

"There's a good chance the person who poisoned the lime was someone known to Joseph. A bar regular, perhaps. Someone no one would notice coming in, casually hanging around, dropping off a lime."

"Dropping off a lime?"

"The perpetrator had to be someone who was in this bar at some point on Monday. Might have still been here when the incident occurred, or might have been in earlier and left. In either case, it's likely that person will revisit the bar. In fact, I'd put money on it. Keep your eyes and ears open for anything suspicious." He handed me another copy of his card, which was just as well, as I had no idea where the first one had ended up. "People often talk to bartenders more openly than they talk to cops."

"Can't imagine why." Even I was nervous talking to Investigator Spaulding, and I had a personal interest in catching whoever was offing bartenders.

He gave a chuckle. "I can't either. Call me if anything strikes you as strange or suspicious."

"All right, I will," I said, remembering the part of the article that said we'd all sleep better if the murderer was off the street. I knew I would.

"Thanks. And if you see me in here, treat me like any other customer."

"All right. But everyone knows you're a cop."

He sighed. "I'm aware. In the meantime, I'd like to talk to Marta Layton for a few minutes, if you don't mind."

"Marta?"

"Don't look panicked. She was here that day. She saw many of the folks who came and went. We have no reason to suspect her at this time."

"So I don't need to get her a lawyer?"

He laughed. "Not yet."

I'd never known a cop to be quite this jovial. But then, I was moving from Los Angeles to New York City, both places where we were bred to be suspicious.

I went over to Marta. "Investigator Spaulding wants to talk to you about who you saw in the bar the day Joseph died. He already knows about most of them. Do you feel okay about talking to him?"

"Sure. I guess."

"If he starts to ask you anything that makes you feel uncomfortable, call me over. Or say you need to get back to work."

"Okay," she said. "But I really do want to catch the son-of-a-bitch who killed Joseph."

"Me, too," I said. "Me, too."

"Hey, are you open?"

The door to the lobby opened. Brent Davis, the newspaper editor, stuck his head around the corner of the small hall.

"Yes," I said. "Indeed we are."

"We're in luck," he said, and three other people followed him in. "Just anywhere?"

"Anywhere."

"We have patrons," I said to Marta.

"Of course we do," she said. "It's Wednesday night."

"Meaning?"

"For some people, it means church. For others, it means the coast is clear."

I grabbed menus as Marta followed Investigator Spaulding to a booth by the wall.

The group of four chose a table mid-floor, likely their table from Monday. Together, they formed a perfect slice of Americana. Brent Davis was the European-American, in khakis and dark shirt under a slim black sweater. With him, to my surprise, were Avantika Azni, proprietor of the Cardamom Café, wearing an eye-catching red and gold sari, along with the young black woman who'd been here on Monday evening and had been visibly distressed at Joseph's demise. She was the one Suzanne insinuated had stolen Joseph from the "girlfriend" who'd been crying in a booth along the wall.

Completing the foursome was a gentleman of Asian extraction, wearing a designer ecru silk suit I would have expected to see in Beverly Hills rather than in Tranquility. The look was completed by an equally expensive haircut and a killer tie.

"Need menus?"

"Usually, we'd say, just the usual," Brent said, and the others nodded solemnly at the thought that the person to whom they'd say it was gone.

"Fill me in tonight, and from here on out, you can say that," I replied.

"You're taking over for Joseph?"

"Yes. At least for a while."

"Glad to have you," Brent finished. "Everyone, this is Avalon, um—"

"Nash," I responded.

"Nash. You know Avantika from the Cardamom. But I'm not sure you've met Jerry Raker, or Addie Moon. They're in from L.A. to help co-ordinate and market the Tranquility's first-ever film festival."

"It's in August, right?" I asked.

"Yes, around the corner, in planning, that is."

I'd heard of Jerry Raker. He was a big deal in publicity in the indie film world, and his husband was a well-known pro-golfer. But I had no interest in pointing out the fact that I knew who he was or that I, too, was from Los Angeles. It would defeat the purpose of being here.

"I hear you have the films selected?"

"Yes. Jerry and Addie were able to persuade a number of interesting filmmakers to submit their new works."

"Exciting."

"Very," said Addie. She was a striking woman, hair straightened and gently curled, large expressive eyes. She could have been an actress. But there was something else. Something haunted. "We're just sorry about losing Joseph."

"He was helping you?"

"Brilliant fellow," said Jerry.

"So, you're staying on," said Brent. "Looking for a place?"

"Signed a lease this afternoon," I replied.

"Great! Where? If you don't mind my asking."

Small town, everyone will know soon enough, I figured. Plus, I wanted folks to know where to look should I suddenly go missing. "Up Main Street, around the bend," I said. "A place off Cherry Lane called Mill Pond."

With that, I had everyone's complete attention.

"Mill Pond?" said Brent. "The place behind the wheel house… across the bridge?"

"The cottage there," I said. Then, more cautiously, "why?"

Avantika, Addie and Brent turned to look at Jerry. Brent said, "Jerry is an expert in the Golden Age of Hollywood. In fact, he has a new biography coming out of Pepper Porter."

"This is all very fortuitous," Jerry said. "Pull up a chair."

"I'm working," I hesitated, though my collecting tentacles were vibrating like crazy.

"It's only us, and we're happy to wait."

I pulled up a chair and leaned in.

"Everyone knows Pepper Porter did a lot for this town, and lived here, at MacTavish's for the last decades of her life."

I nodded, grateful Philip had filled me in.

"Fewer people know that Sally Allison grew up near here. She also used Tranquility as a respite."

"Salty Sally?" I asked, immediately intrigued.

There's no other way to say it: Sally Allison was a hero of mine. She was a woman who knew her mind and spoke it in days when women were supposed to "know their place." Sally was also a luminous star, in some ways the polar opposite of Pepper Porter, as Sally was known for her legendary sense of humor and her forthright use of language. She made hit comedies and musicals, appearing opposite many of the great leading men of the era. Her name and memory were kept alive not only by her body of work, but by a popular short street near Graumann's Chinese Theater, Salty Sally Alley, named for her after her death. My friends and I frequented Salty Sally's, an old-fashioned ice cream parlor and eatery there, when we were in high school.

"When Sally's contract came up, as a point of negotiation, Big Al—the studio chief—had the studio buy some property and build her a country retreat."

"Mill Pond?" I asked.

"The very same. The Lodge at Mill Pond was once the site of parties like Hollywood hasn't known for decades."

"Really!" This was getting more interesting all the time. "Sally died young, didn't she?"

"Yes, indeed. She was sailing from Maine to Florida one summer when a white squall hit. All but one on board were lost. Terrible tragedy."

"Wasn't she married—?"

"To Clifton Taylor."

"Classic love story."

"Yeah, well..." muttered Jerry.

"Yeah, well?" asked Addie. "Story goes that it was true love."

"Maybe it was," said Jerry. "I just can't imagine anyone loving Cliff Taylor for long. Although maybe Sally really was his soulmate, as the publicity went. More likely she died before it could all go south. Anyhow, legend has it that Mill Pond is guarded by an old Hollywood friend of hers who keeps everything exactly as it was the last time she walked out the door."

"The fellow who guards the entrance is named Fenton," I said.

"Yeah?" said Jerry. "How old is he? If he was a contemporary of hers, he'd be in his…" quick calculation, "seventies by now."

"Entirely possible," I said.

"So, did Salty Sally Allison and prudish Pepper Porter have joint parties? They were big at around the same time, right?"

Jerry chortled. "Wouldn't that have been something? No, they had one of the most famous feuds in Hollywood history. Pepper had a certain sense of decorum. She thought Sally was uncouth. Sally thought Pepper had a stick up her ass."

"What's the story behind Mill Pond?" I asked. "Has it been empty since Sally's death?"

"I believe that an old friend of Sally's lived there for a while, Betsy somebody. Raised a family, even. But that was decades ago. And they probably lived in the guest cottage."

"Seriously? I'm living across from Sally Allison's house? It would make my month. Possibly my year!"

"Well done!" said Jerry, enthusiastically. "When can we visit?"

I laughed. "How about when I feel comfortable with this Fenton fellow? I think if a passel of cars crossed the bridge tomorrow, he'd be livid. Just a hunch."

"We'll walk. Quietly. Coffee? Tomorrow morning?"

"I haven't anything in the house. Barely tea."

"Tea is fine. We'll all have eaten. What time?"

Brent wasn't going to let Jerry steamroll me, and was gauging my reaction. I didn't want to annoy my landlord. On the other hand, Jerry did have a lot of knowledge and a great perspective. I'd love to hear his Sally Allison stories. I think, secretly, I've wished I'd lived in the Golden Age of film. For me, it had a sheen the current Hollywood climate of politics, back-stabbing and broken dreams never had. I never thought I'd get this close to yesteryear. Right place, wrong decade. If only I could reach across.

I sighed. "All right. But it will have to be low key. When is good?"

"When does the crew arrive here? Ten-thirty?" Jerry asked Brent.

"Set up at ten."

"Then how about Mill Pond at nine?"

"Okay," I said. "Tea at nine."

"Terrific!" Jerry's eyes were aglow.

"So no one has lived in the main log cabin since Sally's death?" I asked.

"No one. Legend is, this Fenton fellow keeps it as a shrine."

"Okay. That's spooky."

"The town is spooky," said Addie. "Has spooky stories, anyway."

"The town?" I asked.

"Okay, the inn. This inn."

"We're counting on it," said Avantika, with a smile.

"Yes," said Jerry. "We are."

As they spoke, Glenn MacTavish entered in his tartan and jacket. I jumped to my feet. "Want to order drinks?"

"It's okay," Brent said. "Glenn, we forced her to sit. Turns out she's rented the guest house at Mill Pond."

"Interesting," he replied.

As I headed back to the bar, I took out my phone and Googled images of Sally Allison. I chose a head shot that made me smile. It emphasized her wide almond eyes, a smile that hid secrets she looked willing to share, even the small scar across her left cheek, obtained when she fell from the top of an apple tree she'd climbed as a kid. I made it my wallpaper.

Behind me, I heard Brent talking to Glenn. "I caught Chef Paul earlier. I ran the idea by him of having a special menu for the film festival. I think it's safe to say he's not on board."

"Don't worry about it," replied MacTavish. "It'll be handled."

Behind the bar, I took a breath and started to make drinks for the table. As I did, Addie came over and slid onto a bar stool. "Hi," she said.

"Hi," I answered. "Want to change your order?"

"No, just wanted to say hello."

"Sure." I glanced over to the booth where Marta was talking while the inspector took notes. I took a breath and went for it. "You were here the other night, weren't you? When we found Joseph."

She studied me for a minute, deciding where the question was coming from. It made sense to make Addie's Bay Breeze before starting on Jerry's Rum Runner.

"Yeah," she said, "I was."

I set the tall cranberry drink down in front of her. "Forgive me for asking, but were you seeing Joseph? A couple of women thought you were."

She looked startled. "No, I wasn't. I don't know why anyone would think that."

"You were upset. And Joseph seemed like a smart guy, so it could have been. In any case, I'm sorry."

"He *was* a smart guy. He saw a real future for this town. I know some folks disagreed, but it kills me to think anyone was dangerous— and deranged—enough to do something like this."

"What do you mean, a future for this town?"

"He was very supportive of the film festival, for example."

"And the possible artists' colony?"

"Yes."

"Why do you care what happens in Tranquility? Aren't you from L.A.?" I asked.

"I am. But I work for Jerry, and Jerry loves this town. Wants to help build it up. The whole Pepper Porter connection, and the Sally Allison connection as well. Wants to make it the new Sundance. Or Toronto."

"And some folks want to keep it small."

"And dying. But, anyway, the film festival seems on track. Jerry's happy."

"You work for Jerry?"

"I'm his head publicist."

"Wow. Congrats."

"Thanks."

Usually, I'd follow up with leading questions about how she ended up in her current position, and I was curious. But Addie hadn't come over simply to chat. Something was on her mind.

The air was heavy between us.

"You're Anna Nash's daughter, aren't you?"

Crap. *Crap, crap, crap.*

"Yes," I said. "You know her?"

"Not formally. But there are still few enough out-and-proud female comedians working in mainstream pictures that I follow their careers more closely than others. And we did some marketing for one of her films. Talented woman."

I took a deep breath. "So."

"So."

"I really, really don't want people to know where I am for a while," I said.

"Reason?"

"Let me get to know you a little better before I spill my guts."

"Deal. Does anyone know where you are?"

"Not yet."

"Have you let them know you're all right?"

"Not yet."

"You know they can trace phones and credit cards, things like that."

"I do know. But thanks for the tip. Do you think Jerry knows who I am?"

"He likely could figure it out if he put his mind to it. But I don't think he's put his mind to it. It occurred to me because I've read your name, and it stuck with me. Avalon. I like it. The island where King Arthur found Excalibur. But I won't tell."

"Thanks." I took a breath, and headed over with the drinks.

On and off through the evening, I thought about Addie, and what they say about a secret: if one person knows, it ceases to be a secret.

The festival crew stayed for a few hours, talking animatedly. Tourists came in, and a few town regulars. All in all, a fairly easy first night.

I closed up at 10:30, and walked out into the chilly April darkness. I crossed the street to the train station. Two men, not travelling together, waited for the 11 o'clock train to Montreal.

I walked over to the platform and stood with them. It wasn't long before the headlamp of the engine swept around the bend.

I turned on my phone and went to text messages. *I am fine. I need some time. Please don't look for me. I'll contact you when I'm ready. I'm doing well. Decided to go in a different direction.*

The train stopped. Both men got onto the second car; I chose the third. There were a good number of empty seats. I slid into the window seat in an empty row. There was a *New York Times* on the middle cushion. I picked it up.

"This is the Zephyr to Canada. Next stop, Plattsburgh, then Montreal. Passports will be required."

I pressed the send button on my phone.

The doors had made their first chime when I stood, raced back, slid through the closing silver doors and landed, winded, on the platform.

No one seemed to have noticed.

The train pulled away from the antique street lights that bowed over the station platform. I waved good-bye to the passengers, and to my phone, nestled between two seat cushions, under the *Times*.

The night was suddenly still. I felt safe walking home.

My pace quickened as I neared Mill Pond. Now that I knew the history of the place, I wondered what had become of Sally Allison's friend Betsy, who had raised a family here. I'd love to talk with her, to find out how she'd known Sally. I'd love to collect any stories she may have.

Was it Betsy who'd instructed Mr. Fenton to rent out my house? I tried to remember what he'd said. He'd been out of town for two days—which, if true, took him out of the running for Joseph's murderer—and got the message to rent out the place upon his return this morning. Was the message from Betsy, or from a local real estate agent? Did Betsy usually live here but decided to spend a few months in Saratoga? It didn't seem likely. If she was a recent occupant, wouldn't there be catsup in the fridge, or coffee in the cupboard? Something to show someone besides a maid had been there in the last few years?

It sure seemed like was only me and Fenton and the ghosts of Hollywood past.

It was beyond dark when I headed past Mr. Fenton's take-out window and back towards my cottage. I had planned on using the flashlight on my phone to illuminate the path. I added buying a burner phone to my mental to-do list.

The moon was half full, and enough light filtered through the tree-lined lane that I could navigate.

I made it safely across my little bridge, into the house, where I turned on a light, kicking off my shoes. As I turned back to lock the front door behind me, I glanced across the pond to the lodge, which I now knew to be the site of many a Hollywood hullabaloo. I tried to imagine what it would have looked like in those days, with car after car pulling up. I was sure someone would play the ukulele. Or the banjo.

And then I froze. I could swear I saw a shadow moving inside the house.

I waited a moment, staring, but saw nothing else.

A town of spooky stories.

Indeed.

The Late Train

Ingredients

1 ounce vanilla vodka or regular unflavored vodka (vanilla vodka brings the sweetness and the sense of comfort and warmth of a strawberry rhubarb pie)
1/2 ounce orange liquor
2 ounces fresh strawberry puree
1 ounce fresh made rhubarb simple syrup or rhubarb shrub

Method

Mix and shake all ingredients together creating a frothy consistency and serve in a rocks glass. Finish with fresh cut strawberries and an orange twist.

Fresh Strawberry Puree:
Remove stems from strawberries and dice into small pieces and blend in food processor until you have a silky smooth consistency.

Rhubarb Simple Syrup:
Bring equal part of sugar and water to boil. Add cleaned and chopped rhubarb to boiling and then lower temperature on stove top to a simmer let simmer until you have a nice nape. Let mixture cool and strain with cheese cloth and pour into desired storage container.

7

Suite Seven

I awoke after a night of jarring but unremembered dreams, dedicated to the idea of confronting MacTavish to find out about the other dead bartender.

It was early, and I had to spend this crazy energy in a positive way before hosting the morning tea. Marta mentioned one of the places Joseph frequented was the Golden Ticket gym, on the lower floors of the Golden Sunrise Hotel. It was 7 a.m., the sun was up, and I decided to check it out.

The hotel was on the northern end of the pond, close to my place. The Golden Ticket gym was built on two floors, each with walls of windows overlooking the budding trees surrounding Fretful Pond. The space was scented with the air of sweat and intention, and lined with workout machines of every description. It was bustling with before-work users. They offered a one-week free trial, and I signed up.

"Hey, Avalon, see you in a few," said Brent Davis, finishing up on a stationary bike, and heading for the men's dressing room.

I chose an elliptical and set up a book I'd brought along. The young woman on the machine next to me looked familiar. She seemed European-American with a copper undertone that undoubtedly helped her tan. Her black hair was in a workout ponytail, black fitted short sleeved workout shirt over running tights. It was clear from her toned physique that she worked out often. But most interesting was the book she had propped open on the machine's book deck: *Anne of Windy Poplars*, the fourth in the *Anne of Green Gables* series. Also of note were the fantastic nerdy socks she wore on which dragons toasted sticks of marshmallows with their breath.

My biological father sent me the Anne series in the years before I'd understood the term "biological father." My grandmother next to me on the bed, smelling of tea and nutmeg, reading them to me at bedtime, was one of the outstanding memories of my childhood.

I opened my e-reader and flipped to *Anne of Windy Poplars*, turning the tablet towards my neighbor briefly, letting her see the book cover, and proceeded to climb onto the next elliptical. She smiled and paused, removing her earbuds. "Hannah," she said, "Race that Knows Joseph."

"Avalon," I countered. "Nice to meet you."

The Race that Knows Joseph is code, in Anne-speak, for people who are kindred spirits: kind and creative and recognize each other at hello. We smiled at each other, members of an anachronistic but ongoing secret order. "You just join the gym?" she asked.

"Yeah," I said. "New in town."

"Great. We need more folks who know Joseph."

I had the feeling Hannah and I could be hangout buddies. "Come here often?" I asked, then laughed. "I mean, it seems like a good gym."

"Yup," she said. "Almost every day. Clears my head."

"I'm here for the head-clearing, myself," I said.

I was taken by the thought of a friend who wasn't also a suspect. Someone who Knows Joseph—but not necessarily the dead Joseph. That was a different tribe.

Hannah finished her workout before I did, took a long drink from her metal water bottle, and threw her towel around her neck. "See you around, I hope," she said. Then, "Oh, hi, Phillip."

I turned to see to whom she spoke. Walking past her was hotel-painter Phillip, not in his coveralls but in gym pants. And that's all. No shirt, not even a towel around his neck. And, boy, was he muscled. I tried to guess his ethnicity, and landed on—"no clue". Gingerbread. Sculpted. Smiling.

Then I wondered why people often describe darker skin tones in terms relating to coffee or cooking. I didn't know how to describe mine. It wasn't peach or rose or even tan. As a point of interest, I do have the exact skin tone as Greta Garbo. A cinematographer once informed me that his incident light meter was set off Ms. Garbo's skin tone, and claimed I was the first person he'd met for whom no adjustment was needed. I can more successfully describe my hair. The same way Eskimos are said to have fifty words for snow, the Swedes have as many for blonde. Or perhaps that's L'Oreal. I find it personally satisfying to use spice colors in my descriptions. For my own hair, I've settled on yarrow with turmeric undertones.

In any case, Philip saw me and waved. I scrambled to get back into the rhythm of the machine. I didn't know why I was so thrown off by normal people. I guess for too long, I'd been bouncing around between L.A. and death.

By 8:45, I was showered, dressed and headed home. I spotted Mr. Fenton as I approached his abode. He was watching me through the window as he washed his dishes, jacket off, shirtsleeves rolled up, suspenders in place of a vest. The house was so thin that virtually every window was ripe for observing. My own personal Gatekeeper. Joy.

Within moments, Brent, Addie, and Jerry arrived together, jaunting up the sidewalk at nine on the dot. Okay, Jerry was jaunting, the other two were keeping up. I fell in with them and kept up the pace, our greetings fleeting and sideways, so I could move them past the Gatekeeper without incident.

Once down the lane and past the turn to the clearing, I stopped.

"Sorry," I said. "Didn't want to have to chat with Mr. Fenton."

"Got it," said Brent.

"Nice morning," said Addie.

"Holy shit," said Jerry.

He had stepped into the clearing. The pond, the waterfall, the trellised cottage, and the log lodge—I saw them anew with Jerry's eyes. Many would call it a storybook glen, but to Jerry it was a time vortex back to the Golden Age of Hollywood, the entire place set-designed. Cue the bluebirds.

"Mama, I'm home," he whispered, in a voice laced with awe.

"My place." I pointed, and we headed up the hill. At the top of the rise, without warning or hesitation, Jerry did an about-face and took off for the lodge.

I launched after him.

By the time I reached the lawn, Jerry had ascended the tall stairs to the screened-in front porch. To my horror, he opened the door and walked right in. "This place is all that and an Oscar!" he said over his shoulder. "Even the porch furniture is fabulous!" Then he walked up and tugged on the front door. Thank goodness it was locked.

This did not stop him from walking window to window, cupping his hand to block outside light and peering inside. "Sally," he whispered. "Sally Allison."

I grabbed his elbow, dragging him through the porch as big as a great room, and down the wooden stairs.

"Are you trying to get me kicked out?" I spat. "I just moved in!"

"Sorry. Not sorry," he muttered, but in a Technicolor voice dipped in wonder.

He was still in a trance as I moved them through my little cottage and out onto the back terrace, still half expecting Mr. Fenton to come barreling, tearing my lease to shreds.

The morning was quiet except for a busy pair of chickadees.

I got them settled, then went inside and plugged in the teapot.

Back outside, with cups of steaming tea before us on the white wicker table, surrounded with convivial company, I let myself relax. The pixie dust that was the first harbinger of spring wound through the air, the same feeling I'd gotten when going outside in Southern California in February or March. The unexpected warmth, the giggle of nature.

"I can't believe I'm sitting here," said Jerry. He had his phone open. He was sketching Sally's lodge with a stylus.

"When does your biography of Pepper Porter come out?" I asked.

"The films of Pepper Porter will be the centerpiece of the film festival. The book officially comes out in September, but my publisher is making early copies available."

"Perfect synergy," said Addie.

"And what's up with Suite Seven at MacTavish's?"

The three of them exchanged glances that seemed slightly hesitant.

"Since Pepper lived at MacTavish's..." Addie started.

"The idea was to make a new documentary about Pepper Porter, to premiere at the festival, and tie the book and the town together. Brent has worked with PBS on a national level before, and they are funding the shooting of the film."

"But even I have to admit there just isn't enough to warrant a new documentary," Brent said. "No new angles, and everyone of interest to Pepper's story is dead. But before we give up—and the minutes are ticking—"

"Since everyone of interest, including Pepper, is dead...our last-ditch effort is to go in that direction!" said Jerry with a laugh. "There's been so much talk over the years about Pepper's suite, we've convinced the Ghost Seekers, from the television show of the same name, to shoot an episode there," said Jerry.

"Our best chance of getting a quote from Pepper," said Addie.

I couldn't tell how tongue-in-cheek the remark was.

"Our last hope," said Brent. "In fact, we should get going to meet the set-up crew."

"I'll head over with you," I said. "I need to talk to Mr. MacTavish."

We dropped off the teacups in the kitchen and headed out together into the April day.

Two black SUVs and one white rental truck filled with camera equipment were parked curbside at MacTavish's Seaside Cottage when we arrived.

I left my companions and stepped into the lobby, scanning for my employer. "You. You!" the words were loud, pointed and accusatory. It took a moment to realize they were hurled at me—from Chef Paul—bearing down on me with the ferocity of an injured bull.

I purposely affected a friendly, lackadaisical air. "Oh, hi! How can I help?"

"The fucking chargers!" He skidded to a stop inches from my face.

"Phone... chargers?"

"The gold chargers. Wine and gold-colored chargers! You have them."

I raised my hands in a "search me" gesture, as I was obviously charger-free.

"They're in your storeroom. I need them yesterday!"

"I'm sure neither Marta nor I would have spirited away your chargers."

"It was that idiot Emberg," he snarled through gritted teeth.

"May he rest in peace," I said, and stood a moment, looking at the ground. He could do nothing but wait. With fumes pouring out his ears. "Okay. Your chargers are in the bar storeroom. The problem?"

"Your fucking keys!" he snarled, as if I was purposely toying with him. Which I would have been more than happy to do if he wasn't doing the job so efficiently by himself.

So I had the only key to the pub's storeroom. Good to know. Together Chef Paul and I went through the Breezy's kitchen, and into the darkened pub. I led him through the back hall, pulled out my keys, and opened the door. The storeroom was a large room with three long rows of metal shelving units freestanding and others, including wine racks, fastened to the walls around the outside. I'd take a full inventory as soon as I had the time.

I left Chef Paul banging his way around looking for his chargers and headed back to the concierge, Dale, in the lobby. "Mr. MacTavish?" I asked.

"He went up to Suite Seven," Dale said, then in a low voice, "that's where they're going to film!"

I did my best to look surprised at the news, then headed back that way.

This time, I gave a little nod to Pepper Porter's portrait as I passed.

Suite Seven was off the main corridor at the end of its own in a short hallway, with thick, plush carpeting. The heavy wooden door was shut but not locked. I opened the door and called, "Mr. MacTavish?"

No response. But the lights were on, so I ventured into the small entrance hall, which, in turn, emptied into an expansive living room with a wall of windows overlooking Lake Serenity. Outside, a balcony with marble balustrades ran the length of the wall, a table with two chairs set for tea inviting the visitor outside.

One of the windows was open and a sheer curtain danced softly with the breeze.

It was then that I caught a smell: Sulphur? Curiosity drew me farther in. Beyond the sofas and chairs and small dining table was the bedroom hallway. The smell seemed to be coming from the larger of the two bedrooms. Now I spotted smoke as well.

I ran down the small hall and into the suite's master bedroom. It boasted immense curved windows overlooking the lake and surrounding mountains. No wonder a Hollywood star would retire here.

The smoke enveloping the room was white-gray, curling and rising and thickening. Where was it coming from?

Then, on the other side of a coffee table, I saw a heap in the middle of the floor—magazines and newspapers and even wood on top. The room smelled of lighter fluid, the kind you poured on charcoal.

It was recently lit, the magazines on the bottom sputtering and sparking, sending flames exploring the tinder above.

I heard a rustling. Someone was here.

"Mr. MacTavish?" I asked.

No answer.

What to do? I saw a hotel phone on the nightstand and ran for it.

I didn't make it. As I rushed around the side of the king-sized bed, I tripped. Over Glenn MacTavish.

He was sprawled on the floor, a pillowcase tied over his head, blood pooling on the floor beneath his abdomen, where he'd been shot.

I took a step back.

And then, a rustling of curtains. But before I could turn around, there was a strange, sickening feeling from my neck down my side, like a long band of hot molten silver.

And then there was nothing but blackness.

Suite Seven

Ingredients

1 1/2 ounces white tequila
1/2 ounce orange liquor
2 ounce fresh blood orange juice
Juice of 1/2 fresh squeezed lime
Dried sage (for rimming)

Method

Dip rocks glass in fresh lime juice and dip into a sugar and dried sage mixture

Shake all ingredients, creating a nice frothy texture and pour in rocks glass over ice.

This cocktail can be made fresh over the winter months as blood oranges are in season at this time. You can also buy blood orange juice in some gourmet grocery stores.

8

Bloody Handprint

I awoke. Disoriented, slightly nauseous.

Fire crackling. Otherwise, silence. Was my assailant still here?

I lay still and the room continued to be quiet. Smoke filled the air between the dresser and the ceiling. It settled farther and farther down, closing in on the last layer of oxygen above the floor. Just past my head, lay Glenn MacTavish, still bleeding.

I had to get up. Somehow.

I pushed myself onto my hands and knees. Still dizzy and somewhat sick, I crawled over to Glenn and forcefully pulled the rope free. It hadn't been knotted, just twisted enough around his neck to keep him from breathing while someone cinched it.

I finally wrenched it free and pulled the pillowcase off over his head.

He was breathing.

Apparently, I had surprised the assailant before the deed was finished.

But who would asphyxiate and shoot Glenn MacTavish?

I had to get us both out of the fire. I tried to grab him under his arms, but he was too heavy for me to move.

I pulled myself over Glenn and reached for the phone. I hit 0 and counted the seconds until the operator answered. "Suite Seven," I said, "There's a fire. And Mr. MacTavish has been shot. Get help!"

Not willing to simply wait and let Glenn be overcome by smoke, I stood and lurched from the room. One of the tall windows in the living room was now fully open. I could only assume the perpetrator had fled through it.

In the hallway, I called, "Help! Someone help! Fire! Fire!"

No one was in the private corridor, or, indeed, the wider one heading back toward the lobby. I staggered forward, using a hand against the wall to keep my balance.

"Help," I said.

Then Philip was there, not yet in painter's coveralls, and not with Whistle. Just Philip.

"Help," I said.

"Holy Christ," he said.

I looked down and realized I was covered in blood.

Philip ran towards me.

"There's a fire. And Glenn MacTavish has been shot!"

"What? Where?"

"Suite Seven. Hurry. Please."

He helped me sit down and knelt beside me. His t-shirt and jeans were now covered with crimson. "Are you all right?" he asked.

"Yes," I said. "Go help Mr. MacTavish!"

"Stay," he commanded, as if I was Whistle.

I did not stay. I sat for a moment then got up and headed back for the suite.

Philip was in the bedroom.

Glenn was groaning.

As I came to crouch over him, he opened his eyes.

"Thank God," I said. "Thank God."

"Should we drag him out of here?" I asked. The smoke was making it impossible to see, and painful to speak.

Before he could answer, the sound of heavy footfalls approached from the living room. Firefighters had beat the ambulance, but only by moments. We turned Glenn over to them, and Philip and I staggered back out into the hall.

Once free of the fire, my legs buckled and I slid down the wall. "What happened?" I asked. "Who shot Glenn? Who knocked me out? How did someone knock me out?"

Philip put an arm around me and I pulled in oxygen. Within minutes, Glenn—and I—were being wheeled down the hallway. He was strapped onto a long stretcher. Paramedics had forced me onto one that sat up. The fact that the blood I was covered with wasn't mine didn't go far with them after I admitted I'd been temporarily rendered unconscious. "Observation," they said. "Smoke inhalation."

Two officers walked along with us. "Anyone we can call?" They asked Glenn. The younger one asked. "Family, or a pastor?"

Glenn, who still seemed fairly out of it, murmured, "Reverend Bricksford."

Then we hit the lobby and seemingly joined the cast of a Fellini film.

The crew from Ghost Seekers was there with all their equipment, confused at being kept from their destination. Brent, Jerry, and Addie were arguing with the officers who weren't allowing people into the hallways.

Investigator Spaulding strode through the midst of this. He did the human version of screeching to a halt in front of me. "You again?" he said.

Not the most reassuring words ever.

The paramedics were intent on wheeling me through. I argued that I was not injured and did not need to be put into the waiting ambulance when Chef Paul came charging across the lobby at a speed that made our earlier encounter seem downright leisurely.

"How could you?" he bellowed in a voice that echoed off the lobby walls.

Startled, Investigator Spaulding body-blocked the portly chef as he launched himself towards MacTavish. Spaulding nodded to the ambulance attendants, who rushed us out.

As we left the lobby, I looked back to see Chef Paul waving a large, professionally manufactured sign that read, "Pepper's" in blue letters with marquee light bulbs inside.

There was only one ambulance. Obviously, Glenn outranked me in terms of triage, and they loaded him in first.

A female paramedic undid the belts over me, and a man already aboard helped me step up into the back of the ambulance. They got me settled on a side seat and shut the doors. As they did, I saw Investigator Spaulding leaving through the lobby doors and getting into his unmarked car.

We took off.

They'd been able to staunch Glenn's bleeding. He was hooked up to several poles, with what I assumed were saline and blood running back into his veins. His dark hair, usually thick and wavy, was plastered to his head with sweat. They'd given him something for pain, but he was still awake.

As the paramedics called in all their information, I heard the word, "stabilized", which was a freaking relief.

I leaned in close to him. "In much pain?" I asked.

He shook his head.

"Do you have any idea who…?"

Again, he shook his head.

"Did he shoot you first? Or…the head thing?" I was getting right to the point, but I knew I didn't have much time. Once we were back at the hospital—or even once the paramedics returned, the frank conversation would cease.

"Shot me, and when that didn't knock me out, he put the pillowcase over my head from behind and wrapped the rope around it. Did you see him? How did he get away?" he asked.

"I didn't see him. Didn't know he was still there. There was some pain on my neck, and I passed out. I don't think I was out long, just long enough for him to escape."

"Thanks for getting help," he said.

"This is scary," I said. "I've got to know: who was the other bartender who died?"

"Oskar Ahlström. Killed the same day Pepper died."

"Oh. So it was a while ago."

"Nearly twenty years."

"How was he killed? Not poison, I hope?"

"He was shot. Nearly point blank. Was dead for a couple of hours before anyone found him."

"Do you have any idea what's going on now? Or who's behind this?"

He shook his head.

One of the paramedics came back and scanned the machine that gave Mr. MacTavish's vitals. He took the info back to his partner.

"Why would someone be after you? Is anyone mad at the MacTavishes?"

"Maybe not after MacTavishes…maybe I just walked in and surprised him."

We were nearing the hospital. Of all the questions I wanted to ask, what came out was: "What was Chef Paul on about?"

"Need new restaurant. So much about… Pepper Porter… Joseph… new chef, new menu, new décor… call it Pepper's… Ready for film fest… film f…"

"Joseph? What did Joseph have to do with it?"

No answer. His concentration was nearly gone.

"Was Chef Paul in on it?"

"He…suspected…"

The drugs were really kicking in, and I knew it. Didn't stop me. "That's nothing to feel guilty about. You're trying to keep the MacTavish tradition going."

His eyelids were closing. His next words were a whisper. "I'm not really.."

Too tempting. And I was already working off of an adrenaline rush.

"Not really what?"

"A MacTavish," he finished. "My parents couldn't…I'm adopted…but I'm trying…"

It occurred to me it could be a fire-able offense to pump one's boss for information when he was in Space Cadet City. But I wasn't a master collector for nothing. And hell, we'd both been attacked by some crazy person.

The ambulance turned a fast corner, and Glenn MacTavish gave a groan, then completely passed out.

The hospital came into view.

Two things came to me then, clear as day.

1. I have no insurance.
2. Ambulance rides are very expensive.

The vehicle stopped. The back doors swung open.

I hopped down and out of the way as the stretcher was removed. Then I turned to slip away around the side of the ambulance.

"Miss! Miss!" cried the male paramedic.

"I was only comforting Glenn. I'm fine."

Two nurses joined him, and they all stood, looking at me. I glanced down.

"Oh. This isn't my blood."

"But you were rendered unconscious at the scene. There may have been smoke inhalation. We need to check you out."

"No, thank you. I'm fine. No smoke inhalation. Just riding with Glenn."

Investigator Spaulding spoke from behind me. "I believe she is refusing treatment."

Apparently, those were the magic words.

They looked at him. He had his badge out, for emphasis.

They looked at me again, then turned and followed Glenn's stretcher into the emergency room.

"Are you really all right?" the detective asked.

"Yeah. I am."

"Great. Let's talk."

We followed a few paces behind the stretcher through the emergency room entrance. Investigator Spaulding stopped and conferred with the doctor who had Glenn's chart.

"Reverend Bricksford is here," said a nurse. I remembered Glenn had asked for his pastor. He was surprising me a lot today.

The door opened, and the Reverend Bricksford came swinging through. My mind zipped through connections, but it was the white collar that took me back to Monday, the day Joseph died, when the Chamber of Commerce members all came in to the bar to eat. Reverend Bricksford had been with them. Wearing a skirt and panty hose.

But my brain kept computing. Even with her hair pulled back and a serious expression on her face, I saw that it was Hannah.

Elliptical using, Joseph-Knowing, Hannah.

Hannah was a pastor? Damn. One new hope of the day snuffed out.

Then Hannah Bricksford saw me. Her first response was a smile of recognition. Her second was of horror.

The shirt again.

I left abruptly, turning a corner and running full into a nurse carrying a tray of medication. I was able to stop and steady the tray before everything went flying. The nurse glared at me, regained her composure, and continued on her way.

I leaned back against the wall to stay out of the way and catch my breath.

That's where Investigator Mike Spaulding found me. He stopped.

He said nothing. I sniffled.

Instead, he reached into a shirt pocket under his brown sweater and handed me a clean linen handkerchief.

"Come on," he said.

He took me to a conference room. It was rectangular, perhaps twenty by twelve. One wall had long windows, the shades down. There was a red sofa and two yellowish chairs against the windowed wall, and a white table in the middle. He turned on the lights. Then he picked up his walkie-talkie and called for an Officer Shelton to come in.

"How is he? Mr. MacTavish, I mean," I said.

"They say he's in serious condition, but they're hopeful. They'll know more after surgery, of course. So…"

Officer Shelton rapped on the door.

"Ms. Nash, we need your fingerprints, to rule out your prints from the perp's in the bedroom of Suite Seven," he said. "Is that all right with you?"

"As long as they're destroyed, and not put on file," I said. I'd never been arrested, but I had close friends in a demographic that found it useful to know the ropes.

"Agreed."

Officer Shelton had the fingerprint kit, and she was the one to use it. She was fast. Afterwards, she gave me a square package containing a lemon-scented finger wash to remove as much of the ink as possible.

"Get these to Roger right away. Oh, but Miranda," he said. "Then can you do me a favor?"

She stopped. He held out two twenty dollar bills.

"As soon as you've handed off the prints, can you go to the hospital gift shop? I seem to remember that they have t-shirts. Everyone will feel much better when Ms. Nash is a bit cleaned up."

She nodded and left.

It didn't escape me how he'd used his own money to buy me a clean shirt. Admittedly my take on police culture was a bit skewed, having family of various ethnicities in Los Angeles and New York City, two mega-cities. We were always careful to say we supported individual police officers—just not the culture which sometimes ran amuck with a sense of illegal entitlement.

But here I sat with a highway patrol investigator, a black man, being kind to me and not making a big deal of it. I wondered what the culture was within the local barracks—and how he navigated it.

"So," he said. He sat down at the table in the spot next to me. "Please tell me what happened."

"I was looking for Mr. MacTavish. The concierge told me he'd gone to Suite Seven, so I went over. The door was slightly open and the lights were on, but I knew they were going to be filming there, so I didn't think anything of it."

"Filming?" He was taking notes.

"You know. The ghost people."

He looked at me for further explanation, but I had none. I shrugged.

"All right. The door's open and you…"

"I went in. I'd never been in Suite Seven before, so after I called for Mr. MacTavish and got no reply, I looked around. The living room, the kitchen. Then I smelled something—the lighter fluid, I guess. And I saw smoke."

"So you…?"

"I followed it down the hallway to the bedroom, where I saw the pile of magazines and newspapers set on fire. I went to pick up the telephone by the bed to call for help when I…"

"When you found Glenn MacTavish?"

"Tripped over him, actually," I said.

He stopped writing and looked at me. "This is important, Avalon. I need for to you describe exactly how Glenn MacTavish was when you found him."

I'd kept it together pretty well until then. But there was something just… horrific… about what I'd seen.

"He was lying face down on the floor with blood beneath his abdomen. There was a pillowcase over his head and a rope on top of the pillowcase around his neck. I think I surprised someone who was in the middle of choking him." I had to stop and remind myself to breathe. "Glenn told me someone shot him, but when that didn't kill him, or even knock him out, the assailant put the pillowcase over his head and used the rope to cut off his air."

"When did Glenn tell you this?"

"In the ambulance."

"What else did he tell you?"

"That he never saw his attacker."

"Okay. Back at the scene. What happened next?"

"I undid the rope and started to get the pillowcase off his head when I felt something really weird on the side of my neck. It was like… I don't know how to describe it… it went all the way down my side, like, somehow, inside my body. I blacked out."

"Did you feel someone actually touch you with something—either a weapon or a hand?"

"Maybe so. It was very odd."

What kind of maniac would shoot Glenn? And at point blank

range? Although that phrase resonated. In the ambulance, Glenn had told me that Oskar, the other bartender, had been shot at point blank range, nearly twenty years earlier—with a less happy outcome.

And who would knock me out—someone they didn't even know? I put my hand to the area to feel for any kind of puncture, but there was nothing.

"Do you mind?" Investigator Spaulding stood and walked behind me, gently sweeping my hair to the side. "Here?" he asked, exerting pressure with his thumb, at the exact place where I was still sore.

"Yes. That's it. Exactly."

"When I saw the slight bruising, I suspected," he said. "There's a way to make a person lose consciousness and collapse quickly. It's a way to interrupt blood to the stem of the brain. It isn't safe, if you don't know what you're doing—or if your victim is standing. Because of that, the technique isn't taught much anymore. It was more widely used by military police in the past. But it only knocks someone out momentarily—allowing an advantage, or an escape. Which seems to be what happened, in your case."

"Great. So what do you think? Did someone lure Glenn up there to shoot him? Or did Mr. MacTavish and I interrupt someone intent on setting a fire? And why would someone set a fire in Suite Seven? To stop the Ghost Seekers?" I was thinking as I spoke.

Spaulding took over. "Any ideas why someone would want to keep the Ghost Seekers from filming there?"

"Hmm. Well, they don't only film, they try to communicate with the ghost—in this case, with the ghost of Pepper Porter. Could someone want to keep them from talking with her?"

Mike Spaulding leaned back. "Are you messing with me?"

It sounded far-fetched, even to me. "Or... someone wanted to keep the Ghost Seekers from filming... because it would bring attention to the hotel? Or because it would bring the wrong kind of attention?"

"You said Glenn MacTavish was on board with it."

"Yes, he's even going to close the Breezy and bring in a new chef to re-do the restaurant into an upscale bistro called Pepper's, to take advantage of the connection."

"Okay. Back to the scene. You woke up…"

"I woke up and got to the phone and called for help. I made sure Glenn was still breathing, then I ran into the hall to try to find someone. Oh—one of the long windows to the balcony was open. I assume that's how the assailant left."

"And what happened in the hallway?"

"No one was there, at first. I guess they were all in the lobby helping the Ghost Seekers unload their equipment. I called for help, and when I got to the larger hall, Philip Young was there. He came back with me to see if we could help Glenn."

"Do you know why Philip was there?"

"He works at the hotel. He paints the rooms."

"Was he there working?"

I thought back. He hadn't had his painter's coveralls on. Just jeans and a shirt. And, come to think of it, Whistle hadn't been anywhere around.

"I assume so. I was so relieved to find him. To find anybody," I said.

"Did it occur to you that he appeared…a little too fast?"

"You mean, like, he climbed out the window, ran fully around the back wing of the hotel, in through the front door, up through all the halls, and then found me?"

I tried to make it seem as outlandish as it sounded to me.

"Or someone opened the window to make us think he went that way."

"I would assume that whoever did that to Glenn couldn't get out without some blood spatter?" I said, sitting there, Exhibit A. "And… I assume the hotel has cameras?"

"Asking," he said. "Just asking. And while we're chatting, here's another question. What do you know about Joseph?"

This caught me off guard.

"I knew him for half an hour," I said.

"Since then," he said. "Certainly you've heard people talking."

"Not much," I protested. "I got to town on Monday. It's Thursday."

"Nothing? Nothing about if he was seeing anybody, or… who might have cause to be angry with him?"

"On that first night, it was intimated to me that he had been seeing someone named Sophie, but…" Wait. No reason to implicate Addie in this. She'd said she wasn't seeing Joseph, anyway. "But it was implied he and Sophie weren't really together. And…as to who might have something against him? I have heard that Chef Paul isn't the most inventive chef ever, and that Joseph had a hand in deciding to close the Breezy. Glenn wanted someone new by the time of the film festival. Apparently, Joseph agreed. And…"

I felt bad giving information that made anyone seem suspicious. Still, dozens of people had seen Chef Paul screaming through the lobby. He wasn't exactly a slow burner.

"So Paul knew?"

"He suspected. And, this morning, he found the new sign for Pepper's in the bar's storeroom. He was running after us, waving it when the ambulance came."

"Seems odd to be quite so open about it if he'd murdered Joseph."

"But if he murdered Joseph, and Glenn was still going ahead with the plan anyway…"

"Anybody else mad at Glenn?"

"That's all I've heard. I mean, I've only been here three days, but I already know that half the town wants to build a new artists' colony, and the other half doesn't. Still, it doesn't seem reason for murder."

I hoped Spaulding felt like I was giving him what information I had. I was. Almost.

There was a knock on the door and Officer Shelton entered carrying a paper bag, which she held out to me. I opened it to find a pink t-shirt that said, "Lake Serenity," with three butterflies.

"Thanks," I said. "Nothing with skiers?"

She shook her head. "I guess they figure if you're at the hospital, you might be done with skiing."

Investigator Spaulding nodded at a door which led to a small bathroom. Inside, I pulled the bloody shirt up over my head, and replaced it with the butterflies. I didn't dare look at myself. I scoured my hands under the sink's faucet, and returned as quickly as I could to the room.

"Question," said Mike Spaulding. "May we have your shirt?"

I had no plans but to get rid of it as soon as possible.

"To make sure the only blood on it is Glenn's."

I didn't want to be any more upset than I already was, and decided to clear the air.

"Am I suspected of anything?"

It surprised me how much his look softened. "No," he said, quietly. "No, you're not, except of being in the wrong place at the wrong time. You've gotten an erroneous view of what this town is like."

And then I was looking into Mike's—Investigator Spaulding's—eyes, and it hit me, like a runaway semi tractor-trailer on the downside of a hill. He was a Collector. I'd just been collected.

Of course, his reasons were much different. But that's basically what an investigator does—collects stories and figures out how they fit together. Who's telling the truth and who's covering? Who's obscuring the facts and who else is seeking to uncover them? Who is telling partial stories?

The answer to that last question: basically everyone.

Including me.

"Well," I said, recovering. "If the local police detective thinks it's a nice town, I guess it must be."

"Not perfect," he said. "By a long stretch."

I offered the bloody shirt. He opened a plastic bag and I dropped it in.

"There is one other thing," I said.

"Yes?"

"The magazines and newspapers that were burning to start the fire. They looked like old movie magazines, from Pepper Porter's time, maybe? You might take a look at those that didn't burn."

"Interesting." Spaulding gathered up his things. "Oh," he said, his tone once again clipped and professional. "After the incident this morning, I tried to call you. No luck. Do you have your phone turned off?"

"Um," I said. "Battery's dead. Might have to get a new phone."

"I'd appreciate it if you kept your phone working. Tell me if you wind up with a new number. And make sure you have a working phone sooner rather than later."

As we left the room together, he added, "Nice town. But people are turning up dead."

Bloody Handprint

Ingredients

1-1/2 ounces of white tequila
1/2 ounces of orange liquor
1/4 of a fresh squeezed lemon
1/4 of a fresh squeezed lime
2 ounces of fresh beet juice puree

Method

Finish cocktail glass with salt and pepper rim.

Shake all ingredients together and pour over ice in a cocktail glass

Beet Puree: Roast 5 medium beets. After roasting, put beets onto a cooling rack and let sit until beets are warm. While beets are still warm remove the rough outer skin of the beets (rubber kitchen gloves are highly recommended for this process as the beets will stain your skin a dark magenta color.) Put beets in a kitchen blender and puree until you have a nice velvety smooth nape. This should be plenty of beet juice puree for about 6 margaritas.

Please note, and perhaps warn drinkers that this cocktail is made with beets which can stain skin and clothing.

9

Midnight Caller

I am no fan of hospitals, as they've held only bad news for me. I successfully slid through this one and out into the now cloudy April day before I realized I had no idea where I was or how to get back to town.

I sighed and went in search of Investigator Spaulding. A nurse pointed me to a small waiting room where I found the detective in the midst of a whispered conversation with Mayor Arthur Bristow. At least, Art Bristow was whispering—hissing, really—and Investigator Spaulding was taking it in.

The mayor barely glanced at me—obviously a person of no importance—and continued his harangue. "Don't you see? She was there. She had motive and opportunity. Isn't that what you're looking for?"

"I do see the opportunity," Spaulding said. "It's the motive I'm having trouble with. You're going to have to help me out."

"Drugs. Drugs make you do crazy things."

"You're saying Marta Layton is on drugs?"

"Look what she did to Polly! Last time you and I met in this hospital, my daughter nearly died! And who even knows what Marta's sexual orientation is? Or, you know, people who have that Goth look, they're into all kinds of crazy things!"

"I'm sorry, what are you citing as her motive to kill Joseph?"

"Instability!" he yelled. "And you!" he wheeled to look at me. "How can you keep her working there? Let her go at once! Fire her!"

Before I could reply, the hall door opened and the Reverend Layton swung in. Marta's father.

"I came as soon as I heard," he said. "Another tragedy! I can't believe it."

The mayor stepped away, became immediately sober and controlled, and said, "Yes, yes. What is our town coming to?"

Investigator Spaulding turned to me, a bit of residual annoyance on his face. "Yes, Avalon?" he asked, his tone again even. It was the first time he'd called me by my first name.

"Where are we? How's Mr. MacTavish? And what's the best way back to town from here?"

He took a quick look at the two men. Then he said, "Glenn MacTavish is just out of surgery. It went well, he'll make a full recovery. But he won't be able to talk for at least an hour. Or two. Let me run you back to town."

"You don't have to…"

He rolled his eyes at the conversation behind him and said, "I need to check in back at the crime scene."

His sedan was unmarked, for which I was grateful. Once inside, he asked where I wanted to go. "Back to MacTavish's," I said. I was disconcerted by what the mayor had said about Marta—had I missed that much? I wanted to talk to the young woman herself to get her take on what was going on. And, honestly to nip any suspicions in the bud.

"What the mayor said back there about his daughter Polly being in the hospital. Was that true?"

"Yes," Spaulding said. "Polly was hospitalized. And she nearly died."

"Were drugs involved?"

"Yes." We were at a stop sign. He turned to look at me. "Do you have anyone you can talk to about all this? About finding Joseph and Glenn?"

I noticed that, when he was asking questions in an official capacity, he sat straight, and his face looked at you straight on. Now, however, it was angled slightly. It softened his jaw and widened his eyes. The effect was disconcerting.

"Do you?" I asked.

"Do I what?"

"Have someone to talk to about all this?"

"Touché."

He pulled into the circular drive at the inn, parking across from where people were allowed to pause for ten minutes while they checked in. "Listen. Call me if you think of anything pertinent to the investigation."

He had his hand on the door handle.

"Okay," I said. "Here's one thought. You know the other bartender I mentioned who was murdered? Turns out he was shot to death, about twenty years ago. The same day Pepper Porter died. Just for grins, maybe you could check the ballistics on that murder weapon against whatever gun was used to shoot Glenn MacTavish today."

"Really?" he said.

"For grins."

We both got out.

The two black SUVs with Ghost Seeker logos had been moved to the side, and the unremarkable truck that held their camera equipment was across the street. The two patrol cars had also been moved from the front drive.

As I entered the lobby, Marta hurried through the side revolving door. I checked my watch. It was a little after two o'clock. She was still carrying her backpack.

"Avalon…" Breathless, her carefully created nonchalance nowhere to be seen. "What's happened?"

"Come on. Let's talk," I said, corralling her towards the door to the bar. I unlocked it quickly and pushed her inside, relocking it behind us.

"What's going on?" she asked.

She still wore her school clothes—a baseball jersey styled shirt with a navy center and sky blue arms, which did admirably bring out the blue in her hair.

I saw no signs of "Goth" at all, unless you counted the tattooed barbed wire around her left wrist. But it led me to believe that our mayor used his words—and, very possibly, his thoughts—non-specifically.

"What's going on?" she repeated.

"Someone shot Glenn," and, at her horrified expression, I added, "He'll be all right. He's out of surgery."

"What? Where? How did it happen?"

I briefly filled her in. "Now I need to ask you something. What happened with Polly?"

Marta looked stricken. She sat for a minute, pondering. "Why?" she finally said. "Why are you asking?"

"Mayor Bristol was at the hospital. He was acting like he thought this might all be tied together."

Confusion replaced consternation. "I don't know how to talk about it." Then she made a decision and said, "Come with me."

If I wanted answers, it was clear I should follow her, and so I did; behind the bar, into the kitchen and out the back door. She was walking quickly, staying a step ahead. We stayed on the inn side of Main Street. Past the Olympic arena and the hotel, she made a turn up a street called Maple, which headed up at a steep angle. Perhaps an eighth of a mile up, past the service roads behind Main Street, we made a right onto Forest.

This was an older road. There were mailboxes at the end of unpaved driveways that disappeared behind rows of old growth pines. Marta headed up the second one. Again, as at my place, one had the feeling of being much farther from town than one actually was.

Beyond a wooded front yard, we reached a smallish Craftsman style house, sturdy and likely built in the early twentieth century. Stone pillars rose from the ground on either end of a cement porch that ran the front of the house. The front door was heavy and wooden, flanked by multi-paned windows. It was a small but lovingly built abode. The driveway continued around the back, I assumed to a garage. We went up the front walk.

Only after she'd knocked on the door did Marta show any sign of second thoughts.

There was immediate yipping, and the carved door with the rounded top swung inwards.

"Hi, Marta," said Philip Young. "And Avalon." He was surprised but not unhappy to see us. Whistle, on the other hand, danced in pure excitement. "Come on in."

The living room was decorated with hand-crafted wooden furniture and a loomed rug in front of a stone fireplace. Someone had a good eye.

"So, crazy morning," he said to me. "Do you know how Glenn is?"

"He's out of surgery, and apparently doing well."

"That's a relief."

"Have you spoken with the police?"

"Oh yes," Philip said, easily. "For hours."

I assumed he was exaggerating, but was still impressed by his blithe tone.

Marta was becoming more anxious by the minute, and she dove into the first pause. "Avalon asked about Polly. She said Mayor Bristol is trying to tie Polly's overdose to whatever's going on now."

"Really? Sounds like him," said Philip. He plopped onto the sofa, and I claimed a comfy chair. Marta remained standing, nervously shifting her weight from one foot to another. There was something else, too. One look at her face as she glanced at Philip—the same stupid, moony way I'd once looked at a young man named Crispen—and I knew another part of the mayor's throw-anything-against-the-wall list of accusations was also off-base. I wondered if Philip was aware of how she felt. Given, he was a good seven to ten years older than she, but he was certainly crush-worthy, as he'd proven this morning at the gym.

"I didn't know how to explain," she said.

Philip was thoughtful, his long oval face not showing an expression of worry, more of concern. He finally locked eyes with me, deciding how much to trust me. How much story to tell.

"Polly is not happy at home," he began, choosing his words carefully. "Her father believes she is troubled."

"I can't imagine having Art Bristow for a father and *not* being troubled," I said.

The fact that I had my own opinion of the mayor allowed both Philip and Marta to relax slightly.

"At one point a little over a year ago, Art dragged Polly to Marta's dad, Pastor Layton, for counselling," said Philip.

"When I walked past his study, I could hear her crying," said Marta. "I felt bad." She sat down now, on a loveseat facing my overstuffed chair and continued. "I waited outside until she was walking home, and then I walked with her. She was really freaked out and sad. I tried to cheer her up. I don't think I did a very good job, but we did kind of become friends."

"She seems quiet," I said, remembering her intention to not be noticed at the Cardamom. It had occurred to me that, with Polly's svelte frame, porcelain skin, blonde hair, and long lashes, if she had any confidence at all, she could likely be popular.

"Yeah. She doesn't really have any friends," said Marta. "Well, me. I try to be a friend. But back then, she felt like she couldn't really talk to anyone. Everyone was on her case, judging her, and they didn't even really know her."

"You mean, everyone like her father. And your father."

"Yeah. Anyway, last May, like, a year ago, I was supposed to meet her after school at the library, but she never showed up. As I was walking to work later that afternoon, I found her purse at the bottom of the giant luge that slides onto the ice on Fretful Pond in the winter. I climbed up and found her passed out. I didn't know what to do. I ran and got Philip, and he couldn't wake her up, either."

Apparently, Philip's trust in me gave Marta the courage to talk.

"I wasn't sure whether to call an ambulance or call her dad or what," said Philip. "But since the slide is close to MacTavish's, I ran and got Joseph. He climbed up, saw her, and called 911. Then he used his shirt as a mat, held Polly on his lap, and slid her down so the paramedics could get to her right away."

"Was she... on drugs?" I asked.

"*On* drugs, no. That day... that day, she stole Vicodin and Percocet and Valium from her mother's medicine cabinet and proceeded to attempt suicide," Philip said. "If Marta hadn't found her when she did, Polly would have succeeded."

"How can the mayor blame Marta for that?"

Philip shrugged. "Well, it certainly can't be *his* fault. Polly must have fallen in with a bad lot."

Marta checked the time on her cellphone and stood abruptly. "I need to run home and change before work," she said.

"Okay," said Philip. "Still on for tomorrow?"

"Yeah. I have early leave from school."

"See you then."

Marta headed out.

"What's tomorrow?" I asked. Surely, they weren't dating?

"Come here," Philip said, a sudden sparkle in his eye. "Let me show you." He offered me a strong hand for the second time that day, and pulled me to my feet.

We went through his kitchen, which was small but well-equipped, and into a small hallway. Across from a door that led outside, I stopped, looking at a batch of signs propped together against a wall. They were identical, featured a smiling photo of Joseph, and read: *Vote Joseph Emberg for Mayor. Ensure A Bright Future for all of Tranquility.*

"Joseph was running for mayor?" I asked.

"What? Oh, yeah. It was almost impossible to convince him, but finally he got so mad at how Art Bristow treats his family... specifically Polly... and how he has an iron grasp on this town, that he was willing to go for it."

"Art doesn't abuse his family does he?" Even though I disliked the mayor, I was hoping he wasn't a criminal.

Philip thought for a minute. "If you count emotional abuse, then I guess I'd say he does."

"Who convinced Joseph? To run for mayor, I mean."

"Brent and Addie and, well, me. Brent would have the newspaper endorse him, Addie was running his campaign, and Avantika was financing it."

"Avantika, from the Cardamom Café, was financing it?"

"Yep. I don't know what we'll do now that he's gone."

"Did Mayor Bristow know Joseph was going to run?"

"I don't think so. The election isn't till November. We were going to roll out in early June."

"Besides almost everybody liking Joseph, did he have any credentials?" I asked.

"Yes. You should ask Addie. She knew the most about him, since she was running the campaign. And Avantika wouldn't back him unless she knew he could do it."

We came to a door at the end of that small hallway. He opened it.

Suddenly the hall was flooded with light. Curious, I followed him through, and stood on a step up, overlooking a room the size of the rest of the house put together. The wall across from us was nearly all glass, sending natural light to every corner of the studio before me.

For that's what it was: an artist's studio. Large canvases lined the wall to the right, and completed paintings of all sizes—some under a foot in length and some nearly seven feet long—carefully jostled each other against the opposite white wall.

"Some of these," Philip said with the pride of a mentor, "Are Marta's."

"Wow," I said, "so you're not just a painter, you're—"

"A *painter*," he said, and laughed.

The colors, shapes, and boldness of the completed works drew me down, but even as I stepped toward them, I was surrounded by the smell. The scent of paint, of starched, stretched canvas, of turpentine. I ricocheted back in time, back in sorrow, back in horror. A thunderclap of darkness enveloped me. And, for the second time in my life—the second time that day—I passed out.

The next thing I knew, I was sitting in the small hallway, Philip beside me, his arm around me, the door to the studio closed, the mayoral signs stashed out of the way. I was shaken, and shaking. Wow. I'd never had a true flashback before. The part of me that wasn't an overwhelmed lump was interested.

We sat in silence. Once my trembling began to abate and I was once again breathing normally, I said, "Sorry."

"Want to tell me what's up?" he asked.

This time, I searched *his* face, weighing the issue of trust.

"I had a best friend. A brother, really, named Winsome Reilly. We grew up together, in a group that were friends at school—a private school in Los Angeles. Winsome was a talented painter. We all messed around with getting high in high school. Well, I only smoked weed, and it didn't make me mellow like everybody else, it made me paranoid, so I didn't even really like that. Anyhow, after high school, Winsome started doing meth. It got pretty bad. But his family and his group of friends were so tight, that folks came back from all over to hold an intervention."

"Two questions," said Philip. "First, was the intervention successful? And second, his name was Winsome?"

I laughed. "I grew up in some pretty crazy celebrity circles. Somehow giving your child a weird name proved that you were celebrity enough your fame would protect your kid from ridicule. Trust me, I got off easy with Avalon. Frankly, so did Winsome. And, second, yes, the intervention did work. Winsome went into rehab, and when he came out, he was his old self."

"But…"

"But time passed, and suddenly some of those other friends of his were hanging around. He'd started using again. He swore he could handle it, though everyone knows meth…won't be 'handled.'"

Philip sat quietly, respectful of the gravity of the story.

"One Friday, Winsome and I were meeting for supper and a movie. He never showed. I drove past his studio on the way home, and the lights were on, so I went in. He was there. Dead. Already dead. An overdose. He had been dead for a couple of hours, at least. I hadn't realized that the smell of an art studio could be enough…I'm sorry, Philip. Your work looks amazing. I've never had a flashback like that before."

"Don't be sorry. You've been through a lot lately. I'm sorry to hear about Winsome. Do you have any photos of his artwork?"

I wasn't expecting that question, and I went to pull out my phone, which was no longer there. "If you can go online, his website is still up," I said. He handed me his phone, and I found it, navigating to some of my favorite of Winsome's pieces.

"Wow," said Philip. "Nice."

"Thanks. Yeah. He was pretty good. Do you have any of yours I can see?"

"You mean, on my phone? I'm assuming we should skip the studio for today. No. wait. Come on."

I followed him to the guest bedroom. There, on one wall, was a large painting, maybe five feet by six feet. It was of a countryside, with a man and a woman on a horse, and a large dove, and a sky full of lambs. It wasn't like anything I'd seen. The rich colors, the sizing of the elements reminded me of Chagall, but the themes and the colors were somehow exotic. It evoked an immediate emotional response, one of longing and hopefulness at the same time.

The intensity of my reaction terrified me.

But Philip was standing there, expecting me to talk. I couldn't. *Ask a question, you can always ask a question,* I told myself, but even that required effort. "When did you start painting?"

"I think I've always painted, and partly because it runs in the family. My mom dabbled, but my grandfather is a well-known painter in India."

India. That was the influence in the colors and the shapes of the subjects in the painting.

"You've obviously studied."

"I went to Columbia undergrad and the École Nationale des Beaux Arts for my MFA."

As he spoke, it occurred to me there was something familiar about the painting. "Is there—is one of your paintings in the Cardamom Café?"

He smiled. "Yes. It means a lot to Avantika to be a patron of local artists. She paid top-dollar for that painting. On purpose."

"She hangs local artists? I didn't see any works by Michael Michel."

I was trying hard to hold it together, but with every ounce of blood in my veins, I wanted to bolt.

His expression was bemused. "She feels Michael's paintings are ubiquitous enough around here."

"Look," I said. "I've got to go." I checked my watch and saw that, indeed, I did need to get to MacTavish's to open. This day was turning out nothing like I'd expected.

"Okay," he said. He was clearly confused, and even hurt, that I hadn't said one specific thing about the damn painting.

"Thanks," I said, trying to leave on a positive note.

"For what?"

"Well, this morning, for starters."

"No problem. Any time you find someone who's been shot, I'm your man. And thank you. It'll take several good coats of paint to cover those bloody handprints. More work for me."

He looked concerned, and I realized I was trembling. He walked me to the front door. "You know your way back?"

I nodded. As I started down the steps, I saw a young woman heading toward me. She was perhaps six inches shorter than I, dark hair in cornrows on the top, then let loose into a profusion of thick locks that passed her shoulder. Her skin was milk chocolate and flawless. We traded hellos and she continued up the porch stairs. As I turned at the treeline to wave goodbye, I saw her curve naturally into the side of Philip, his arm casually slung around her shoulder, him suddenly very tall in comparison. He gave me a brief wave, then they smiled at each other and disappeared inside.

Crap. What was their pillow talk?

He knew too much, he'd seen too much. Worse, he held in his hands my vulnerability. He could tell her things that would make her feel sorry for me.

To keep from thinking of other things, as I walked, I made a list of Reasons to Hate Philip, which started with:

1. He knows things I never meant to tell.
2. He enjoys sex too much. Okay, this one I was extrapolating, but from the easy way his girlfriend melted into him, my educated guess said there was no angst in his lovemaking, no bargaining or game-playing, he would come to his partner with joy and make certain they both had a fantastic time.
3. Worst: his artwork terrified me. He wasn't a collector, he was an expresser. He felt things deeply, he plumbed emotions— likely his own and other people's, and recorded them with color and shape in a way that drilled down into you.

When numbers one and three were added together, they equaled the fact that, whether he recognized it or not, Philip Young wielded extraordinary power over me.

Some people, having a day like this one, might consider calling in sick to their job. Not me. My bar had always been my haven, my safe place.

I entered the bar the way I'd left, via the kitchen door. Whenever I took a job as a bartender, I made it a point to find a place to stash my bartenders' kit and a change of clothes. The kit because most bartenders carry a special shaker that is a personal statement, as well as tools of the trade that might not be different than those provided but somehow work better for us. Usually the kit contains bar spill mats, too, which catch extra liquids. Bars provide them—a lot of liquor distributors give them out—but again, length of bristles and personal preference as to design give a sense of ownership of your space, which is important.

I liked Joseph's spill mats. They were from Maker's Mark and were heavy and well made. To start, I'd continued using them as an homage to him.

More to the point on this Thursday, it was a relief to have a spare black shirt and pair of pants in my kit, which was in the storeroom. I found the storeroom locked and my keys sitting in a lump in the middle of the bar. A statement from Chef Paul.

I grabbed them and ran to change, knocking over the Pepper's sign as I shoved the storeroom door open. Yet another statement. Thankfully, the sign didn't break. It took both hands and throwing my shoulders into it to move the sign. I finally got it out of the way, wondering just what kind of situation I'd walked into the middle of.

Marta ran in at two minutes to four, wearing her black waitress outfit. "Ready," she said.

I finished counting the cash drawer and nodded. "Okay. Let's go."

Word about Glenn's shooting had travelled around town. More than a dozen people were waiting in the lobby for us to open. Many of them were townsfolk I'd seen on the street but not at the Battened Hatch. They took tables, but—one by one—each group sent a delegate over to the bar to ask for water or napkins as an excuse for the chance to ask me about finding Glenn.

As I didn't know these folks, I kept the answers simple and didn't go beyond what would certainly be in the next day's papers. Yes, I'd found Glenn shot, in Suite Seven. Someone had set a fire. I called for help, and help came. Glenn would be fine. No idea who did it. End of story.

Before long, my equilibrium had returned.

It was after seven o'clock when Suzanne Turner from The Spice Trade came in and sat at the bar. She politely said hello. Remembering how she'd helped run Michel's reception, I was afraid her arrival was precursor to the advent of the mayor and/or Michael

Michel or even the Reverend Layton (whom I had never seen in the bar, which perhaps allowed it to be Marta's safe space). So I was relieved when, instead, Suzanne was joined by the petite, well-coiffed Gillian, the friend with whom she'd been drinking the night of Joseph's demise. Gillian had exchanged her pink jacket for one in mint green. The two women embraced briefly.

"Damn strange times," said Suzanne sadly.

"I'll drink to that," said Gillian. "In fact, I'd like to." She turned to me. "I liked that cocktail you created the other day. Have any new specialty drinks tonight?"

"As a matter of fact I do. In the mood for sweet or savory?"

"Savory."

"Along the lines of the Bloody Mary?"

"Sure. What've you got?"

I did the mixing, careful not to let them see the secret blend of ingredients. I knew it looked like a Bloody Mary. But it was tastier. I added a celery stalk for emphasis.

Gillian eyed it, and smelled it. "What's it called?"

"It's a Bloody Handprint."

"Seems fitting." She sipped. "Well done," she said, and took another long draught. "Well done."

Suzanne stayed with a gimlet. "Let's talk about something besides Glenn. And Joseph," she said. "Bloody distressing."

"Sure," said Gillian.

"Any unusually promising young skaters?"

"There are five who might go the distance. Three of them are talented and competitive beyond belief. Come on over some afternoon this week and see them skate. We have some real potential in that rink."

Aha. Gillian was a skating coach. And, from the looks of her, I guessed she might have been a competitive skater herself at one time.

I broke my own rule and surreptitiously Googled her. Yep. Gillian Petrakov. Bronze medal, three decades ago.

"Polly's still skating?" asked Suzanne, as she ordered a second drink.

"Yes. She's getting good."

"But not Olympic material?"

"She's not interested in that level of headache," laughed Gillian. "And good on her for knowing it."

I left the women comparing notes on movies and shows they'd recently streamed.

"Polly ice skates?" I asked Marta, who was behind the bar putting ice in water glasses.

"Yeah. It's her form of exercise, I think. She uses it to burn off anger."

"So, what's the deal with Suzanne?" I asked, casually. "She seems a little sane to be hanging out with the mayor. She also seems a little more torn up about Joseph."

"Suzanne?" Marta looked over. "She's okay, I guess. I don't know her all that well, but she does seem nice. She knows I paint. She actually offered to pay so I could go to a private boarding school that has a good painting program."

"Really? You didn't want to go?"

"I was willing to check it out. But my dad said no." She tried to sound nonchalant.

"And no is no."

"I wasn't sure I wanted to go," she answered carefully. "It's about choosing your battles."

"Philip says you're a good painter."

She actually smiled.

By ten p.m., most patrons had cleared out, likely disappointed not to get any more juicy information about the shooting.

"Another gimlet," requested Suzanne. Gillian had left half an hour before, but Suzanne still sat, finishing a chicken Cesar salad. "Last one," I said. "Closing early tonight."

All of a sudden, I was overwhelmed by exhaustion: physical, emotional, and mental. The day, which began so promisingly with the stint at the gym, had been encroached upon by evil. A dozen times I'd told the story of finding Glenn, but suddenly it hit me that I'd been attacked, also. Someone I didn't know had been behind me. He'd knocked me out. He'd had a gun. He could have chosen to kill me. At the very least, he left me to die in a fire.

"Marta, go on home," I said. "Tomorrow's a school day."

"Sure you're all right to close up?" she asked.

"Yes. All the checks in?"

She nodded. "

"All right. Good night." I didn't take a lot of pleasure in sending her home to her father, but she seemed fine with it. Maybe, despite my own encounter, he wasn't as manipulative as Mayor Bristol.

As if she'd read my thoughts, Suzanne said, "He's a good man, you know."

"Sorry?"

"Reverend Layton. He often gets the short end of the stick. It was very hard for him to lose his wife. She died three years ago. He goes to the cemetery. Sits by her grave at dusk. Stays until dark. I've heard him talking to her."

Suzanne was slightly slurring her words.

"You're not driving home, are you?" I asked. I didn't yet know the taxis in town, but I knew I'd have to call one.

"No," she said. "It's not a far walk. And I think I'll call Jeff."

"Jeff?"

"Runs the local cab company."

"Ah. I should get his number from you."

"Sure," she said, and wrote it on a bar napkin. "You're a good bartender." This was proffered in that "I love you all *so much*," voice that some folks affect when they're snockered.

"Tim loves that girl," she continued. "But he doesn't know how to handle her. He can't move on, you see, until he feels Marta is looked after." She lowered her voice to a whisper. "It's what he talks to his dead wife about."

"How did she die?" I asked, almost dreading the answer.

"Cancer," she said. "It took a long time. She was e-mace-iated."

Hate to say I was relieved, but I was relieved. At least there hadn't been another mysterious offing.

"Suzanne, I've really got to get to bed, and you should, too. It's been a hell of a long day."

"Want to share my cab?" she asked, after texting Jeff the Cabbie.

"Thanks, but I have to close up."

She left and I locked the door behind her. I'd already closed out the register and cleaned the work station, leaving it pristine and set up for the next day. "Joseph, are you here?" I asked. It would be comforting at this point to feel a benign presence.

Nothing.

I walked out through the lobby, feeling the need for company and lights as long as I had them.

It was a twenty-minute walk down Main Street to my lane. But tonight the glow of the streetlamps wasn't friendly and welcoming. The streets were deserted, and the wind was blowing through the trees in an attempt at a howl.

The tall ladder that led up to the luge track by the lake cast long shadows. I pictured Polly huddled at the top, her backpack left below, perhaps as a last cry for help.

I felt alone, and menaced.

Even Mr. Fenton's lights were out. He was no doubt abed in silk pajamas.

It was nearly a new moon, and the oaks along the lane, once so inviting, now fingered the sky like talons.

I purposely didn't look at the lodge that belonged to the tragically-killed movie star. If there were ghosts there, I didn't want to know.

I cursed myself for not leaving a welcoming porch light on for my return.

The large old key fit into the door and it swung open. Who was the key kidding, anyway? Anyone who wanted to could break into this cottage. The person from Suite Seven, for example.

Whoever killed Joseph, for example.

Whoever killed Oskar, for another.

What kind of idiot was I not to have a phone?

Especially somewhere so removed. A cottage where no one could hear you scream.

I slid silently through the front door and sidled over to the fireplace in the small living room, where I grabbed the poker. Then I went room to room, turning on each light, checking for intruders, and clicking them off as I moved on.

No hidden figures lurking.

I locked up and turned off the other lights, turning on the bedroom lights just long enough to change into a sleep shirt. I hated turning the lights off again, but I did, willing the shadows from the trellis against my window to lead me into sleep and into morning.

They didn't. I lay alone and frightened in the dark.

Remembering the feeling of the hand on my neck, blocking the blood flow in my artery.

Remembering the feeling of being overwhelmed by horror, by darkness, in Philip's studio.

Remembering Winsome, who knew me better than anyone ever had.

Remembering holding his cold body.

The sound punctured the hem of my consciousness as a small intrusion. It grew louder and more central to my thoughts. And then I realized what it was.

Horrified, I stood up, grabbing my pillow in front of me and picking up the poker I'd dropped beside the bed. Then I went to stand barefoot in the hall, staring at the ghost-phone that had no dial or dial tone. The phone that hadn't rung for forty years.

The phone that was ringing now.

Midnight Caller

Ingredients

Apple Cider
Goldschlager

Method

Heat fresh apple cider.
Pour over 1 ounce of Goldschläger.
Settle in for the night!

10

Ghosts

In the movies, terrible things happen to young women alone who pick up phones at night.

I somehow knew it would be a gravelly voice. It would be my attacker.

Would not picking it up stop him, though? If he was waiting for me, there was a very long way to run to get to the street. How could I even get across the bridge?

No. *Please, God, no.*

But I couldn't go through the next hours not knowing. That would be worse.

I picked it up. "Hello?" I said.

"Is this Avalon?"

It was a woman's voice. "Yes."

"I have some questions for you."

"Yes? Who is this?"

"Your landlord."

My landlord. The person who had instructed Mr. Fenton to rent out my cottage.

Was it Betsy? It had to be. Why would a run-of-the-mill realtor call at midnight?

"Are you the person who raised her family here? The friend of Sally Allison's?"

"Yes. We need to talk. Now."

"It's late. And it's been a hell of a day."

"You're up. And I'm up. And I've got some questions."

I was up because she was freaking calling me.

"Okay. What are your questions?"

"Why don't you come over and we can talk?"

"Come over?"

"To the lodge."

"You're there? Now?"

"Yes."

It was a corded phone—the short cord was the old fashioned kind, wrapped in a smooth cloth casing, brown and satiny, so I couldn't walk to the window, but when I looked that way, I could see light shining.

"This is strange. Come to a remote house, by myself, in the middle of the night. Should I be frightened?"

A throaty laugh. "My dear, of all the things you need to be, frightened isn't one of them. You'll be back safely, very shortly."

"All right. Give me a minute to dress."

The phone went dead.

I needed to get either an alarm system or a dog to warn me of imminent peril.

Seriously, what was I doing? Going out in the dark, without a phone to call for help? To a landlady who wanted to meet in the middle of the night? Adding potential vampires to the list of Tranquility's dangers now, were we?

Maybe I shouldn't have left California.

My mind careened straight back to holding Winsome's body. The weight, but not the warmth. And all that happened after.

No, nothing was as dangerous as that.

Even tracking down a murderer here in New York. All he or she could do here was kill me, right? So far, no one had threatened my immortal soul.

I pulled on some clothes, ran a hairbrush through my hair. I turned on the living room light and porch light, then headed out the door.

Lights also blazed from the lodge. Even so, I put buying a flashlight on my list as I made my way through the shadows down to the bridge and crossed it.

I walked across the blue-black shadowed lawn and up stairs I'd already traversed once today.

The porch was a well-designed outdoor room with circular carpets and crème colored sofas in half circles dotted with green and blue pillows, facing comfy chairs. Two steel fire pits defined conversation areas. Three chandeliers made of deer antlers gave even lighting, awaiting a swinging party which would not arrive. If it was kept as a shrine, at least it was kept clean.

I knocked on the carved wooden door, and it immediately swung open.

"Come in, come in." I entered a wood-covered great room, a huge stone fireplace dominating its far wall. A gigantic chandelier crafted from an old wagon wheel holding electrified candles was centered above the open space perhaps 20 feet above. Hallways led off to either side. Yup, exactly like the cabins people went to in the movies when they went to "the country."

The woman admitting me was perhaps two inches taller than I and could best be described as willowy. She wore black pants and a black sleeveless shirt with some sort of long chiffon floaty-thing over it. Her hair fell softly to curl at shoulder-length. It was white and silky, gold still sprinkled through it. I didn't think it was a rinse, but what did I know? Even the word 'rinse' was pushing my salon knowledge. Still, it was easy to see how she could have been a friend of the movie star's back in the day. I felt I should apologize for her loss, although Sally

Allison had died a good forty years ago.

"Hello," I said. "I'm Avalon Nash."

She knew that, obviously. My name was on the lease, and she'd called me Avalon on the phone.

She extended her hand. "Mrs. Chander. Pleased to meet you—and sorry to disturb if you were abed, but I have to ask…was there someone here this morning?"

Shit. It had been such a crazy day it seemed like the tea I'd had with Brent, Addie and Jerry was a month ago, not this morning. "I'm sorry, yes. A friend, a great fan of Sally Allison's. He got away from me and ran over. It will never happen again. I promise it won't."

"Really? Who was this fan?"

"His name is Jerry. A publicist from Los Angeles. He's here helping with the film festival. He's written a new biography of Pepper Porter, and being invited to my place was almost too much for him. He knows all about Sally's life and career as well as Pepper's. But I won't bring anyone back here again if you don't want me to. Please don't make me move out. I love the cottage—it's like it was meant to be."

First thought: what the hell, Avalon? You're not an apologizing or pleading kind of person, though admittedly one who was currently tired and overwhelmed. In the moment it took her to answer, however, my thoughts careened through a 180-degree turn. Maybe breaking my lease was the best thing. Maybe I should get the hell out of this crazy town.

"Meant to be? How do you mean?"

"The moment I knew I needed a place, I tripped over the for rent sign. I only came this way because I was fleeing Reverend Layton."

She threw back her head and laughed. "There has to be a hell of a story behind that."

"I was walking a dog for a friend, and Whistle—that's the dog—

peed on his lawn."

"Indeed," she said, "That would do it. So you're new in town."

"Yes. Arrived on Monday."

"From where?"

"Los Angeles." Another time, another life. "I'm a refugee from Hollywood."

"Oh, dear. Young Hollywood. Tell me truthfully, had you ever even heard of Sally before you rented this place?"

That brought a genuine smile. "Oh, yes. My friends and I went to Thornton Academy. There's this little street near the school, and not far from Graumann's Chinese Theater—well, now it's somebody else's Chinese Theater—named Salty Sally Alley. On the alley is a diner, an old-fashioned soda fountain, I guess. It's called Salty Sally's. We used to go there all the time. There are posters from her movies on the walls, and a jukebox with songs from her records and movies. Our sophomore year we made it a thing to watch all her movies. They were great. And we had the best times at Salty Sally's."

"Did you watch *Banker's Holiday?*"

One of the classics. "Yes."

"Do you remember the character of Crofton Hughes—the second male lead?"

"The one who was engaged to Sally's character but loses out?"

"Yes, exactly. Played by Rutherford Fenton."

It took me a moment to understand what she was telling me. "You mean...Mr. Fenton? From the house out front?"

"Indeed. He cleaned up pretty well in his younger days."

"Why did he give up acting to live here, alone, all this time?"

"First off, roles weren't exactly rolling his way. *Banker's Holiday* was his zenith. Second, he was stuck on Sally."

"Did she know it?"

Mrs. Chander looked at me, confidingly. "My dear, you're a

woman. Don't we always know?"

"I don't... well, sometimes we see what we want to see."

"Yes. But we *know*."

I wasn't going to argue. But I didn't want to think about it.

"How many movies was Mr. Fenton in with Sally?"

"Three."

"Did he move here when she did?"

"A little afterwards."

"How did all this fit in with Sally being married to Clifton Taylor?"

"Oh, dear. Those were different days."

"In what way?"

"If you're going to ask about things long past, we need to start pouring whiskey," she said.

I should have stopped her right there. I should have pled my case for keeping the cottage and asked if I could come back at a decent hour, on a day when I hadn't been knocked out, to hear stories.

But the chance to collect Sally Allison stories!

Mrs. Chander was true to her word about pouring whisky—and she had the good stuff. Balvenie, Batch 7 Speyside Single Malt. $5,000 a bottle. I'm not a big drinker, but when presented with the opportunity to imbibe Balvenie, why would I not? I wasn't driving home.

Usually I was the one dispensing the drinks, not the other way around. Still, it was time for questions. I gathered my courage and asked, "Are you Betsy? Were you a friend of Sally's?"

"It seems someone's done her homework. Sorry to disappoint, but no. I'm Lee. Lee Chander. I do know Betsy, though."

"Did you know Sally?"

"Guilty as charged."

From her gossamer look, it seemed entirely possible she could have been Sally's contemporary—though, if so, she'd aged well.

"Are you from here? Did you grow up here? Is that how you knew Sally?"

"Yes, I'm from Mountain Pass, the next town over. We went to Whiteface Mountain High."

Of all the stories I wanted to collect, Lee likely held many of the top 50. But why did she have to call at midnight, after the longest, most hellish day ever?

"You were saying? About Mr. Fenton being in love with Sally, but her being married to Clifton Taylor?"

The whiskey singed a silky burn down my throat.

"The studios were losing control of their stars' personal lives, but if the public turned on someone, it was still career suicide."

"So you're saying...certainly Mr. Fenton respected Sally's marriage bonds?"

"It's complicated."

"I'm discreet. Complicated is my bread and butter."

She raised her glass for a toast. "And Philip trusts you."

"What?"

"If you were walking Whistle, he must. Anyway, Sally was never one of those women who thought she needed to be with a man to be complete. The late 50s and early 60s were prime time for a sassy woman in Hollywood. The more she didn't need a man, the more men fell at her feet."

"But she didn't fall for any of them?"

"Crushes, yes. Flirtations, by the score. Falling for them? They were boys who refused to grow up. Even the grown-ups. Pretty boys in costumes. Until..."

"Clifton Taylor?"

"Cliff." Lee snorted, and poured herself another glass. "Cliff was all man—at least, that's how he thought of himself. Six-foot-three, hairy as hell. Women swooned worldwide. Still, his reputation preceded him in Hollywood. No one wanted to work with him. He was egotistical and overbearing. Did I mention self-centered? And then, Sally and Clifton were hired on the same picture. They came armed for turf wars, which commenced with a battles of wits. Came at each other with both barrels blazing. Fireworks on set. Chemistry like you wouldn't believe on screen. And soon, inevitably, fireworks in bed.

"During the shoot of the second Allison-Taylor film, *Midnight Madness*, a runner called Sally to a large soundstage. I was visiting at the time, acting as Sally's personal assistant. We followed the page to the set, but it was odd—completely dark and deserted. Even the runner left. Then, suddenly, a drumroll. The lights switched on, and the place was awash in black and white. Cliff had paid the choreographer to create a gigantic production number using all the chorus dancers, costumed in black and white, and, get this—he had Frank Loesser write the song. It ended with Cliff walking Sally to the top of a huge staircase, where he got down on one knee and presented her with the largest sapphire and diamond engagement ring in captivity."

What an extravagant image. "She said yes?"

Despite Lee's story, which would have captivated me at any hour, I was fighting to remain conscious.

"Of course. And the assemblage went straight into the coda."

Lee stood and strode over to the art deco wet bar. She picked up a framed photo and brought it back. Sally Allison and Clifton Taylor at the top of the silver staircase, with two dozen matching dancers, hands, top hats and eyes raised to the deities above.

"What if she'd said no?" I asked, aghast.

Avalon, pay attention. Sally's friend is drinking and talking! Your dream has come true.

But my temples hurt from the effort of keeping my eyes open.

Lee laughed again. "I guess we'll never know."

And neither would I. Before she finished the story, I passed out, sound asleep, on the sofa.

I awoke to sun streaming in through a skylight I hadn't noticed the night before. Mrs. Chander had covered me with a soft blanket, my head was on a pillow and my slippers were on the floor. Aromas of morning cooking and the crackle of bacon sputtering wafted in from the kitchen. I felt safe and rested.

It would be rude to disappear and run home, so I stretched and rose, found the guest bathroom, then followed the sounds into the high-ceilinged kitchen, with windows that looked over the forest and the running brook.

"Good morning," said Mrs. Chander. She wore ecru silk pajamas, with a short silk floral robe tied atop. Her hair was pulled back, bangs tucked up into a scarf. "You seemed all in, so I let you sleep. Sounds like you'd had a best-over day."

"Yes, I'm hoping today will contain considerably less free-flowing blood," I said. "Thank you for letting me crash."

"I stand with you in that. Don't go until you've had breakfast. Although, as you've noted, I'm a night owl. It's supper for me. I'm making fresh blueberry waffles. Unless—don't tell me you're one of those carb-free creatures."

"Heck no. Carbs are us," I answered. "And the waffles look fabulous. But I don't want to intrude."

My hostess grinned. She moved in an easy, swooping way that felt elegant.

"You'll find me to be a fraud in the cheffing department. I make fantastic waffles, then my expertise is exhausted. So enjoy these and be impressed, there's nothing coming behind them."

"Deal," I said, hungrily eying the meat she was forking from the pan onto drain paper towels to drain. "The bacon looks is perfectly crispy."

She beamed. "See there? You've doubled my talent in one sentence. So. You called yourself a refugee from Hollywood. Does that come from attending Thornton or are any family members involved in the industry?"

I was hoping to get her talking again, and thought it a fair exchange to tell her about my mom, about the cabarets and comedy clubs in New York, her stint on the *Daily Show* and our subsequent move to L.A. so Mom could be in movies. Growing up on sets, thinking Craft Services was a food group, falling asleep at the dining room table at home as Mom entertained her cadre of talented companions.

"I personally know several generations of kids who'd 'Amen, sister!' everything you've recounted," she said. "How about you? What's your superpower?"

"I'm a bartender," I said.

"Any schooling after Thornton?"

"Yes. I went to NYU for two years. But I wasn't ready."

"For what?"

"To come back to the city. To know what I wanted to do."

"What did you study?"

"Theater. And sociology. And poly sci."

"Ah. Sounds like a craft bartender's course-load to me. For the meantime, anyway. Okay, breakfast is ready in five minutes."

"If this is your supper, would you like me to bring you a drink? A Bellini, maybe, or Bloody Handprint?"

"Bloody Handprint?"

"It's a spin on a margarita I served yesterday, although I don't have beet puree. I could see what ingredients you have."

128

"Sure. Feel free to play at the bar. But you've only got five minutes till everything's ready. You'll have to be a Super Bartender."

I turned in the doorway. "Mrs. Chander," I said, "what I've just told you, about my mom and growing up in Hollywood and all...could you keep it between us? I'm...taking some time off, between coasts."

"Whatever you'd like. I've found that secrets have their time. You'll know it when the time is right."

"Thanks."

The bar was well-stocked. I couldn't exactly make a Bloody Handprint, but did a different, more-interesting take on a traditional Bloody Mary. Lee had set the photo of Sally and Cliff's proposal on top of the bar. I picked it up and studied it. Cliff looked happy and proud. Sally had an expression between happy and bemused. I was sorry I had sent off my phone with the wallpaper of the laughing photo of Sally, the happiness apparent in her eyes, the mouth ready to spill secrets of her own. It had been a joyfully revealing picture.

An actual dinner bell rang. "Waffles!"

I grabbed my offering, the spicy tomato concoction, and headed in.

Her breakfast plates were blue and yellow, and she set them on a table in a breakfast nook next to floor-to-ceiling glass, also overlooking the sparkling stream.

"So this is it?" she took the glass and drained a long draught. "Fucking fabulous, my dear. Will you tell me what's in it?"

But I was having trouble catching my breath. I am not a nervous person. Very little puts me off my game. Yet, in the last twenty-four hours, I'd been repeatedly thrown for a loop.

As I was now.

"Coffee?" My hostess stood over me with a white porcelain coffee pot. I looked at her smiling there, still gorgeous though make-up free.

And I let myself study her soft hair, bangs held back by her multicolored headscarf...and the scar, still barely visible, from when she fell from the apple tree.

"When will your secrets have had their time?" I asked softly. "When will it be right for you to speak up, Mrs. Chander... Sally?"

Waffles and Sympathy

Ingredients

1 1/2 ounces cake vodka
1 ounce blueberry schnapps
3 ounces lemon-lime soda
1/2 ounce grenadine

Method

In a shaker, add ice, cake vodka and blueberry schnapps. Shake and dump everything into a cocktail glass. Add more ice until glass is filled 3/4 full. Pour sprite on top. Pour grenadine down the side of the glass.

11

Back in the Day

The. Silence. Pulsed.

Breathed.

Usually, I could read situations well. Not this one.

Was I *trying* to get myself thrown out of Willoughby?

Finally, she took another gulp. "Damn good drink," she said. "Damn good."

"Should I not have asked?"

She cut into her waffle. "Eat," she said. "It's getting cold."

I poured warmed maple syrup over my waffle and sliced into it. It melted in my mouth. "This is fantastic," I said, indicating with my fork.

"I am rightfully proud," she said. Then, conversationally: "How did you know?"

"The scar. The apple tree."

"Fuck. You do your research. That will teach me. First time, ever, I let someone I don't know spend the night, and she knows about the freaking apple tree."

"It wasn't research," I said quietly. "You meant something to me. Like a mentor I'd never met. Someone who stood up for herself. Who refused to play the game. Who had a sense of humor. Also, remember my superpower is that I'm a bartender. I keep secrets all the time. It's in our Hippocratic Oath. As is the pledge to never to give away the top secret Blue Martini recipe."

She gave a deep sigh. "Well, I'll tell ya. Sally's secret wore out its welcome long ago. Almost everyone with whom I closely interact knows the truth. And, who really cares now? Cliff is dead and gone. And you're the one person in town who can read a scar that isn't Harry Potter's. So, we keep each other's secrets, unless otherwise released to tell, capiche?"

"Capiche."

I started breathing again. "So... how?" I asked. "Why?"

"Cliff." Her eyes narrowed. "You're sworn to silence," she said. "If you tell anyone, I have a fixer. Fenton is my fixer."

"Trust me," I said. "No need to call a fixer."

"Make me another of these, and let's sit in the great room."

Sally bussed the dishes, and I whipped up an even stronger version of the last drink, which I handed to her as she arranged herself comfortably on the sofa.

"Cliff was a crackerjack," Sally started. "Clifton Taylor in love with you is overwhelming."

"I can only imagine."

Sally sat for a while, staring into the peppery vodka concoction. "Our engagement was written up in all the magazines. Everyone in the world knew. If YouTube had been around, the proposal would have gone viral. There were probably Tibetan monks offering prayers for us. Wedding date set, caterers hired, flowers bought, dress designed. Gossip columnists itching, photo mags ecstatic. Only one thing we didn't have...a marriage license. Cliff always had an excuse not to go get one. Until, finally, he admitted...he was already married. Told a whopper of a tale about how he'd been tricked into matrimony, she was a shrew, they hadn't lived as husband and wife for years..."

"He was married?"

"Yes. But meanwhile, the studios and the public were insistent we make it legal. It had become a national frenzy. So we had a wedding. A beautiful, unforgettable, over-the-top, anything-but-legal wedding."

"Please. Don't leave me hanging."

"Yep, Cliff was a crackerjack. Turned out he didn't have a wife. He had three. At least, three women who had wedding photos and thought they were his wives. I knew better than to make the same assumption. Here's the ultimate irony: when I realized what kind of masher he was, the studio wouldn't let us 'divorce.' Seriously. I was stuck in a fake marriage."

"Did Clifton ever live here?"

"No. Perhaps that's why this lodge has always been my safe ppace. After *Gemma in the Gloaming,* I was done with Hollywood. Not with acting; I love acting and dancing, but oh, the games and the people that surrounded the whole process. Done. After the last day of filming, I up and left. I did have to train it from here into New York City to do some looping, but that was all. It wasn't long thereafter that my good friend Preston Fielding had the idea of sailing along the east coast, down to Bequia in the West Indies. He was the only survivor of the trip."

I tried to decipher the emotion behind the words. Relief? Regret? Some of each?

"Were you even there at the beginning of the trip?"

"Of course. There are many photos of me waving good-bye to those ashore at the marina as we sailed off. Rutherford picked me up off Cape May, New Jersey. Preston lost his boat off the coast of South Carolina."

"I'd guess they never found your body."

"No."

"Did Clifton know?"

"He was jim-dandy at garnering sympathy as the handsome widower. Lord, he was beside himself at the funeral. What tangled webs we weave."

"But did he know you weren't really dead?"

"Oh, who cares? He certainly didn't. Didn't wait around for a death certificate, either. Guess he figured, since we weren't actually married, there wouldn't be any inheritance. I moved to Paris, cut my hair, started speaking French, and fell in love. Truly in love, this time. With a tempestuous, fantastic Indian painter. Saif Chander."

The look on her face when she said his name was gentler and more expansive at the same time.

"Saif and I have had a wonderful life together. It wasn't quiet and it wasn't easy but it was sure worth it, on every level. We had a son and a daughter, Bennett and Rena. They grew up in Paris, New Delhi and here. They went to school here. Guarded by Rutherford Fenton, overseen by my friend Betsy Pullman—who many assumed was their mother, even though their last name was Chander, and hers was not. I was often here, also. Saif spends much of the year in India, and I spend that same time in the U.S. I came and went as Lee Chander. Sal-*lee*. I grew up a town over and some of my old friends were wise to the game, but they kept the secret, God bless them.

"Our family always meets for summers in Paris. Parents and kids, husband and wife. Husband and wife." She smiled. "Saif thought he'd never marry. He was so dedicated to his art, to his work, he had no time or emotional space for dependents, or so he'd announced. He never could have traversed the waters of conventionality, but we were never a conventional family. Which worked splendidly for all of us."

"Philip is your grandson?"

"Yes. How did you put that together?"

"You said you'd trust me since Philip did... although, Philip trusting me seems to go a long way with many folks in this town. And Philip told me his grandfather was a well-known Indian painter. So, is your husband... is he still alive?"

"Yes, dear. Certainly is. And it's almost summer." She was grinning now.

"Did Pepper know?"

"Did Pepper know what?"

"That you were alive after the accident? Married? A mother?"

"Yes. Pepper knew I was alive and well and living in Paris. She visited me there once. I'm not sure she knew I married Saif. We never discussed it. She knew I had children, and that they weren't lily-white, which was something worthy of comment in those days. But for some reason, she kept things to herself. I'm not saying we didn't drive each other crazy. We did. That wasn't manufactured. But we shared an odd background no one else could possibly understand. She was the only other person around here who called studio heads by their first names, who understood the absurdities... what that level of fame can do to a person. We did share grudging admiration. It would have helped if she drank."

Sally drained her glass.

I brought the conversation into the present. "I'm sorry to be asking this, but did Pepper's death ever seem suspicious?"

Sally looked at me, more curious than surprised. "No. Oskar, who died the same day, yes. Perhaps you heard about him. He was shot, so that was out of the ordinary scheme of things. But Pepper... she had a bad heart. Always. When she was a teenager, the doctor told her she'd be on bedrest her entire life. That, if she decided to make pictures, let alone sing and dance, it would kill her. Six months before she died, she was given two months to live. None of us were surprised when she died. Sad, yes. And I *was* sad. Pepper somehow softened toward the end. We'd become allies if not friends. She took a part of my past with her. There was no one else to whom I could say, 'remember when?' and name some crazy Hollywood shenanigans. But no one needed to kill her. Her heart did the job. Why do you ask?"

"You might have heard that someone killed the bartender at the Battened Hatch last Monday. And shot Mr. MacTavish yesterday. People have mentioned there have been other incidents in the past."

"As I said, Oskar was killed and they never caught anybody. But I do firmly believe Pepper went on her own."

"So it's only the bartenders who are murdered," I said ruefully.

"You should probably mention that to whoever takes over the position," she said.

"Whoever takes over the position—that would be me." I stood slowly. "Thanks again for letting me sleep over. So, you're not going to kick me out if the cottage?"

"Darling, in the day, we would kill to have a good bartender living next door."

"Pleased to be of service, Mrs. Chander," I said.

Back home, I showered and felt more clear-headed and ready to face the day. It was 10:30—too late for the gym, but still early by bartender time. One thing I enjoy about working evening hours is having most of the day off. Most people have their kick-back time after work. Mine was before. By this time yesterday, I'd already found Mr. MacTavish and been assaulted.

I decided to go and see how he was doing. We'd been through something together, and I hadn't talked to him since the ambulance ride. Part of why I felt close to him was because he'd confided some personal things—but he probably had no recollection of having done so. That was tricky. How much did he know that I knew?

In the kitchen I found the items I'd been carrying when I'd gotten home the night before, including the napkin with Jeff the Cabbie's number on it. I turned it over, made a decision, and walked back over to Mrs. Chander's. She was surprised to see me but fine with letting me use her landline to call a cab—apparently the number came up as 'private' because Jeff, who answered on the second ring, had no idea where I was calling from. I made arrangements to meet him out front in fifteen minutes.

Perhaps inspired by Sally's flowing garments, I dressed in shorts and a flowery top, planning to change for work later. The April day was supposed to be in the mid-sixties, and I stopped back at the cottage to pull on a jacket, just in case.

Jeff's cab was parked at the curb out front on Elm. As I approached the guardhouse, though, a dark figure appeared in my path. He affected a self-important stance, but I didn't notice because I was analyzing his face, trying to put together the older stranger with the movie actor of forty years past.

"Did I not make clear that, were you to live here, you were to mind your own business?" he asked. He sounded appalled. "Yet you brought a group of outsiders up yesterday."

"They weren't outsiders."

"I know who they are, and what they're doing. I know exactly. And you, you brought them here, and even let them go up to the cabin!"

"I… that is, only one of them ran up, and only for a minute." He really could put a person on the defensive.

"And *you*! Were you up at the lodge this morning?" His dudgeon was high.

"Yes. She makes lovely blueberry waffles," I said, continuing by him, without breaking stride, and got into the car.

Glenn MacTavish was in a private room, large windows overlooking the parking lot. It figured that in this land of lakes and mountains, the hospital would be carved out on the only flat, uninteresting parcel of land. Wouldn't anyone convalesce faster with fantastic views? In any case, I carried a large visitor's pass. Apparently, I was the only one of Glenn's guests who bothered to get one.

One bouquet of flowers and six bottles of whisky done up with various wrappings of bows and balloons dotted his nightstand. Brent Davis, Jerry Raker, and Addie Moon were on one side of his bed, Investigator Spaulding on the other. Glenn, in the middle, looked older than I'd seen him, and wan—but then, hospital gowns do no one any favors. He was hooked up to fluids and monitors, and his hair was styled with the hospital half-wash, his usually-pristine beard unshapen. I felt a wave of grief. Having Glenn well and in charge apparently meant more to me than I'd recognized.

"They do have a point, Michael," Glenn was saying. "Suite Seven wasn't a murder scene, and you've had more than twenty-four hours to investigate and fingerprint and clean up the fire and whatever else. The inn also gave you all the surveillance video that we have."

"We've spent months arranging this investigation with the Ghost Seeker people," argued Jerry. "They've come with the crews and equipment, and they agreed to stay one more day. If they can't get into the room today to set up for filming tonight, they're gone."

Investigator Spaulding looked unconvinced.

Glenn overrode.

"Go ahead and do it," he said. "It's my property and you have my permission." He turned to the detective. "What else can you hope to find by keeping the room sealed off?"

"All right, I'll call over. Give us an hour. The room will be unsealed at noon."

"Yes!" said Jerry.

Brent was already leaving, cellphone in hand.

"Thank you," Addie said, and she gave Glenn a happy kiss on the cheek.

Investigator Spaulding saw me and smiled as he shook his head.

"Call me if you think of anything else that might be pertinent," he said to Glenn. "Anything at all."

Glenn nodded.

The elevator at the end of the hall dinged. The detective gave it time to close with the film folks aboard before heading out to catch the next one. As he left, he nodded his head sideways as an invitation for me follow him. "Listen, Ms. Nash," he said once we were in the hallway, "We're allowing the bar to be open, but stay on your toes. Tests are back from the limes. They were soaked in pure nicotine, one of the most lethal substances on Earth. As far as toxicity goes, marijuana is a 1, couldn't kill someone with it if you tried. But nicotine is a 5, nearly off the charts. A woman once killed her husband by simply putting some in his aftershave."

"Damn. How does one come by pure nicotine?"

"It's not that difficult, if you know people who have access. It's an unusual instrument of death, so we're thinking someone chose it specifically because he or she did have access. Just be careful."

"Thanks for the heads' up."

"One more thing," he said to me under his breath. "Do me a favor and don't find any murder or shooting victims today, all right? I know you've been in the wrong places at the wrong times, but I don't like having to convince the captain."

"I'm all for a day clear of crime scenes," I said.

"Say, got that new phone yet?"

"Soon," I said.

He gave me a look that said, *Who doesn't have a phone?* Which was a valid point. Then he left with an over-the-head wave, and I headed back to see Glenn.

Glenn was alone in the hospital room with Hannah Bricksford. She was here in her role as minister, as she wore creased trousers, blouse, suitcoat, and white collar.

"I think we've got the details for Joseph's service nailed down," she said.

"Should I wait outside?" I asked.

"No, I'd like to talk to you," said Mr. MacTavish. "Just give us a moment to finish up."

"So Joseph's family arrives tomorrow night, and will stay at the inn?" Hannah asked.

"That's right."

"Both parents, mother and father?"

"Yes. And two sisters, one brother and their families."

Hannah took off her glasses and sat in the seat next to the bed. "This must be awfully hard for them. How do you wrap your mind around something like that? Especially when we don't know who did it, or why."

"Yes. It's hard for any of us to wrap our minds around."

Hannah put a comforting hand on his arm. "I know you loved him a lot."

"Aye. He was wise, and quiet and strong. And always there. I counted on him being there."

"Do you know much about his life in Iowa?"

"His father was the mayor and an attorney. Joseph took the bar exam himself. His parents wanted him to be next in line…for the law firm, for politics, but he had no interest. And he knew he was bisexual. Might have found a nice woman and settled down, but maybe not." Glenn gave a small laugh and wiped a tear from his eye. "He still thought that might happen someday. He was great with kids. But, back in Iowa, he knew he'd always be a disappointment as Richard Emberg's son, so he left town before even getting the results of his bar exam. Didn't know where he was going. Didn't know what he was going to do. Ended up in Tranquility by mistake, he used to say, because it's where you change trains."

I hope he didn't notice that my breath stuck in my throat. This was becoming a little too Twilight Zone. Maybe when I was dead, the next bartender would arrive at the station, thinking she was only changing trains…

There was a lot of emotion behind Glenn's words. "He and I…we never had an exclusive arrangement. But he was always there for me. With a word of advice or a bit of humor, or a wider perspective. He was always there."

"Did his family know about your relationship?"

"I don't think they knew anything about his life in Tranquility at all. They sent him Christmas cards, so they had his address. But they never visited. They took his leaving as desertion."

"I wonder what they'd think if they knew he was running for mayor after all," I asked.

Glenn and Hannah looked at me like they'd forgotten I was there. "I saw his signs at Philip's house," I said. "It sounds like he would have made a good mayor."

"It took them months to get him to agree to run," said Mr. MacTavish. "But he didn't care much for Mayor Bristol."

I nodded, keeping my mouth shut, perhaps too late.

"Okay," said the Reverend Bricksford, closing her planner and standing up. "It will be a lovely service. I'll make sure to talk to the family after they arrive."

"Aye. Thanks."

"And you'll be discharged by Sunday?" She sounded doubtful.

"Yes, I'm going home tomorrow. The doctor wanted me to stay an extra day, but I insisted. I'll be at the funeral, never worry. Though I might need to skip the dancing after."

"Take care of yourself. We can't do with you down for the count."

"I will. Never worry."

Hannah took his hand, bowed her head, and said quietly, "Lord, heal and comfort Glenn, and Joseph's family, and this town. May we seek to show love and work for justice, as you command." She looked up, smiled at him, and headed out.

Once she was gone, I moved to Mr. MacTavish's side. "How are you feeling?"

"Listen," he said. "Those things I told you in the ambulance—"

Ah, so he did remember.

"Those aren't meant to be public knowledge."

"I never thought they were."

"Nor was the discussion to which you were privy just now."

"I understand."

"Very well. Was there something else you wanted to see me about?"

The parade of visitors had worn him down.

"I mostly wanted to make sure you were healing well, that you'd be all right," I said. I took a deep breath. "And I wanted to know if, after thinking about it, you had any idea who was in Suite Seven, or why they'd attack you. And me." I'd gained nothing by downplaying my own role in the incident, even to myself.

"I don't, lass. I am hoping it wasn't personal. That whoever it was didn't expect either of us to come in before the fire finished any chance of filming."

"You think it was about the filming?"

"Well, we've never allowed filming before. There's never been a fire before."

I nodded. "But why?"

"I can't think of a thing. Except for the ghost legends. First of all, there is no ghost in Suite Seven. And, if there was, what would it matter? Move a glass of water or appear in a dressing gown—who cares, really? It would be nice if something happened when the Ghost Seekers were there, to have MacTavish's on the show and all, but a fire makes no sense. Not to mention… we need to stop these things happening at MacTavish's. One incident might be interesting, but people attacked in rooms? It doesn't sound good. We've already had one family cancel because of the 'drama.' It's fine if we have a ghost, not so good if we have an attacker."

"Did you know Pepper Porter?"

"Aye. She died when I was ten years old. Before that, she was a big presence at the inn. A big presence in the town. A gracious lady."

"She got along with everybody? Your parents? Others around town? It was fine with folks that she brought in the Olympics? She got along with Oskar?" I didn't want to push too hard. But there were questions.

"I know what you're thinking, but rest yourself. The Olympics she helped bring to Tranquility saved this town. She was a great friend of my parents. I was a lonely child, and she made me feel special, especially after my mother died. My mother didn't die suspiciously, I see that question coming up. Mother was ill for quite a while with multiple sclerosis. It was a hard, sad time, and Pepper really helped. As to your final question—Pepper and Oskar the bartender got along famously, even though she didn't drink. She had no reason to wish him ill. I'd stake my life on it."

"And you're definitely going to close the Breezy and replace it with Pepper's?"

"Yes. Should have sacked Chef Paul years ago. He's had one menu since he arrived, and only half of it is worth eating. Joseph talked me into hiring a new, young chef, several years out of the Culinary Institute. She's been working under some great chefs and is ready to open her own place. She's fine with calling it Pepper's. She'll be here late next month."

"So it's a done deal. The sacking of Chef Paul?"

"Again, lass, don't go around telling everything you know."

"I won't be the one giving Paul any bad news," I promised.

"'Aye, that's up to me," he said with a smile and a sigh. "Thanks for coming by. More to the point, thanks for interrupting someone doing away with me. Do try to stay alive. I'd hate to be out another barkeep." His eyelids were drooping.

"It is my plan to stay alive," I said, and left, letting the door close quietly behind me.

Back in the Day

Ingredients

2 ounces vodka
1 1/2 ounces fresh blueberry puree
1/2 ounce lavender simple syrup

Method

Shake all ingredients over ice and serve chilled straight up in a martin glass. Finish with a fresh lemon twist.

Blueberry puree
Blend and puree one pint of fresh blueberries (blend on a low speed and blueberry puree tends to become gelatinous if blended on a high speed.) Blend until blueberry puree is nice and smooth.

Lavender simple syrup
In a medium sauce pan add 3 cups of water, 1 1/2 cups of sugar and a handful of fresh picked lavender with fresh buds. Bring these ingredients to a light simmer until you have a nice desired nape over your stirring spoon, or a nice sugary coating on spoon. When you have a nice consistency of sugar to water after a light boil let sit for about 20 minutes so your lavender oils absorb into the simple syrup. Before transferring the hot liquid into an easy pour container make sure this is completely cooled as sugar will give you severe burns. You can leave the fresh lavender in the simple syrup or you can remove by straining the lavender simple syrup through cheesecloth.

12

Collared

This time I'd paid more attention to where the hospital was in relation to the town. As I left Glenn's room, I debated whether to walk it—my guess was forty-five minutes—or to call Jeff back with his cab. I was leaning toward walking when the elevator arrived. I entered and pressed L. Just before the doors closed, the Reverend Bricksford ran aboard, heels clacking.

"You didn't make it to the gym this morning."

"No," I said. "Late night."

We stopped a floor down, and four other people got on. Conversation ceased.

Hannah and I were the last off in the lobby, and didn't talk as we headed for the front door to the parking lot. She stopped outside. "Do you have a car here? Or can I give you a lift?"

Oh, hell. I wasn't completely sure I remembered all the turns to get back into town, and I didn't have a phone with a GPS. For that matter, I didn't have a phone to call a cab.

"No, I don't have a car. I am hoping to acquire a bike shortly. And a phone, for that matter. But if you're going into town, sure, I'd appreciate a lift."

She had a red Prius, parked in one of three clergy spots near the entrance. She moved a stack of books and a take-out bag from Boston

Market off the passenger seat so I could sit down.

We pulled out of the hospital parking lot. "I have a bike," she said. "I mean, an extra. It doesn't have speeds, or anything fancy. It does have a basket. Could you use it? At least until you buy another?"

Well, that was unexpected. And, given that I had no idea where around here one could purchase a bicycle, it sounded helpful. "Sure," I said. "Thanks."

"What happened to your phone? Did you lose it?"

"In a manner of speaking."

"I don't have to be anywhere until after lunch," she said. "Would you like me to take you to Deerfield to get one?"

"Is that the nearest cellphone store?"

"Yes. Verizon. Reception here isn't always good, but that's your best shot."

I didn't want to put her out—or, okay, to be beholden to her— but I did need a phone. And I had no idea how far Deerfield was.

"You're sure you have time?"

"Nothing I'd rather be doing. We folks who know Joseph stand together." She smiled.

Crap. She was going to hold the *Anne of Avonlea* thing over my head.

"So Joseph's funeral is Sunday?"

"Afternoon. Yes."

"And you're officiating?"

"Yes. Joseph was a parishioner. Not there every Sunday, but always willing to help out. He helped build the tutoring center in Deerfield."

"It seems like he was a great guy. I've hardly heard anything negative about him."

"Then you haven't spoken much to…"

"The mayor?" I said.

"You got it."

"I've heard he wasn't a Joseph fan. Nor was Marta's dad, I'm guessing."

"Seems like you've got the lay of the land."

"So, Joseph did have some enemies?"

"I wouldn't go that far. Non-fans."

"Joseph and Glenn were a thing? Did many people know?"

"They were good together. Good for each other. Happy. Solid. Generous. It was fun hanging with them. Somehow neither saw himself as a 'relationship' guy. While I'm sure Glenn is right when he said Joseph would have made a good father if the chance and the right woman had presented herself, I think they didn't realize how much they meant to each other. I wish they had. I wish they had made a commitment."

"Why do you say that?"

"I don't know. They both deserved happiness. To be settled, and sure of someone."

"Is that a necessary thing?"

Hannah looked at me and gave a wry smile. "No, of course not. I was speaking specifically."

"Are you settled and sure of someone?"

"Nope," she said. "Neither. Not looking, at the moment. And doing just fine."

I gave her props for not turning the question around and asking it of me. "Does it make it hard to date—with the collar and all?"

She giggled. "I don't wear the collar on dates. Unless someone asks."

"Really?"

"No," she said, still laughing. "But it takes all kinds. I don't think I'd go out with anyone who saw the collar as a must."

We drove again in silence. The landscape was gorgeous. Rolling hills, and a house here and there. I never would have made it to

Deerfield on a bike. "Real problem with me and dating," Hannah said, "Is, first, I'm happy on my own, and second, you know how they say girls look to marry someone like their dad? Mine set the bar pretty high."

"He did?"

"He did."

Wait…her last name… "Is your dad Samuel Bricksford?"

"Yeah," she said. "He is."

Though my mom wasn't religious, Mormor—Grandma—was, enough for them both—even I had heard of Samuel Bricksford. He was a young African American firebrand back in the 60s, who matured into a well-known civil rights advocate. He spoke to huge crowds, led protests, spoke truth to power. He was a charismatic talking head on television and probably was responsible for getting laws that codified injustice changed. He'd been jailed several times.

"Wow," I said.

"Yeah," she said. "Only child. Not much to live up to."

"But you're—"

"Very light-skinned. I know."

"And you're the pastor here, at Saint Barnabas?"

"For the last three years."

"Are you happy here?"

"Yes," she said. "These are good people. There are problems, obviously—though I'm not talking murder now. Neighborhoods, and communities, where people aren't exactly well-fed and well-educated. We're working on it."

"But you're happy in small city America, not out leading marches?"

"There's a lot here that needs doing."

"This is a pretty white community." I wondered how her church felt about hiring Samuel Bricksford's daughter. The fact that Hannah could pass for white brought up a number of questions on its own.

"Oh, you've noticed?" There was a smile on her face.

I couldn't tell if the answer was the truth or a dodge. We were entering a town now, houses close together and streets crossed in regular blocks. Unlike Tranquility, Deerfield had strip malls and office buildings. The ring of mountains behind served as a backdrop rather than a feature.

The phone store was on the main street, well-lit and airily designed behind plate glass windows. Since we'd arrived before lunchtime, an associate was able to help me right away. My old phone was part of my mom's family share plan, had been for a decade. It was high time I set up my own account.

I left the store with a nifty new smartphone and found Hannah sitting on a bench finishing up a call. It was fun to have the latest gadget, not only as a communication device, but as a new toy. So many apps. So many possibilities.

"Thanks again for bringing me out here," I said as we got back into the Prius.

"Sure," she said.

"Joseph went to your church."

"Yes."

"And you were fine with that? Even though you knew about him and Glenn."

"You mean, that they were together. Sure." Hannah pushed the accelerator—she was one of those drivers who sped up at a yellow light.

"How can that be? I mean, my guess is Reverend Layton would not be okay with their relationship." Like my mormor wasn't. Which played really well with my mom.

"You'd be right about that." She chewed her lip; perhaps was she was deciding how detailed of an answer to give.

"I mean, doesn't the Bible say it's a sin to be gay?"

"I don't believe that, by 100%. Some day, if you'd like, we can talk the specific theology. But my view of the Bible is that it's the story of God interacting with people. We're a little slow, but we're learning as we go along. Moses gave us the starter set. Jesus came to tell us what is really important, which is revolutionary love. Forgiveness. Loyalty. Generosity. Justice. Faithfulness. To 'love the Lord our God with all our hearts, souls and minds, and our neighbors as ourselves.' The rest, as they say, is fine print."

"I'm not so sure Reverend Layton would agree with that."

"Check the attendance on Sunday morning of Grace versus Saint Barnabas. They win. It's easier to get people in the door when you're offering hard-to-get tickets to heaven."

"You're not?"

"In Jesus' view, the Kingdom of Heaven starts here and now. We're not all about the sweet bye and bye."

"Coming back around, how about Joseph? Do you have any theories who might have killed him?"

We'd reached the outskirts of Tranquility, and slowed down to the village speed of 25 miles per hour. Hannah wasn't expecting that question. "No," she said, as she swung into the parking lot of Saint Barnabas. "Scary. I've never done a funeral for a murder victim before. That I know of."

"You don't think it's because…someone knew about Glenn and Joseph's relationship?"

"There are folks in this town who'd say it's against their religion, but I can't believe they'd think that being gay was evil but murder was fine."

"Still, it's odd that the victims of the two recent crimes were Joseph and Glenn, don't you think?"

The Episcopal church was made of the local light stone, with soaring stained-glass windows. We pulled up the driveway next to it which led toward the manse, a newer home. It was one level, with lots of glass, a style popular in the 1960s. "Let me show you the bike."

The bike was blue with a white seat and twin baskets over the back wheel. If I started riding out of town a lot, I'd probably need one with speeds to help me up the hills. But in the meantime, it would cut my work commute from twenty minutes to five.

"Thanks," I said. "I'd love to borrow it till I get another. And thanks for helping me get a phone. Are you this helpful to all the new folks in town? I guess it's one way to grow a congregation."

I felt stupid the minute I'd said it. She'd never once asked me to church.

"Well, I try to be helpful, yes. But there aren't often new people who have the potential to become... friends. Well. You know where I am. We could catch a movie sometime—without me wearing the collar."

I laughed and rolled the bike to a stop outside.

"I mean it," she said, "Lots of people talk to a bartender. But who does a bartender talk to?"

I waved as I pedaled away.

Collared

Ingredients

6 ounces Sparkling White Wine
1/2 ounce Elderflower liquor
1 ounce Honeydew puree

Method

Serve in a wine glass or collins glass over ice. Stir ingredients together (do not toss or shake as sparkling wine will create a fizzing effect).

Garnish with fresh honeydew on a skewer and add fresh honey or a small piece of fresh honeycomb on top of the honeydew.

Fresh honeydew puree:
Cut honeydew in half and remove seeds. Cut the outside of skin off melon. Dice into small pieces and put into food processor to make a nice silky honeydew puree.

Set aside some chucks of honeydew for garnish.

13

Barks in the Night

"They're perfect! So perfect, I could weep," a cameraman was saying as I rounded the corner that led to the shorter entrance to Suite Seven.

The hallway was jammed with people, lights and equipment. It was 11:30, and Investigator Spaulding's orders had been followed, opening the suite to the camera crew.

Brent Davis and Jerry Raker walked past, skirting the lights and cameras, deep in conversation with one of the on-screen ghost seekers as well as a man with a button-up shirt and loosened tie, whom I guessed to be a producer.

I heard a small bark and turned the opposite direction to find Philip leaning against the wall, holding Whistle. I came and stood next to him, in the easy manner we'd cultivated. When I remembered all the layers of our various interactions, I moved a step away. He didn't seem to notice.

"They wouldn't let me scrub off or paint over your handprints," he said.

"In fact, they sound ecstatic," I responded.

"Recently dried blood is a perfect lead-in to a spooky story," he responded. "Fame, murder, and pillowcases, all down the same hall."

"Speaking of fame," I said, trying to remain calm and conversational, "I spent the night at your grandmother's."

Philip was startled. He stood up straight and looked at me, tensing enough that Whistle looked up at him.

"She made me blueberry waffles for breakfast."

"She invited you over?"

"Yes," I said, remembering the drama of the situation.

"Do you have a minute to talk?"

"Sure," I said. "Though I'm supposed to open the tavern at noon, and I'm running a little late. Could we talk while I set up?"

"Yeah," he said. He let Whistle down onto the floor and she happily paraded with us down the hall.

"There's a lot I'd like to know, at some point, about your family. I mean, as much as you're comfortable sharing," I spoke distinctly but only for his hearing. I tried to sound normal and not at all impressed.

"What? Oh, yeah, sure. Whenever."

The lobby was full of people watching the Ghost Seekers come and go. We passed through and slipped into the pub, which I re-locked behind us.

Something else was on his mind that trumped the fact I knew that Salty Sally was not only alive but was his grandmother. What could be that important?

We turned the corner out of the entry hall. Being alone with Philip was suddenly fraught. He knew things about me, and my vulnerabilities, no one else here knew. I nodded him to a barstool, and slipped behind the bar. Yes, I was getting ready to open, but it also provided a barrier between us—a "Johnny Carson desk," as my mother referred to such things, giving me distance from the other person and the upper hand.

"Want anything?" I asked, because he was sitting at my bar, and it seemed polite.

"Nah," he spoke. "Thanks."

What was my problem? How had Philip, my first friend in

Tranquility, become dangerous to me?

Philip sat quietly, waiting for me to stop fussing with the clean glasses. When I finally stood still and looked across the bar, his face seemed drawn and unshaven, his tousled hair unkempt.

"Something's going on around here," he said quietly.

"Ya think?"

"Whistle woke me up at 2:30 this morning, barking," Philip said. His dark eyes were troubled. "She never does that. She was barking at one of the bedroom windows. The shade was down, and I assumed shadows from one of the trees were bugging her. I'd just gotten back to sleep when she leapt off the bed and started barking at the closed bedroom door."

I got goosebumps listening to him talk. Things must be getting to me more than I thought.

"Did you get up?"

"Of course. When I opened the bedroom door, Whistle went running to the front door, growling, threw herself against it, and then went to a front window. I thought... I thought I heard footfalls run down the steps, but by the time I got there and turned on the porch light, there was no one there."

"Did you call the police?"

"No. It seemed a little crazy to say my dog was barking and I might or might not have heard footsteps."

"Did you look around outside?"

"Outside? No. I went around and made sure all the doors and windows were locked. This morning, I looked around. I didn't find anything. No telltale footprints, but it's a stone walk; who would know? No one left a message and none of the windows looked like they'd been pried."

"Could it have been a friend? Marta, or Polly, or someone who needed somewhere to go, but decided not to wake you?"

"Possibly. The thing is," he started but then trailed off.

"What?"

"I have a bad feeling about this. I know it sounds crazy, but I feel like someone wishes me ill. Like I'm not safe."

"In that case, you need to tell someone. Investigator Spaulding."

"I guess. There isn't much to go on. Police can't mobilize because someone has a bad feeling."

"You should tell them someone was at your house in the middle of the night."

"No proof."

"Cite Whistle." I opened the bar's deep wine fridge and began checking how much was left in each bottle for by-the-glass pours. We needed more Pinot Grigio.

"Could do that, I guess." She'd been playing around the feet of his bar stool, and he scooped her up.

"And maybe stay somewhere else till this all gets resolved? At your girlfriend's, or your grandmother's house until this all blows over. You'd feel safer. I would, too. Did you grow up at the lodge?"

"I grew up in the cottage."

"Where I'm living?"

"Yes. My brother and I shared the second bedroom. I think it's an office now. Tight quarters. But it worked."

"Wow," I said. "I thought there was good energy around that place."

"I can't leave my place. The art studio is there. What if someone broke in and defaced the artwork? The pieces aren't only mine. I feel very protective."

"Yet you feel you're in danger."

"I wouldn't go as far as being in danger. I'm... uneasy."

"I'm uneasy, too," I said, heading back toward the tall wine cooler. "I wish I'd felt more uneasy before I went busting into Suite Seven yesterday. I guess my radar isn't the best. By the way, did you know that Joseph's funeral is on Sunday afternoon?"

"Yes, Marta let me know. And it was in the paper yesterday."

I had to start reading the local paper on a more regular basis.

Whistle was nudging Philip's chin with her nose, and starting to squirm. "Looks like someone needs a walk," I said.

"She does," he said. "Thanks for letting me talk. See you later."

"Be careful," I said.

Philip was such a steady, common-sense person that his apprehension bothered me. I proceeded back to the storeroom where I kept my clean bartending outfits. The hallway had only a small overnight work light on, and it was a challenge to meet key to keyhole, but I did it and swung the door open. I turned on the overhead light, as the storeroom had little natural light, its only window high up and facing away from the inn, out over the water.

I felt a breeze and looked toward it.

The window stood open.

Damn.

A cursory overview didn't show anything missing or out of place. I decided to set up the bar and do a more thorough inspection.

I went to the shelf where I kept my folded black trousers and an assortment of black blouses and shirts. I picked up the top shirt, ready to pull off my flowery top, when I heard the rustle of paper. There was a sheet of typing paper, folded into fourths, sitting on top of the next shirt. Trembling, I picked it up. It read:

You are the reason he is in danger. Fuck off.

Barks in the Night

Ingredients

2 wedges of orange
2 wedges of lemon
2 wedges of lime
.5 oz of real Maple syrup (not log cabin or Aunt Jemima)
1.25 oz of Woodchopper Maple Birch Whiskey by Lake Placid Spirits. If regular whiskey is substituted, add another teaspoon of syrup.
Splash of soda water

Method

In a rocks glass muddle (1) wedge each of the citrus and the maple syrup, once muddled top glass up with ice. Pour In 1.25oz (1 shot) of the maple whiskey. Flip glass into shaker and shake gently. Fill the now empty rocks glass with ice and strain shaken mixture into the glass. Top off with a splash of club soda and garnish the glass with the remaining wedges of orange, lemon and lime! Enjoy!

14

Daytime Secrets

Seriously? It was my freaking fault? That *who* was in danger? Who? Glenn? Philip? Joseph, who it was already too late to do anything about?

Winsome?

Give me a break!

What was I doing that would put someone in danger?

Was this from Firestarter Guy?

If so, why? What had I done to provoke him or her? I went with Marta to Philip's house. I ate blueberry waffles with Sally. I visited Glenn at the hospital. I drove to get a phone with Hannah. What was the big freaking deal?

Who had a key to access the storeroom? Only me. And Glenn. Could someone have climbed in the window? It was pretty high up. Or had Chef Paul made a copy of the key when I'd loaned him mine?

I fished my new phone out of my pocket. With slightly trembling fingers, I dialed.

"Spaulding." He answered on the third ring. He sounded official. Of course, he wouldn't recognize my phone number.

"Detective," I said, "It's Avalon Nash. I have a new phone. And someone left me a note."

After the call, I took a photo of the note with my phone, then put it back where I'd found it—as Spaulding had requested. I finished changing clothes and headed out to the bar.

Rusty, who filled in during Marta's school hours, stood in the dark by the bar, looking confused.

"Oh, there you are," he said. "I think we'd better hurry and open."

I hadn't had time to finish my set up and get into my Zen zone, but I turned on the lights and followed him over to the entrance hallway. When I opened the door to the lobby, forty-seven people stood waiting to come in.

Okay, maybe not forty-seven. At least twenty. Apparently, word had gotten around Tranquility that there was a television crew at MacTavish's Seaside Cottage and many citizens had a sudden urge to drop by. Maybe Glenn was right: a documentary about Tranquility and MacTavish's actually would help business.

Those waiting streamed in, and we got busy.

When Investigator Spaulding and two uniformed officers arrived, I barely had time to take them back to the storeroom.

I told Investigator Spaulding I had no idea who left the note, or to whom it referred. As far as I knew, I was doing nothing to put anyone in danger. If someone wanted to successfully threaten me and stop me from doing something, he would have to be more specific. Sheesh.

Marta arrived at 1:30, out of school for the weekend. I've seldom been so glad to see anyone in my life.

Just after the lunch rush, around two p.m., Addie Moon and Jerry Raker came from the set-up for the Ghost Seeker shoot and slid onto bar stools.

"How's it going?" I asked. "Think the Ghost Seekers will find anything?"

"Here's hoping," said Jerry. "Pepper Porter never did mind being in the public eye. Maybe the old girl will rally."

"Any new specialty drinks?" asked Addie.

"Here is today's list," I said.

"The Bloody Handprint?" asked Jerry. "Boy, you get right to it."

"It's what happens when there's a wifi printer in the storeroom. I can change the drink list as often as I like."

"Most bartenders just use a chalkboard. But the Bloody Handprint works for me," he said. "I was looking for a drink more savory than sweet. Not too much jalapeño?"

"Only the required amount."

He also ordered the tortilla soup.

Addie ordered a Cesar salad and a raspberry Bellini.

"What are they rigging in Suite Seven?" I asked.

"Video cameras from many angles, including in the bedroom and the bathroom. Infrared cameras, too. They're also gonna do several EVP sessions, where they talk to the spirit and listen with a very sensitive digital recorder. You can often hear things on playback not noticeable to the human ear."

"Somebody said they're going to do another hotel room, too?"

"Yes, if they come all the way to town, they want to up their odds. There's a room way back on the third level where a rich tycoon died. He was old and simply passed in his sleep, but he has an interesting life story, and a good part of the Ghost Seekers program is telling the stories behind the hauntings."

"Ah." It is a part of the hotel (and cruise ship) industry seldom discussed. People die in the rooms. It happens.

As I served their food, Brent Davis came and sat beside them. He wore a navy blue suit, a white shirt and a gold tie. And a wedding ring. I'd heard he had a wife and a grown son. He was the local part of the documentary trio, and I tagged him as settled but adventurous at the same time. "So," he said, "will one of the Ghost Seekers sleep in Pepper's bed after they finish shooting?"

"Yes. They're going to wrap it up around one a.m. and then one of the female on-air Ghost Seekers will sleep in Suite Seven, see if a ghost will sit on the corner of the mattress."

"Here's what I don't understand," I said. "If they're really interested in finding ghosts, why don't they stay at a place for a week—or at least two or three days? If I was a ghost, it's completely likely I'd be taking the night off when they showed up for a few hours."

"Main reason is they don't have the resources to go through all that footage, or to cut their locations in half to more deeply investigate just a few," said Brent.

"Also," Addie added, "it's like those shows that rebuild entire restaurants or houses in one week. Part of the viewer's thrill is 'can it really happen?'"

"Interesting," I said, turning as Brent called me over to order a chicken Cesar salad.

"Back in a bit," said Jerry. "I've got to change into camera-appropriate clothing. They're going to interview me for background info on Pepper."

He gave a small salute and headed out.

"How did it go with the PBS execs in Albany?" Addie asked Brent, once Jerry was gone.

"About how I expected. Even with the interesting stuff in Jerry's book, there isn't much that's new. No real reason to dust off Pepper Porter. I'm guessing they'll pull the plug this week."

"Even if Pepper shows up in a ghost video?" Addie asked, hopefully.

"It would be five minutes of new footage, if that. We're not doing a supernatural video."

"How about the angle of both Pepper and Salty Sally living in Tranquility? Their feud?" Addie pressed.

"Nothing new there, either," Brent said, loosening his tie. He seemed downcast. "Avalon, give me a Stella Artois."

"Coming right up," I said.

By three o'clock, the pace had slowed. The Ghost Seekers were doing their thing in halls sealed off from the general public. Someone ordered a second gin and tonic, but everyone who'd ordered food was already served and eating.

"Marta, want to do the gin and tonic for table six?" I asked.

"Sure." She was a fast learner—a great observer, so making the drinks was a sensible next step.

"As a matter of fact, could you hold down the fort for half an hour?" I asked. I wanted her to start to have the confidence to run the place by herself. I also wanted to be able to buy myself some break time. Just now, specifically, I wanted to bike home for a minute. Half an hour seemed practical.

"Really?" she asked. "Sure."

We put each other's numbers in our phones. She showed me again that she had the bartender recipe app we'd decided was the most helpful. I'd handmade a bottle of mixer for the Bloody Handprint.

I got my blue bike from the back hall and reached Mill Pond in five minutes, riding up the path and over the bridge, before leaning the bike against the steps to Sally's lodge.

I was on the porch before I heard voices inside. Shoot. My first thought was one of disappointment; Sally had a guest. I'd been hoping to catch her alone. My second thought was of curiosity. Who else in the town knew she was here, that she was Sally, besides Mr. Fenton, me and Philip?

I paused inside the porch, off to the side of one of the conversation areas. The voices sounded close enough to be coming from the great room, which was right in front. By shifting slightly, I could see Sally seated on the plush sofa to the left of the huge fireplace. She was talking to a man who stood before her, but whose back was to me.

His head was hung, as though he'd been giving her bad news or making an apology.

She didn't seem depressed or anything, though. In fact, she seemed perky and in control. She was questioning. He was answering. Then he laid down over Sally's lap. She said something else to him, not in anger, though she was clearly in control. A nod of ascent from the man. He jumped with the first swat, somewhat less with the second. She wasn't playing around. He was really "getting it."

My cottage. I had to get my bike and get to my cottage.

I stashed my bicycle in back of the house and put the kettle on, then I sat, with my cup of tea, and watched out the front window. How long could I wait? After fifteen minutes, I was on the verge of heading back to work when the porch door opened and a man headed down the steps. He seemed almost light of foot, his head held high, although he did step a bit gingerly.

It was Tim Layton. My first thought: that will teach him to yell at me and Whistle.

This was a crazy town.

It was getting close to the time I'd promised to return. I was feeling less sure about barging in on Sally. I wondered...

The handset to the old black phone was heavy in my hand. There was no sound of ringing. But a few minutes later, a voice said, "Yes, dear?"

"Mrs. Chander? It's Avalon. I was wondering if I could stop in for a minute."

"Of course. And you must call me Sally."

This time, she was alone at the lodge as she invited me in. "Tea?" she asked.

"No, I need to get back to MacTavish's. I'm on break."

She sat on the sofa by the fireplace and offered me a spot. I chose one on a neighboring loveseat. "This does sound interesting," she said. "If you've come away on break specifically to talk to me."

The first sheen was off the idea, but I overrode my palpitating heart and opened my mouth.

"I wanted to know... what we were talking about this morning. Has your secret had its time? Are you committed to being anonymous for the rest of your life? Must no one know that Sally Allison is alive? Now that Cliff is dead, and the studios hold no sway...you are such a repository of history and insider knowledge." She didn't answer right away, and I plunged on, trying to present my case before nerves overtook me. "It's just that...if you had ever considered re-emerging, this would be the perfect time. The upcoming film festival will really help Tranquility; and there are some nice and talented folks, including Brent Davis, who produces documentaries for PBS, and Jerry Raker, who is a celebrated writer. They're doing a documentary about Pepper, but they don't have enough new info to make it worth PBS producing it. Interesting stuff, but nothing new.

"On the other hand... if suddenly Sally Allison was alive, and could tell her own story and the story of those days, it would help them out. And they're good folks. I'm sure they'd follow your guidance about what to say."

The words had tumbled out. I hadn't been looking her in the eye.

Her white-blonde hair had a gentle curl at the bottom, her bangs were back, and she wore a lavender and green scarf on top like a hair ribbon. She looked camera-ready even now.

"You want me to reappear as Sally to help out with a documentary about Pepper?"

"Well, I... didn't know how far you'd want to go. How much you'd want to tell, or help out. Obviously, if you're interested, the *real* story is you."

A darkness flitted behind her eyes. "Have you mentioned this to them?"

"No! Of course not. You asked me to keep your counsel, and I have. I would never. I will never. But they're good folks, and it would help them out."

She held my gaze. There was steel in her stare. "What's in it for you?"

I felt shocked, almost nauseous. "Nothing. I swear. You don't have to do it. Obviously. I'm sorry, we just met. I don't have the right to be asking you anything. Please forgive me."

Geez, I tried to use my powers for good, and see where it got me?

I stood up, wanting to make a quick getaway.

"So, you're keeping my secrets, and there's nothing in it for you?"

"I like this town," I said, "and many of the people in it. I was trying to help out, but I see now how I got ahead of myself. Please forgive me. I'm still hoping there might be some more waffles in my future."

At this, she did the last thing I expected. She laughed.

"It's been quite a while since anyone has asked me to come forward as Sally. I've gotten used to living a quiet life. I don't want that to change. I will consider it, though. There are some stories I have yet to tell."

"Thank you," I said, standing. "And again, I'm sorry if I overstepped."

"Thank you for keeping things to yourself. It means a lot."

I turned to leave. "Was that... Reverend Layton who just left?" I asked. I couldn't help myself, I was dying of curiosity about how she knew him.

"Yes," she said. "Why? Unless... did you happen to arrive earlier?"

Busted.

I have this really annoying truthful streak. "Yes," I said.

"Again... I can trust you to keep what you saw to yourself?"

"You mean..."

"That he got a good thrashing."

"Yes. Of course."

Sally's eyes were sparkling now. Timmy grew up with my son. Was slightly younger than Ben, but always tagged along. Once, when they were still in elementary school, they pinched some candy they really wanted from a general store in town called Otto's. Those were the days before time-outs and all that. So I had the boys return it to Otto and pay him. Then we came back here and I took Ben into the back room and gave him a spanking he wasn't likely to forget. Afterwards, Tim asked if I could spank him, too. He was indeed wracked with guilt about stealing and said his parents wouldn't even take notice when I called them. So I did."

She stood and walked me to the door. "While I understand time-outs and the like have their uses, and certainly abhor parents who abuse their children in the name of punishment, there is something to be said for a good spanking. You confess your misdeed, you pay for it right then and there—and all gone. Never comes up again."

"He still comes to you?"

"Oh, not often. Only when he has something he feels he really needs to pay for. Then he leaves feeling much happier. "And I admit, I do enjoy it. Our Timmy does need taking to task every now and again." Her eyes narrowed. "But that's all there is to it. I'm in no way a dominatrix, and certainly don't want that word to get out!" This time, she burst into fits of laughter.

"Of course not. Not a word, I promise."

"Not that I think this particular spanking will do him any good. Like Catholic confession, one has to quit the sin, not just want to quit the sin. And, even though he still feels he should be mourning his departed wife, he's a long ways from falling out of love—or lust— with the charming Reverend Bricksford."

I had my hand on the screen door, and I went through it onto the porch. I skipped down the stairs to the bicycle, and went after the kickstand with a vengeance.

Was I supposed to believe all Layton had to feel guilty about was misplaced feelings of lust? Could it be that he had something darker that needed repentance?

And, seriously. How many secrets was I expected to keep around this place?

Daytime Secrets

Ingredients

2 cups lemon-flavored sparkling water or club soda, chilled
1/2 cup citrus-flavored vodka, chilled
1/2 cup fresh lemon juice
1/4 cup sugar
1/4 cup orange liqueur
Crushed ice
Garnish: lemon slices
Makes on pitcher

Method
Combine first 5 ingredients in a large pitcher. Serve over crushed ice.
Garnish each serving with a lemon slice, if desired.

15

Nighttime Secrets

It continued to be a spectacularly busy night at the tavern. According to talk at the tables, everyone in town—having noticed nothing about television crews—spontaneously decided to have a drink at the Battened Hatch.

We chased everyone out at one a.m. I locked the doors and made a quick stop to check the restrooms. As I came back toward the pub where Marta was cleaning tables, I noticed the door to the smoking porch was open. My breath caught for a moment. Could it be Joseph was still present, somehow?

Ridiculous. Get a grip, Avalon.

Not surprisingly, that door, and that porch, held an energy that reverberated deep inside me.

I walked purposefully over and opened the door far enough to let me step outside.

I wasn't alone.

A woman stood looking out over the lake. Her hair was just below shoulder length, and she wore a long dark jacket over a sweater and pants. I could distinguish no colors in the night.

She heard me approach, looked at me quickly, and turned back to the lake.

"I was saying good-by," she said.

"To Joseph?" I asked.

"To Joseph," she said.

My memory clicked. She was the woman sitting in the booth, crying, the day Joseph died. "You're Sophie," I said. "You and Joseph dated."

"Yeah," she said. "You could say that."

"Was it... more than that?"

"Yes," she said. "You could say that."

She'd been in tonight with one of those original friends. Sophie had imbibed two Vanilla Ginger martinis. I didn't push. I waited.

"Joseph and I met in an improv class. Turns out we each drove two freaking hours to Saratoga to take the class. Joseph was great. Hysterically funny, fast on his feet, his mind was just so clever. And deep." She sighed. "I don't know what you've heard about me—if you even have—but everyone around here thinks I'm, I don't know, mousy. Boring. Sometimes, even I feel that way. But when I'm on stage, or doing improv, I become a different person. It was a riot when Joseph and I discovered we were both from Tranquility. We started driving to class together. We fell in love through improv class. So in love."

She wiped tears from her cheeks. "Even here! Even home in Tranquility where I'm just regular me, not a size 2, not an Olympic champion or a mover and shaker, Joseph loved me. He made me feel so smart, so funny. Yes, I knew he was bisexual, but when we were together, he promised, we were really together."

"So, what happened?" I asked.

"He wanted to get married. Wanted to have children. I... I don't know. Children were never part of my plan. I couldn't imagine it. Even with him."

"So you broke it off?"

"It seemed the only kind thing to do. Let him go find someone else, someone who did want kids."

She looked out at the lake again. "But we never did stop loving each other. A week before he died, he came over to watch a movie, like we used to. We watched *A Night at the Opera*. The Marx Brothers. We both loved old comedies. He asked if I might ever change my mind. I said that maybe I would. That made him happy. We kissed when he left. We were going to watch another movie last Monday night after he closed up. We never got to."

"I'm so sorry," I said again.

"Who would kill him?" she asked, and I had no answer.

Sophie looked at me. It was true; she wasn't a skater-size-2, or even size 10, but she was attractive and seemed kind.

"I still don't think I want kids," she said.

"Believe me, I understand," I said. "Listen, we're closing up now. But stay out here for a few more minutes if you'd like."

"Thanks."

I went back inside. She gave a small wave when she came through a few minutes later.

Marta and I were almost done counting the cash drawer when the Ghost Seekers arrived. We looked at each other and reluctantly opened the door.

Three of the on-air crew members and six of the technicians and crew came in and ordered drinks. They'd left two of the on-air team members to sleep, while being recorded, in the two rooms they were investigating. They were jovial and tired. They would have no idea if they'd caught ghostly activity until they reviewed all the tapes and videos in the upcoming days.

They were good tippers and great raconteurs, regaling Marta and myself with behind-the-scenes stories of previous investigations. By 2:15, they'd all shuffled off to bed.

Marta and I locked up and were heading out through the empty lobby when a young woman emerged from the hallway back to the rooms. She was almost staggering. "Are you all right?" I asked. As I did, a young man, one of the Ghost Seekers crew we'd served earlier, came running in from the street door to meet her.

"Stella, you look awful," he said.

"Was she the one…" I started.

"Who was sleeping in Suite Seven, yes," the crew member said.

Marta and I looked at each other. What had happened?

The crew member put his arm around her, protectively. "Sorry," he said, "she gets these migraines sometimes." Then, to her, "Come on. Come on back to my room. Let's get you some meds."

"But the investigation," she objected.

"I've already turned off the cameras. We've got enough. Come on."

The young woman looked like she was truly suffering, and I was glad someone was there to help her.

"Are you sure you're all right?" I asked her. Then, "It's a migraine, not a mean ghost?"

"Not a mean ghost." She buried her head in the gentleman's shoulder. He scooped her up and carried her toward the rooms.

As they left, Marta put a restraining hand on my arm.

"What?" I asked.

"Suite Seven's empty," she said.

"Yes?"

"And he turned off the cameras."

"So?"

"Let's do one ourselves."

I'd never seen her so excited. "One *what*?"

"An EVP session. Where you talk to the ghosts."

"But we don't have equipment."

"I have a really good digital recorder. That's all an EVP recorder is. It can capture the full spectrum of sounds."

I must have looked hesitant.

"Come on," she said. "If I was a ghost, I'd rather talk to local people than some television types, wouldn't you?"

"Maybe not if I was a famous actress," I said. But then, who really understood ghost psychology?

Marta dug through her bag and removed the tape recorder. Her eyes were alight. "Come on," she said. "Just for a few minutes."

The whole thing seemed amusing. Or crazy. Or slightly scary. Why would it be scary, unless I had the slightest inkling there might be a grain of truth to any of this? In which case... "Oh, all right."

We headed back through the winding hallways to Suite Seven, where the door stood open.

"Do we turn on the lights?" I asked.

"No," she said.

Together we went in. She was carrying tea in a white glazed mug which she set down on an end table in the living room. We discussed which room to start in, the finalists being the living room and the master bedroom, where the most recent assault had taken place.

We decided on the bedroom.

Marta carefully set the recorder on the dresser and we settled in. "You want to talk first?" she whispered.

"I don't think it matters." I started. "Pepper, my name is Avalon, and this is Marta. We work here at the hotel. I'm the bartender. Marta is, too. I know you didn't drink, but If you're still here, we'd like to talk with you."

We waited a minute or so, as Marta said our silences would be important. She'd apparently been reading up.

"Thanks for all you did to help the town and the inn," I said. "You're warmly remembered."

"But stuff is happening, and we maybe need your help," Marta said, conversationally. "Two days ago, Glenn MacTavish, who owns the inn, and Avalon here, were attacked. Right here in your suite. We're trying to figure out who. And why."

"And the bartender, Joseph, was killed," I said. "I know another bartender, Oskar, was murdered here the same day you died."

"I think we should ask yes-no questions," Marta said.

"Like what?"

"Did you know that Oskar died?" she asked. Then we waited. Nothing. "Do you know who attacked Glenn and Avalon?" Again nothing. "If so, was it a man?" We sat in silence. "Did his name start with 'J'?" Marta said.

"Why 'J'?" I asked.

"Don't know, came to mind," she hissed.

We asked questions the Ghost Seekers folks wouldn't know to ask, for maybe 20 minutes or so. Then we decided to be quiet and let the recorder go on for a few minutes.

Which meant we promptly fell asleep.

It was nearly 3 a.m. when we started awake.

"Did you hear that?" asked Marta.

"Yeah," I said. "What was it?"

We got up and groggily headed into the living room.

Everything was as we'd left it. Except Marta's cup of tea was on the floor, newly fallen, the glass shattered, and now-cold liquid was seeping into the carpet.

"Oh, no," Marta said, and grabbed some nearby cloth napkins, soaking it up.

Then we realized how odd this happening was. No windows were open. The hallway door remained shut. We stood and looked at the cup.

No explanation possible.

I took a picture of the fallen cup on my cellphone.

"The recorder shut off," she said.

"We should probably go," I suggested.

We left the room, her carrying both the recorder and the empty tea cup.

She went out through a side door which put her closer to home. I continued through the twists and turns to the lobby. It was deserted. Even the desk clerk was back in the break room.

I headed out into the quiet of the dark early morning.

Which was when I found Whistle, turning in circles, beside herself, waiting outside the front lobby door. She was not wearing a leash.

She saw me and bounded over.

"What?" I said. "What is it?"

She yipped, frantically.

Oh, no.

No, no, no.

She turned and started running.

NIGHTTIME SECRETS

Ingredients

1 ounce Stoli Salted Karamel
3/4 ounce whilte creme de cacao
1-1//2 ounces heavy cream

Method

Shake together. Rim glass with frosting, dip into praline crumbles.

16

Missing

I called Whistle and she came, bounding into my arms. I stuffed her into one of the back baskets of my bike and pedaled as quickly as I could up the big hill toward Philip's house.

I arrived to find the porch dark, and the front door standing wide open. There was one light on, back in the master bedroom, the door of which was also ajar.

"Philip?" I called, though I knew he would not answer. "Philip?"

I grabbed my phone and called 911. After reporting suspicious activity at the house, I hung up and called Investigator Spaulding directly.

"I'll be there right away," he said. "Avalon, go back out to the road. Do not go inside."

"Okay," I said, and walked, carrying Whistle, back to Philip's mailbox. My heart was thudding, but I couldn't be the one to find... whatever. Not again.

Within five minutes, a car arrived. Within ten, the scene was ablaze with lights swarming with vehicles.

Twenty minutes after he disappeared into the house, Investigator Spaulding came to find me where I sat on the front steps holding Whistle, who was snuggled down into my arms.

By this time, I was hopeful. No ambulance had come. No coroner had arrived.

Mike Spaulding sat down next to me.

"He's not here," I said.

"No, he's not."

"Any sign of a struggle?" I asked.

"Yes."

"Blood?"

"No."

"But you think he might have been taken. Kidnapped."

"It's likely he did not leave the house of his own free will."

That sounded bad.

Lights were on throughout the house now, a team of crime scene investigators doing their thing. Spaulding had his ever-present pad and paper at the ready. "What brought you over here tonight?"

"I was leaving MacTavish's Seaside Cottage—"

"What time was this?"

"Around 3:30 a.m."

"You were just getting off work?"

"No. The Ghost Seeker woman had to leave Suite Seven because she got a migraine. Marta and I went in to do an EVP session." Now it sounded silly.

"EVP?"

"Electric Voice Phenomena. You know. For hearing ghosts." His facial expression didn't change, but I could tell what he was thinking. "It seemed like a good idea at the time. Anyway, as I was leaving, I found Whistle out in front of the hotel. She was frantic. I knew she'd never be out by herself if Philip was around. So I brought her back up to Philip's house, and found the front door sitting open. I called 911 and I called you."

"You immediately suspected something was amiss?"

"Earlier today, Philip told me he thought someone was after him for some reason. He thought he'd heard someone on his porch last night. He was uneasy."

"Did he report this to anyone?"

"I don't think so. He felt hearing someone on his porch wasn't much to go on."

The detective flipped shut his notebook. "Follow me," he said. We walked around the side of the house and up into the small hallway between the kitchen and the studio. "Have you seen these before?" He was gesturing at the "Joseph Emberg for Mayor" signs.

"Yes," I said.

"When?"

"When I was here with Marta. Day before yesterday."

"Were you aware Joseph was running for mayor?"

"Not before that. They weren't going to launch the campaign until next month."

"Who? Who was going to launch the campaign? And why did Philip have signs?"

I wanted to help the detective, I did. But I mostly wanted someone to go find Philip. "Addie. And Brent. And others, I don't know. Philip had the signs because he'd designed them. Apparently, Joseph was on the team that wants to open an artists' colony here, and modernize, and everything."

"And who, in your estimation, might have a lot riding on this not happening?"

"Well, I'd guess anyone who wanted someone else to stay mayor," I said. "Which would include the current mayor, and many people at Michael Michel's gallery opening. Michel himself donated at least $10,000 to a nonprofit that supports the mayor's re-election. Look—granted, most of what I know about crime solving is from books and television—but if someone is kidnapped, aren't those first hours very important?"

"Yes," he said. "Yes, they are."

"Did you get the ballistics report on the two shootings at the hotel?"

His notebook slapped shut. "Yes," he said. "And you were right. They were a match. The odd thing was, the bullets were from Wogdon dueling pistols. The kind they used back in the day—the kind that shot Alexander Hamilton. Hard to find. Notoriously unpredictable and hard to aim. Strange hair-trigger setting."

"Hair-trigger setting?"

"It's a way the trigger can be pre-set to fire more quickly, with less pressure. Unreliable to say the least. Also very likely to go off without warning."

"Really," I said. I'm not sure if I was expecting a match. "Were there any dueling pistols at the hotel, on display at any time? Any that have gone missing?"

"That's a good question. I'll check."

"Do you have to wait till morning to talk to people in town who might have a motive to kidnap Philip? What if they have him now? Don't we need to find him before anything happens?"

"Let's see what we find inside. If there are fingerprints, or any other clues…"

"Like tire tracks?" Why weren't they doing something? Everything?

"Listen. No one came here and killed him. They took him away. Which means they want something, and he's very likely still alive. Come early morning, we'll talk to anyone who might have information. That's only an hour or two away. I've sent deputies to make sure there aren't middle-of-the-night goings-on anywhere there shouldn't be. We are taking this seriously. And if you're going to be of any help to anyone, you need to get some sleep."

I didn't move.

"We're on it, Avalon. We're doing everything possible. Get some rest. But… don't leave town."

I'd heard that before. "I won't. But listen, will you please call me if you… find Philip?" This was hitting me in the gut. "Please?"

"I will," he said. "In the meantime, Officer Brooks will take his dog to the shelter."

"No!" I said, holding Whistle tightly to myself. "I mean, I'll keep her. I'll take responsibility."

"Do you think it's what Philip Young would want?"

"I do. He'd never want her in the shelter."

"All right," he said. "At least until morning."

I glanced at my watch. It was nearly 5 a.m. The sky had turned from black to pre-dawn gray.

"Do you need a ride?"

"Thanks, but no," I said. "I've got my bike."

There was a small towel laying in the hallway. I picked it up and put it in the bottom of a basket to make it a more comfortable ride for Whistle.

And then I headed home.

The small town was on the outskirts of morning. A truck lumbered down otherwise silent streets, its giant claw arm picking up plastic containers of recycling. Lights were on in the kitchen of the large hotel on the lake, and as I cycled past the stone church, a lamp flicked on in the adjacent manse. Avantika Azni, wearing a light coat, arrived at the Cardamom Café, keys in hand.

Streetlights ended where Main Street became Elm. All was quiet in Mr. Fenton's house, and nothing broke the darkness behind. I pedaled back and stopped, looking at Mrs. Chander's lodge. No one stirred. I thought about waking her to tell her about Philip, but there seemed nothing she could do except worry. Investigator Spaulding was right. We'd be of more help if rested.

I used the large brass key to get into my cottage. It only then occurred to me I should have taken a leash and Whistle's bowls and food from Philip's house. But when I put her down on my little square lawn, she peed immediately, and then she followed me inside when I called. The house seemed friendlier with her there. I put down a cereal bowl of water in the kitchen and went to sit on the sofa in the small living room.

Something was nagging me. A movie scene with dueling pistols. One I'd seen, although not recently. What was it? A snatch of memory came back: watching an old movie with Winsome and Crispen and some of our female friends. Had it been one of the Sally Allison movies we'd watched together? Yes. It was one where she played a movie actress starring in a movie about people in the olden days. She wore a powdered wig in the movie within a movie. And there was a duel.

My swanky new phone was connected to the town wifi. I went onto the Internet Movie Database and looked up Sally Allison, then scrolled through her filmography. My second guess was correct: a comedy called *The Lass from Lyon*. And there, in the cast list was the second male lead: Rutherford Fenton.

My fingers shook as I dialed the police detective.

"Spaulding," he answered.

"It's Avalon," I said. "I don't know if this is related, but Rutherford Fenton, who lives in the house by the entrance to Mill Pond, was in a movie called *The Lass from Lyon*. He fought a duel in it. Maybe he never gave back the pistols."

"They were probably prop guns," came the answer. "But we'll check into it."

"Thanks."

I got up and checked my door locks again. The sky had added steel blue to the lightening gray. I stretched out on the sofa and pulled a lavender throw blanket over me. Whistle made a nest for herself down by my feet. The little sighs she gave when she breathed helped relax me and ultimately lulled me to sleep.

Missing

Ingredients
Whisky

Method

Take a whisky glass.
Fill it.
Drink.
Repeat.

17

Word Around Town

Strange sounds. Rooting around. Banging.

I opened my eyes to find daylight, grabbed for my phone, and sat up. 11:03.

Holy crap.

The banging continued. I looked down at my feet to find the furball missing. "Whistle," I called.

The ginger-colored dog came prancing in, happy to be with company that was awake. The banging ceased. I had a feeling I'd find the kitchen cupboards standing open. One mystery solved.

But Whistle's presence brought back the black weight deep inside me.

I checked my phone. No messages. No calls of any kind.

Philip was still missing.

What day was it? Saturday.

Saturday. The tavern should open at eleven-thirty. Noon, at the latest.

Glenn MacTavish was coming home from the hospital.

But should he? If someone was still out there, shooting people? Kidnapping people?

And Joseph's funeral was tomorrow. That meant his family was arriving today.

What a mess this town was in. Oddly, I wanted Tranquility to come off well for Joseph's family. I wanted them to know he'd made a good life for himself. It kept me from dwelling on the dread that had settled in the pit of my stomach.

Philip.

Yes, I was envious of him, but that was on me. He had a talent, a fire that burned deep inside him. More to the point, he was a good person. Why would someone wish him ill?

Whistle was on her hind legs, urging me up. Muttering, I headed for the bathroom, and then for the kitchen.

I opened the door to let Whistle out for her early meander while I rummaged for something that would make a suitable dog food stop gap, coming up with roasted chicken I took off a bone.

Whistle came in, happy with the offerings of meat and water.

Philip.

I had to get to work. It was still my first week, for pity's sake, and Glenn—my boss—was home today.

Philip.

I took a quick shower and pulled on my bartender blacks.

I grabbed an apple from the kitchen and dialed the phone.

"Spaulding."

"Nash. Any news?"

"Not yet. I will let you know."

"Fenton?"

"His alibi checks out. He was out of town when Joseph was killed. And he claims he was doing handyman work on your cottage when you and Glenn were attacked." A pause. "Any handyman work done at your place?"

"There was an outside hose that was leaking. I can't tell you for sure when it was patched," I said.

"Can you tell me who else you've spoken to?" I asked. "Any leads you're following?"

"You know I can't comment on an ongoing investigation. But I can let you know that public places, such as galleries, coffee shops and churches have been visited. We've also thoroughly checked MacTavish's Seaside Cottage. Unobtrusively, of course."

"If someone kidnapped Philip, they'd hide him somewhere out of the public's way, though, wouldn't they?"

"That kind of search requires a warrant. Which comes after evidence. That's what we're doing, Nash, looking for evidence. In the meantime, Philip's disappearance could be linked to the note in the pub's storeroom. The pub again seems to be a focal point in what's happening. Keep your eyes and ears open, and continue to let me know if you run across anything. People are… more careful and hesitant when talking to the police."

"But everyone talks to the bartender."

"If she's a good listener."

I promised to do as he asked, and in return, he promised to let me know of any significant developments.

My kitchen cupboards revealed no great possibilities for human breakfast. I decided to stop off at the Cardamom on my way in.

Meanwhile, Whistle sat, looking up at me with hopeful eyes. *Philip*, they seemed to say, *Are you taking me to Philip?*

What to do with Whistle? I couldn't really take her to MacTavish's. Unlike Philip, who worked in empty rooms and halls, I was in a food-handling restaurant with many unknown people coming and going.

Should I leave her here in the cottage and come home on break to feed her and let her out? Could do, except this was a strange place to her, and she might be confused and nervous.

I looked out, past my small terrace at the wooden lodge up on the hill. Sally had mentioned Whistle when we'd talked, leading me to believe they were acquainted.

On the other hand, if I went up there, I'd have to tell her about Philip.

I picked up the heavy handset of the ghost phone. It was nearly a minute before she answered.

"Avalon?"

"Yes. Sorry to bother you, but I wanted to ask a favor. Could you possibly keep Whistle while I'm at work?"

"You have Whistle?"

"Yes."

"Yes, yes, I can do that. Come up."

I locked the doors, called Whistle who happily followed me outside and over to my bike, which I walked across the bridge and up the hill. The little dog was dancing as we climbed the steps. I guessed she'd been here before.

I took a deep breath and knocked.

"Come in, come in," Sally said, beckoning me across the veranda into the lodge. The Pomeranian and I obeyed.

"So you know about Philip," she said.

"Yes. How did you hear?"

Sally was dressed in blue silk pants, a matching top and another opaque duster decorated with hand sewn flowers. It was beautiful.

"My friend Betsy told me. Word around town is that he's missing."

"Yes," I said. "I'm so sorry."

"One thing a woman must do is stop being sorry all the time. Sorry to disturb, sorry about Philip. Instead say something on a positive note, such as, I hope Philip returns soon."

"I do. Hope Philip returns soon."

"As do I." Sally sat on the arm of her favorite chair. I could see lines of worry in her face.

"How did you end up with Whistle?"

"I was leaving MacTavish's at about 3:30 this morning. Whistle was outside, like she'd come looking for help. I knew where she and Philip lived, so I followed her up. The front door was open, and no one was home. So I called 911."

"Oh," she said. "Oh."

"The police said there were signs of a struggle. There wasn't any blood or anything." It was like there was a volcano in my stomach. Should I be telling her this?

Was I getting an ulcer?

"Anyway. If you can keep Whistle till I come home..."

"Yes, of course. You'll let me know if you hear anything?" Despite her positivity pep talk, she looked like a very worried grandmother.

"Should I tell the police you're family? And ask them to keep you in the loop?"

Sally looked thoughtful at this suggestion. "Thank you, dear, but not yet. I will keep my ears open. And count on Betsy and Fenton. And Rachel. And you."

"Rachel?"

"The young woman Philip's been seeing. I am hoping she'll be advised about what's going on."

I don't know why there was a stabbing pain at the knowledge of Rachel's name. It wasn't like I had a horse in that race. Or that I thought he and Marta would make a pair. Their age difference alone made that unlikely, at least at this time in their lives.

"Should someone let his parents know?"

"They do know. They are finding flights."

I nodded. "Oh... I have a real phone now," I said, and gave her my number.

"Keep this private," she said, giving me the number from her own cellphone. "Which reminds me. Before Philip disappeared, I thought about your friends who are making the documentary about Pepper.

If I do decide to go public again after all these years—and I'm not sure I want to, not sure at all—I do need to find the right way to do it. I would need to talk to them—interview them, really—about how they would handle it. How they'd go forward. I could only speak to them with the assurance of strict confidentiality."

"I could arrange that," I said. "I'm sure they'd sign a non-disclosure agreement, or whatever would be appropriate. And I trust them."

"That goes a long way with me," she said. "Now hadn't you better go? Whistle is fine here."

"Yes, thanks. I'm off," I said. "I'll stop back for her after work—that is, if Philip isn't back by then." I desperately wanted to say I was sorry again, but it didn't seem the way to go. "I'll be glad when he's back, safe and sound."

"Atta girl," Sally responded, and she gave me a small smile.

Once again, the Battened Hatch was ground zero for those wanting to hear the latest in town gossip. I saw the folks waiting in the lobby for the doors to open and made a beeline around back for the kitchen entrance. I gave myself ten minutes for prep. Marta wasn't in yet. Rusty, who filled in when needed, was in the nearly-empty Breezy. I would poach him soon if she didn't arrive.

I closed my eyes and took a minute to simply breathe. Then I turned on the streaming music and headed for the door, flipping wall lights on as I went.

Patrons filed in, a veneer of somberness over their shining hope of procuring further scuttlebutt.

Most were people I didn't know.

Addie entered alone, claiming a table for four. The big surprise was that Michael Michel came in and swung himself onto a stool at the bar. "What'll you have?" I asked.

He took a moment to pretend to decide what he should choose.

"Vodka tonic with lime. Grey Goose it is," I said, and he looked at me, surprised, but didn't object.

As I added his tonic, Marta swung through the kitchen door behind the bar. She was upset. "Do you know what's happened to him?" she asked.

"No," I said. "Do you know?"

She shook her head, tears threatening to break loose. "Do you have any theories?" I asked quietly.

Marta shook her head. "No. Do you?"

"About a million, but none that make any sense."

"Same here," she said. "Want me to slice?"

I'd only done one lemon and one lime. "Sure."

"Sixths or eighths?"

"Eighths for the lime, sixths for the lemon," I said, and smelled both pieces of citrus in what had become the new bar ritual.

"They're not letting anyone into his house," Marta remarked.

"How about into his studio? I know a lot of your paintings are in there."

She looked startled. "Yes. Did Philip show them to you?"

"No, we didn't go into the studio," I hedged. "But he said you were very talented, and I believe him."

"If you're talented, why are you mucking about with that kid?" asked Michael Grey Goose. He sounded like he'd started drinking a while before arriving.

"Philip is an excellent teacher," she answered, turning the piquant fruit into perfect wedges.

"Kid, listen to me. If you want to paint, don't waste your time. Your father is a friend of mine. I owe him. I would teach you. You could paint things that people would buy, not just emotional claptrap."

"One of Philip's paintings is in the Cardamom Café!"

Michael gave a grunt that signified, *my point exactly.*

Marta's knife stopped mid-air. I put a calming hand on her wrist.

"Thanks," I said to Michael. "A kind offer. I'm sure she'll keep it in mind."

I took one of the limes, hung it on the rim of his highball glass.

"Skål," I said.

"Skål," he repeated, and he drank deeply.

"I could—" Marta started, venom in her tone.

"You could what? Take some orders? Fabulous idea," I said, removing the paring knife from her hand. "These will keep us for a while."

I glanced down the bar, feeling unexpectedly sad at seeing Glenn's barstool still empty.

Those near it weren't empty for long, though, because the younger "on-camera" members of the Ghost Seeker team soon jumped onto the middle chairs. "What's up, guys?" I asked the three young men and one young woman. The males hadn't shaved—or bathed—since last time I'd seen them.

"We need food and drink fast," said the center guy, wearing a backwards ball cap.

"Yeah," chimed in the second, "technically, we're still up listening closely to every millisecond of recording. We're not allowed to sleep or leave the room."

"But there comes a time of diminishing returns," said the young woman. She had straight auburn hair, which obviously *had* been washed. Huzzah.

"What's fast?" asked the leader.

I showed them the tavern menu and got the men beers and the young woman a Midnight Caller, which she chose off my crafted cocktails menu.

"How's it going?" I asked casually. "Don't you need to do a reveal of ghostly findings to the proprietor before you leave? I guess it's good that Mr. MacTavish is home from the hospital today."

They exchanged nervous glances.

"If we have something to present."

"Pepper Porter apparently doesn't appear on command," said the one in the ball cap.

"If you don't find anything, will there be an episode at all?" I asked.

"You know, sometimes we get all the way to the end of hundreds of hours of footage and then suddenly—bam," said the thin one, attempting to sew hope.

"Bam!" repeated his crony.

I didn't ask if *bam* meant flying cutlery or apparitions or spooky voices. I also didn't ask if maybe sometimes they added the *bam* if it didn't show up on its own.

Momentarily free from drink orders, I disappeared to the back hall and into the women's room. It was during the requisite employee hand washing that Marta slid through the hall door.

"Who's watching the store?" I asked.

She bent down to make sure no one was in a stall, then she said, in the most intense whisper I'd ever heard, "I think he did it."

"Who?" I asked.

She looked me straight in the eyes. "Michael Michel," she said. "He's giving lots of money to have Arthur re-elected. And he hates Philip. Hates his painting, hates his poster design, hates all of it."

"You think he killed Joseph, too?"

"If he knew Joseph was going to run against Arthur, it makes sense. It would have taken someone really driven. He's really driven."

The bathroom door opened. Two out-of-towners came in, chatting and laughing.

"Better get back out there," I said.

From what I'd observed, Marta had good instincts. I didn't want to just let this go. But we also had no proof. Michel was gone by the time I got back, a five dollar tip by his empty vodka tonic. Oh, Mr. Grey Goose. What hath thou wrought?

Jerry, Brent and Avantika joined Addie at their table. The men ordered burgers, the women ordered salads. Only Jerry and Addie drank alcohol—a Sam Adams and a Willoughby Lemonade. They chatted intensely at first, then looked sad, then sat playing with their food.

It was a big night in general, but an especially big night for bleu cheese olives. I grabbed my keys and took the first opportunity available to disappear into the storeroom to replenish the stock. I closed the door behind me. Then I closed my eyes, taking a moment to catch my breath before heading back through the stacks to the bleu cheese olive jars on the back wall.

As I did, the hall door opened and closed.

Someone turned the lock from inside.

Then the lights went off.

Word Around Town

12 oz. can frozen pink lemonade concentrate, thawed
4 cups white cranberry juice cocktail
1 750 ml. bottle extra-dry Champagne
1/4 cup Grenadine
Garnish: pink lemonade or cherry sorbet float ring

Method

Stir together lemonade concentrate and cranberry juice cocktail in a large pitcher. Cover and chill at least one hour. Stir in Champagne just before serving. For non-alcoholic version, add Sierra Mist or Sprite in place of Champagne.

If serving from a punch bowl, add a cherry sorbet float ring by slightly thawing then refreezing sorbet in a round mold.

18

The Lime End

Silence.

I stood, listening.

As noiselessly as possible, I put down the bleu cheese olives and picked up a huge can of regular pimento olives. Back at Thornton Academy, one of our required gym units was self-defense. The instructor taught us, "if you don't remember anything else, remember this: *Stay calm. Break the pattern.*"

Stay calm means, well, stay calm. *Break the pattern* means do something the assailant doesn't expect, which breaks his own planned pattern.

Whoever was with me had cut off outside help and turned off the lights. He had a plan of which I hadn't been aware. He'd broken into my pattern.

Advantage, him.

It was dark. I knew the storeroom.

Advantage, me.

If he was expecting me to freeze or hide, it wasn't going to happen.

I was mad. It was about time someone gave me an excuse to bonk him on the head.

I stalked up the opposite side aisle toward the door. One good thing about bartending is the need for soft-soled shoes.

My assailant was crouching, looking down the aisles, but I'd made it to the front while he was still adjusting to the dark. I brazenly walked across the front as he slowly and dramatically crept down the side.

In one move, I turned on the lights, threw open the hall door, and said, "Okay, Bozo, do I holler for the police or give you a solid concussion with an olive can? Or both?"

"Marta!" I hollered. "Help!"

"What?" she called back, looking down the hallway.

"I've got a perp in here. Call the cops and bring the ghost seekers."

"No. No!" The voice had a French accent. "Don't call! I'm not a perp! I only wanted to talk with you."

Michael Michel stood straight and walked up to the front. I stood in the doorway and pointed across the room at the video camera.

"Just so you know, everything that goes on in here is on the record."

"Damn," he said. "Damn."

"Watch your language, Painter Who Brings Me Home," I said. "Why didn't you talk to me out in the tavern?"

"I wanted to talk to you in private. Please tell her not to call the police."

"Let me see your hands," I said.

He held them up. They were empty.

"All right," I said, and called, "Marta, don't call the cops. But watch the monitor. If he tries anything, hit 911."

I turned back. "What's so important?"

"I think I know who is behind… everything that's going on."

"Oh, good."

"It's Tim Layton."

"Reverend Layton?"

"Yes, I think so. Don't you? He doesn't like Marta working here.

He doesn't like her painting with that lunatic. So he just... stopped it."

"What's your proof? And why are you telling me?"

"I'm telling you because I don't have any proof. I would go to the authorities if I had proof. But, if I'm right, you'd better be careful, hadn't you? Because now you're hiring her."

"So what called for locking me in the storeroom and turning off the lights?"

He stood straight, fighting the effects of too much alcohol, and said, "You are an ungrateful girl."

Then he stalked past me, out of the room, through the bar, and out into the night.

I shivered involuntarily, thankful to be an unmolested, ungrateful girl. Realizing I was still holding a three pound can of pimento olives, I went back and swapped it out for the smaller jar of olives stuffed with bleu cheese.

Could Michael Michel be right? Was it possible that Tim Layton had more to be punished for than a crush on a theologically errant colleague? Perhaps. Likely. But murder?

As I arrived back at the bar, Addie came over to ask for her group's check. "Leaving so soon?" I asked.

"We're expecting a phone call from another of the festival organizers in about an hour. And we have to decide whether to pull the plug on the Pepper Porter doc."

"Now? So soon?"

"Well, it is what it is—a nice, interesting film about the latter days of Hollywood's golden age. It'll be a great thing to have available as a slice of history for folks staying here at MacTavish's. But it doesn't really merit national distribution at this point."

I handed her the tab.

"Say, what was with you and that artist guy just now?" she asked.

"His version is that he locked me in the storeroom to tell me who he thinks killed Joseph."

"Yeah? Who?"

"His guess is Tim Layton."

She tried to stifle a laugh, which only succeeded in morphing it into a snort.

"What's funny?" I asked.

"Only that he doesn't like the Reverend Layton. Sees him as a threat. The clergyman holds a lot of sway in this town. The mayor, and much of the rest of the gang, attends Layton's church, and they listen to him. Nah, if I had to take a wild stab at it, I'd go straight for Arthur Bristol, the mayor, himself. Can't really control his daughter Polly anymore, though not through lack of threats and intimidation. He thinks that Marta and Philip, and probably Joseph, were giving her the courage to find some independence—which they were. And that's on top of the fact that they're in the group that disagrees with his public policies. If Arthur somehow discovered Joseph had agreed to run for mayor—well, look out. He's not the type to suffer in silence. Or without taking action."

"Of course, you were running Joseph's campaign, weren't you? Which leads me to believe the mayor isn't one of your favorite people."

"I do think this town will be much better off with different people in charge."

"Hey," I said, running her business credit card and handing her back the receipt, "Hang out for a minute. All of you."

I quickly filled the three drink orders that had come up most recently—I mean, I carefully handcrafted them—and headed over to the film festival folks' table.

"What's up?" asked Brent.

I pulled up a vacant chair from a nearby table, turned it backwards, and sat down, leaning over the back.

"Here's the thing," I said, trying to sound nonchalant. "If it's not too late to add some footage to your documentary, I might have someone who can give a new take on the Pepper Porter/Sally Allison rivalry. Also, this person has inside information about other things that were going on at that time."

They clearly hadn't been expecting this.

"Wait," said Jerry, "Is it the woman who lived at Mill Pond? Sally's friend? Is she still around? Have you met her? Does she have Sally stories? Did she know Pepper at all? If not, I don't know that it will be much of a help."

"Boy, you are a champ at holding an entire conversations with yourself," I laughed. "You talked yourself into it and out of it in the same breath."

"It's what he does," said Addie.

"She's still around. I've met her and talked to her. And, yes, I believe she does have some as yet untold Pepper Porter stories. But she's been very leery about talking. Hasn't said a word to anyone about Sally or Pepper for decades. She's still not sure she's ready to talk. But she did agree to meet with you, if you're interested."

"Hell yeah," said Jerry. I could see his thoughts streaming at about a thousand miles per hour. "If she knew Sally well, maybe that could be my next book."

Addie added, "He has a way of getting ahead of himself."

"Is there a catch?" Brent asked. He was thoughtful also, his responses more considered.

"You'd have to be willing to sign a nondisclosure agreement to even have a conversation with her," I said.

"Well," said Addie, "Even though it seems unlikely a friend of Sally Allison's would have enough inside info on Pepper to truly make a difference, it would certainly be worth meeting her. But we're nearly out of time. It would have to happen soon."

"When could we meet her? Now?" Jerry was eager to jump in.

"We do have an important call in half an hour," reminded Avantika.

"If you'd like, I'll give her a call and see."

"If she's a night owl, there's no time like tonight," said Jerry. "And yes, we'll sign a nondisclosure."

I stood up and headed back to the bar.

"She'll love us," Jerry called after me.

Grabbing my phone, I headed out to the little smoker's porch. "Evening, Joseph," I said. It made me feel better about being in the spot where he'd died. "Things have gotten a little crazy."

I dialed Sally. "Any word on Philip?" she asked.

"No. Have you heard anything?"

"No. His parents are on their way. They'll arrive tomorrow from Spain."

"Okay. This might not be the best time, but the filmmakers about whom I was telling you would really love to talk to you, as soon as humanly possible. They're about to give up on having anything new for their documentary."

"'About whom you were telling me.' Oh, darling, I do appreciate your good grammar," she said. "When would they like to meet? I'm not really a morning person, as you well know."

"Well… they asked about tonight."

"That's awfully soon. But honestly, anything to keep my mind off Philip."

"How would you get them the nondisclosures?"

"I'll have them up here. If you vouch for them, we'll go with that. How about midnight?"

Back inside, I reported the news, which was happily received. Avantika alone begged off, as she had an early morning at the Cardamom.

As they headed out to prepare for their call, I announced the pub was closing at 11 p.m. I wanted to get home to change and greet the filmmakers before introducing them to "Sally's friend."

Last call was at 10:30. No one objected. In fact, the place emptied out quickly, and Marta flew out of the building the minute I announced closing. I locked the door at 11 p.m. sharp. As I was turning around to empty the till, I heard a knock behind me. I fought with myself but went back to tell the person he or she was too late.

It was Investigator Spaulding. Or, it was Mike, I guess I should say. He was in civilian clothing. I opened the door, and the first thing he said was, "I'm off duty."

"I've closed early," I responded. "But I'll get you a drink while I close out."

He came over and took a stool and I poured him a Rolling Rock while I counted the drawer.

"Any news about Philip?"

"Nothing I can talk about," he said. "But actually, nothing much. Any news on this end?"

"There is no dearth of theories, that's for sure," I said.

"Yeah?" he said. "Tell me a couple."

"Pick any townsperson. Then add the person who he or she likes least. Or envies. Or is annoyed by, and a theory of guilt is born."

"That's not surprising. On the other hand, for some, it becomes a game to pick the least likely person and find a motive."

"Such as?" I asked.

"Okay, for example…how about Glenn MacTavish? Suppose he and Joseph weren't that in love, in fact, he wanted to get rid of him, but couldn't."

"Glenn *was* sitting at the lime end of the bar that night. But wait— how would he shoot himself? Or knock me out? He couldn't have knocked me out while he was lying on the floor."

"What if he had an accomplice?"

"Whom he asked to shoot him with a dueling pistol? Those things are infamous for being unreliable. He could have been killed."

Mike exhaled. "Okay, you're right. Didn't get very far with that one."

"What if someone found the old gun stashed somewhere here and decided to send a message?" he asked.

"I don't know. Do poisoning and shooting go together? I thought those methods profiled different kinds of killers."

"It depends on how many victims you need to do away with. Sometimes you have to get creative." His official phone buzzed. "Spaulding." He listened for a while. "I'm here with her right now."

That didn't sound good. Who was looking for me? And why?

He hung up but didn't speak. Within seconds, his phone buzzed, and he turned his attention to a text he was receiving. He read. And read.

"Fuck," he said.

"What?" I said. "And what does it have to do with me?"

"The police station here got a call from the police in Montreal. Apparently someone in lost and found at the train station has your old phone."

"Okay."

"It had died, but the lost and found people plugged it in to try to find clues to the owner. When they did, they found a series of text messages that were received yesterday."

"Okay…"

"They've been forwarded." He extended his phone to me, and let me take it.

I read the texts in the order in which they would have been received.

I told you that you are the reason he is in danger.

I told you to fuck off.
Stop immediately or he'll pay.
You don't listen, do you? Leave town now.
I have him. He's not hurt much. Yet.
Why don't you fucking answer?
His death will be on your hands. In a matter of hours.
Fucking answer me.
Be on a train out of town before midnight.
Bad decision.

The final message sent was via audio.

Philip's voice: *"What are you doing? What? No. No, please!"*

A gunshot.

A cry of pain and anguish.

Philip's cry.

The Lime End

Ingredients

1 1/2 oz of preferred vodka
2 oz of fresh cucumber lime puree
Finish with sparkling water or soda water

Method

Pour ingredients into a collins glass over ice and stir. Finish with fresh cucumber slices and fresh lime wedge. Do not toss or shake this cocktail, as sparking water or soda water will create a fizzing effect.

Fresh cucumber lime puree:
English cucumbers work best for this puree as there are little to no seeds. If using regular cucumbers, remove the seeds from the fruit. Peel and dice cucumber into small pieces and put into food processor. Add juice of two fresh squeezed limes. Puree ingredients together until you have a nice silky puree.

19

Voice in the Night

Tears rushed down my face. "No," I whispered. "No!"

I looked at Mike, confused and furious.

"It has to be Michael Michel. Those texts were exact quotes of the note left in the storeroom! It had to be him! He tried to trap me in the storeroom again today! He hates Philip. But why is he doing this?" I was nearly shouting.

"Did Michael Michel have your phone number?" he asked.

"He… might have. I worked an opening at his gallery. I might have given the number to him, or someone else there."

"We have the threatening note from the storeroom. You're right, the texts seem to be from the same person. And you said Michael accosted you?"

"Yes! Just tonight! But why? What do I have to do with anything? Why do I need to get out of town? It makes no sense whatsoever! And Philip's shot! When was that text? How long ago?"

"The last text was only an hour ago."

"Can't you find out where it originated? Can't you do stuff like that?"

"It came from a burner phone. Unfortunately, Tranquility is in the middle of a valley. We don't have a hell of a lot of cell towers around here to triangulate. The text did originate somewhere inside about a five-mile radius, which includes all of downtown Tranquility," he said.

"So he's here. Philip—and his kidnapper—are here somewhere, within a five-mile radius?"

"Seems that way. We're trying to narrow down the location. Meanwhile, we'll pay a visit to Mr. Michel."

He turned and left abruptly.

I'd put the receipts into the safe. I grabbed my jacket, ran outside, hopped onto my bike, and headed home.

It was Friday night, and many lights were still on in downtown Tranquility. The movie theater—as well as several restaurants and bars—were still open. Overnight lights were on in Michel's gallery, three huge paintings illuminated in the plate glass window. But what was in the basement? How much evidence did the police need for a search warrant?

As I came to the end of Main Street, the dark gothic church, of which Tim Layton was pastor, rose from the sidewalk and towered over passers-by. There were still lights on in the parsonage next door, three stories in height and equally creepy. How did Marta stand living there?

Even as I wondered, I heard my name.

"Avalon!"

I screeched the bike to a halt in time to see a dark figure running down the hill. My adrenaline spiked. "Avalon!"

It was Marta.

"Thank God I caught you," she said. She stopped then, slightly confused to see tears on my face.

"What is it?" I asked.

"I was listening to our EVP session," she said.

"Not now," I said. "Something else important is happening."

"But *this* is important."

"Marta," I said. "Someone shot Philip."

Her eyes grew huge. "Is he okay?"

"We don't know. We don't know where he is. The police are looking. I've got to go."

She reached out and grabbed my arm. "No," she said. "You have to come listen."

"Tomorrow," I said. "I'll listen tomorrow."

"No," she demanded. "*Now.*"

I paused. Why was I in such a hurry? What was I going to do? Sit alone at home? Work up the courage to tell Sally her grandson had been shot? That was one conversation I did not want to have.

I left my bike by the curb and followed Marta up to the forbidding stone manse. There were lights on in the front living room. But she took me around back and onto a dark screened porch. We went in through what was once the servants' entrance, into a small hallway behind the kitchen.

"The house has a lot of big rooms," she whispered. "But this is where I stay out of the way."

She opened a door made of wood that matched and blended into the wall around it. We went together into a narrow closet. She'd set up a listening desk, with the tape recorder, headphones, a meter which read audio spikes, a pen and accompanying pad of paper with which she kept a list of sounds and time markings.

She sat me down and had me put on the headphones. She pushed rewind to the correct location. I heard my own voice. "Pepper, are you here? Can you hear me?"

The reply came; faint but matter-of-fact: "Unc horse."

"Unc horse?" I said, pressing pause.

"*Of course*," she said.

Then she pressed play. "Who's doing this? Who hurt Avalon and Glenn?"

There was no answer.

Marta held up a "just a minute" finger and fast-forwarded to a numbered spot. She hit play.

There was silence. Then there came shattering noise which I interpreted to be the cup of tea crashing to the ground.

"Good cake," said the otherworldly voice, as if underwater. "Marzipan."

"What?" I said, totally confused. "What about marzipan?"

"*For God's sake,*" Marta corrected. "*It's Fenton.*"

I took off the headphones and pushed back the chair. I stared at Marta. "What? How are you getting that?"

"From Pepper Porter," she said. "I'm getting it from Pepper!"

"Was that Pepper's voice?"

"It answered when you addressed Pepper."

We sat there, staring at each other.

"Play it again."

She did. I could kind of hear the words, "It's Fenton." I could kind of hear "marzipan."

"I don't know…"

"It's Fenton!" Marta repeated.

"Are we hearing that because it's what we want to hear?"

"No," she said. "It's Pepper. Pepper said it."

"Marta, listen, I want to know who's been doing this as much as anyone. We have to find Philip, I know. But I'm not hearing it. Not for sure. We can't go crashing forward because of marzipan!"

"Pepper Porter said it!"

"How do you know?"

Marta had been very agitated, but her body language changed abruptly. She became quiet and centered. "Because Pepper's saying it right now."

"What do you mean? Where is she?"

Marta looked me straight in the eye. "She's right behind you."

I stood up, knocking the chair over, and whirled around. Nobody. Nothing but a dark room.

"She's here? You're sure?"

Marta nodded.

"What's she wearing?"

"Brown skirt. Beige blouse. Orange and gold scarf."

We continued to stare at each other.

"Philip," she said, reminding me of what was at stake.

"You're telling me the truth?"

Again she nodded.

"Okay," I said. "But this conversation isn't over."

"I know. But what should we do?"

What, indeed? Did I call Investigator Spaulding to tell him a ghost was fingering a suspect? Both Marta and I would end up on a list of crazies, and anything else we said would be treated as suspect.

"What should we do?" she asked again.

"The most practical way to see if it's true or not would be to pay a visit to Rutherford Fenton."

"Without calling the police first?"

"Can't call yet. If we find anything, absolutely. We'd better take a weapon. What have you got?"

Together we searched the kitchen. The only bashing instruments were chairs, which were far too large to lug or use effectively. Feeling both anxious and antsy, we went out to the garage. There, we each grabbed a shovel.

Anger at the potential kidnapper and fear for Philip fueled the need for rapid response, as did the desire to quit the manse before running into the good reverend.

I left my bike. Marta and I walked determinedly down the sidewalk, heavy implements resting on our shoulders. Fortunately, both the church and Mill Pond were on the north end of town. One turn in the road, and we were nearly there.

Rutherford Fenton's narrow house sat directly upon both the public sidewalk and Cherry Lane, which entered Mill Pond. It was silent and dark.

"What do we do?" Marta whispered.

Now that we were here, this seemed somewhere between crazy and insane. A ghost led us here? What if someone had set up the voices on the recording? Or what if it was a ghost voice, but it was one of those residual hauntings, a hiccup in time that kept replaying? What if it was Pepper Porter, but she was answering the door thirty years ago, finding out who was bringing tea. "It's Fenton."

But she said, "For God's sake, it's Fenton." With some urgency.

"I think we should call the police," Marta hissed.

"But what if Philip is in there? The police can't go barging in without a warrant. And I don't think ghostly voices amount to probable cause. Whereas, I'm his tenant. I can go in, angry, because my water isn't working."

"At 11:40 at night?" Marta asked. "How do we explain the shovels?"

"Night gardening," I said.

She looked unsure. But she gathered her courage and said, "Okay. Let's do this."

"It has to be me. I'm the tenant. Plus, I need you out here, ready to call 911."

"But what if he finds you? What if he attacks you?"

"Call my phone. Right now. Then we leave our phones on. If you hear anything amiss, if anyone attacks me, or I scream or you lose contact, call 911."

"So you're going in as bait?"

"No! I'm going in to find Philip."

She called my phone, and I answered. I put the phone, still live, into my pocket. Marta backed up against the foliage across the drive.

Going in to find Philip. That was what I was doing. Going to find Philip. Either he was in this house or he wasn't. And no one else could find out. If he'd been shot an hour ago, time was of the essence.

I hadn't been in time for Winsome. I had to be in time now.

If it killed me.

I walked over to the house. It was so thin and tall it felt like it should have been in an evil fairy tale.

If the door was locked, I was prepared to break a window pane with the handle end of my shovel.

I grasped the handle. It turned.

The door swung open.

Crap.

Now there was no excuse.

I entered a small, square living room. The furniture—what I could see of it in the moonlight—was masculine and matching. Like someone had bought it thirty years ago, as a statement about the well-appointed gentleman.

The room was so diminutive that I could see its entirety in a glance. It was empty. I paused and thought. If Mr. Fenton was here, he must be upstairs. I had to be absolutely silent.

If this was my house, and I had kidnapped someone, where would I stash them?

The upper floors were so narrow, yet had so many windows that it seemed dangerous. Even with shades and curtains drawn, some passer-by might see a shadow. Or hear a moan or a gunshot.

I would take him to the basement.

Did this place have a basement?

I snuck across the room to the only inside door. It opened into an equally diminutive kitchen. Again, it was fastidiously neat and well-appointed. Copper pots hung overhead; a professional-level knife block on the countertop. With a glance I could see out the window over his sink—the window through which Rutherford Fenton watched me come and go.

There was an outside door. I knew it led to a tiny landing with two steps down to the backyard.

Next to the outside door was a smaller door. Did it lead down?

It creaked as I slowly pulled it open. Behind it, indeed, was a narrow, curving set of stairs.

What was I doing? Was Fenton asleep upstairs? Was I trespassing? Breaking and entering? Prowling? Did New York State have "stand your ground" laws? Could he shoot me with impunity? Or with a gun?

As I gathered my courage, my phone crackled. "Avalon. Avalon! Fenton's coming! I see him coming up the sidewalk! Heading this way. Get out!"

Fuck! Now what? If I left now, I'd never know what was down in his basement.

If I didn't leave, Fenton would likely discover me in his basement. Unless, of course, I hid down there until the coast was clear.

This chance would never come again.

I stepped down and pulled the door shut behind me.

Voice in the Night

Ingredients

1 1/2 ounces white rum
1 teaspoon simple syrup
2 ounces fresh honeydew puree
lime wedge
fresh sprigs of mint

Method

In a rocks glass muddle fresh lime and fresh mint. Add ice, rum, simple syrup and honeydew puree. Shake ingredients together and finish with soda water and fresh chunks of honeydew and lime wedge

20

Primroses and Poppies

I found the flashlight on my phone and shone it on the steps below.

They creaked.

I hurried.

The small downstairs hall had an earthen floor. Likely, in the olden days, it's where coal would have been delivered—which meant there might be a coal chute. An escape hatch.

The door at the end of the short hallway bore a heavy latch that effectively served as a lock, and could only be opened from the hall side. It was heavy and hard to move. Once I had the latch up, the door didn't open until I put my shoulder to it.

The room beyond was dark and dreary. It *had* been the coal chute. There was nothing in the room but several wooden boxes and the earthen opening behind a grate.

I shone my flashlight around to make certain, but otherwise the room was empty.

I backed out, barely managed to replace the latch, and went to the only other door.

As I did, I heard a door—likely the front door—swing open above me. Then, footsteps.

My heart revved. My breath came in short spurts.

One door. One door and I could turn my attention to getting out of here undetected.

The latch on this door opened more easily. Perhaps it was more frequently used. I swung it open and lifted my phone, letting the flashlight scan the concrete walls of the basement room.

The first thing I noticed was the large dark stain on the opposite wall. As the light hit it, it turned dark red.

Blood.

I followed the pattern down to the floor and swept the light closer.

Which is when I found the body.

I gasped, glued to the spot. I gathered my courage and purposefully shone the light down. The face was turned away from me, but I thought I recognized the clothing.

Terrified, I walked forward.

It was Philip.

I grabbed my phone. "Marta! Call 911. Philip's here. In the basement."

"Is he alive?"

I reached out a hand, slamming back in time to the same action, a different friend. The difference was, Philip was still warm.

"He's lost a lot of blood, but I think he's still alive. Get an ambulance. Hurry!"

I hung up so she could make the call.

There was blood everywhere. On the wall, on the floor, on Philip. There were pieces of paper beneath him, also sticky with it. Lots of paper; onion-skin, I think they used to call it. Brittle. Like a manuscript.

"Philip," I whispered, "We've found you. Hold on. Please hold on. An ambulance is on the way.

I put my hand on his chest. He was barely breathing.

You. Bastard.

I grabbed back the shovel and barreled through the door, leaving it open behind me. Why had Fenton sent me those texts? What was he blaming me for? Why had he shot Philip?

I roared upstairs, letting the basement door bang open. The light was on in the kitchen. I clutched the shovel before me, ready to use it as either a weapon or a shield.

Rutherford Fenton stood in my path, wearing chinos, a button-down shirt with sweat stains under the arms, and a vest. He held the largest knife from the knife block.

Large. Sharp. Shiny. Deadly.

He looked straight at me.

"They're coming," he said.

Behind him, out the window, I saw no police, no ambulance, nothing. Not yet. Up the street, in the dark, I thought I saw movement. Maybe Brent, Addie, and Jerry?

But here, in this kitchen, it was only Fenton and myself.

I opened my mouth to say something, but before I could speak, he tore his gaze from mine and bolted out the kitchen door and down the stairs into the night.

Surprised, I followed him. I saw his dark shape moving fast, running along the side of the path, away from the street. I followed as closely as I could. The shovel was heavy and weighed me down— but it was the only weapon I had. I grasped it and ran.

He crossed the bridge and was nearly up the hill to Sally's lodge when I broke past the treeline into the moonlight. He didn't look back. It was as if I was inconsequential, that I—and even Philip— didn't matter.

Only one person did.

I ran as fast as I could. By the time I finally climbed the hill and arrived at the bottom of the steps to the lodge, I was gasping for breath. I paused only a moment, collecting myself, before charging up the steps, and through the screened porch.

Then I stopped.

Fenton had left the front door open. Through it, I saw Sally emerge from the kitchen, carrying a tray of highball glasses filled with ice, clear liquid, and mint leaves. She wore satin lavender pants with a matching blouse, topped by one of her lovely floaters, sheer white and decorated with flowers in lavender, pink, and powder blue. As I noted her outfit, the terrible thought struck me: *this is what Sally Allison is wearing when she will be killed.*

She saw Fenton, who had his weapon hidden.

"Hello, Ford," she said.

"Sally," he said. "I need to speak with you."

"I'm always glad to talk with you, but just now I'm expecting company."

"At midnight?"

"Yes."

"It doesn't matter. This is more important." His voice was commanding, his tone imperative.

"What?"

"Have you forgotten what I've done for you?"

She stopped her bustling and looked at him, catching that something was amiss. At the same time, she saw me standing in the doorway. Carrying a shovel. She gave a nearly imperceptible shake of the head: she wanted to handle this herself.

"How could I ever forget what you've done for me? I owe you my life. More specifically, I owe you my death." A secret smile.

I shivered, then remembered her other, manufactured, demise, in which he'd played a part.

"Let's have lunch tomorrow and have a good sit-down. Perhaps we'll plant poppies," she said.

"Or primroses," he answered.

It was dialogue from a film they'd done together, in which he'd played her fiancée, with whom she was planning a house and a garden.

"You're lying," he said. "There never were any poppies, were there? And there were never meant to be."

"Rutherford, what's going on? Has something happened? You don't seem yourself."

"It was all a lie, all pretense. You manipulated me, every step of the way. Bitch."

"Darling, something's going on. But since I haven't spoken to you in several days, I can't imagine it actually has to do with me. What's changed between us? Nothing."

Sally looked him in the eye and gave him a winning, personal, it's-just-you-and-me smile. It was the Salty Sally smile, the one that leapt off the screen, assuring you there was no one else as important in the entire world. The smile that warmed the heart of the recipient.

Rutherford lost his footing momentarily in their history, and his own blind hope. Then he snapped back to Earth.

"Bitch," he said. "You bitch. This is how you play me. How you've always played me. I was so blind. Think. Think of everything I've done for you. When the studio wanted you to be with Cliff—and you wanted to be with him—I ran interference for you. I lied for you; I swept you out of back doors, I drove you hidden in back seats. I was best man at your wedding. And then, then, when he started... hitting you, who was it that hit back? Who gave him a black eye? Who shoved his drunken ass out of the limousine?"

"Well, I did," Sally answered. "But you helped, too, Ford, you did. I've always known that. I've always been grateful."

He continued on, as if he hadn't heard her. As his voice got louder and more aggressive, barking coming from a back hall. Apparently, Whistle was in a bedroom, the door shut.

"I helped you pack up, you bitch. I helped you move away. I left

Louise for you, moved here with you. I helped you die, I helped you disappear. Because it was going to be you and me—that was always the plan. Poppies and primroses. We would be married.

"Who kept all your secrets? When you pretended to die so you could cheat on Cliff, when you changed your name, went to Europe? Took lovers, had babies… brown babies. Kept it out of the press? Me, always me!" He was close to weeping, with frustration and anger. "And when Pepper was going to tell your secrets, spill your shame to the world, who stopped her? I was your secret love. Your fixer."

"What are you talking about? I never cheated on my husband. How could I? That hound! We were never legally married! He'd had three wives—still had three wives! We did the fake wedding for the studio, to get the heat off of us. I never cheated on him. I married Saif! He is my husband! And those 'brown babies' you mentioned— do you mean my son and daughter? How dare you? How dare you!"

They locked eyes. He still had the carving knife behind his back.

"Wait—what?" she was processing his words. "What do you mean Pepper was going to spill my secrets? That you stopped her. How did you stop her?"

Fenton's voice had fallen into a rasp. "She wrote that book, that tell-all book! She and Oskar. There was no one to stop them. No one but me. What I've done for you! I've lied, I've stolen, I've killed. I killed Pepper. Killed Oskar. I'm a damned man, damned to hell. And what did you do in return? You spit on me, on everything I've done. You revealed yourself to that stupid girl who rented the cottage. You agreed to spill all, to tell our secrets to those film people. All the secrets I gave my very soul to keep. My soul is black, black as sin. And you're telling me you were never married to Cliff? You were a free woman, all that time? You never wanted me, did you? You led me on, had me do your bidding, but you never loved me. You never loved me."

Sally saw the craziness or the desperation in Fenton's eyes. She changed her tone. "Rutherford. Rutherford. How can you say such a thing? I've always loved you. Always. No one else was there. No one else will ever understand what those days were like, back in Hollywood. Just you and me. The studio heads, the directors, the movie stars—legends to others. Friends to us. First- name basis. That time is gone. No one else can join us knowing this…knowing them, knowing that time, how it was. Alive and colorful and crazy, wasn't it? Only us. Only you and me."

He was no longer hearing her. He snarled, "You will never marry me. You will never have sex with me. But I have discovered there is something more intimate. Do you know what the most intimate act is… between two people?"

Fenton grabbed her arm and pulled her to him. They were toe to toe, eye to eye. "The one thing that guarantees our names will be linked together for eternity. No one will ever speak of you again without mentioning me. No one will watch a Sally Allison movie without remembering Rutherford Fenton. Ever."

Sally tried to pull free, but before she could, Fenton spun her around in a choke hold and brandished the knife, pulling it up to her neck. In slicing position, both her jugular and carotid arteries exposed.

But as they both spun around, to Fenton's surprise, he found me standing in the doorway.

Shit. Now what?

Break his pattern, break his pattern. One wrong word, one thing interpreted as threatening, or demeaning, and Sally was dead.

"Wait," I said. "You're Rutherford Fenton? The Rutherford Fenton who starred in *Gentleman's Passage*? You were great in that! And *Fortune's Cookies*? Wow. I had no idea." I purposely named two B movies he'd starred in on his own, without Sally. "It's really you?"

Rutherford Fenton stared at me.

"Mr. Fenton," came another voice. I looked behind him, shocked to find Jerry Raker coming through the door from the kitchen. "Mr. Fenton, you don't need to do anything else to be linked with Salty Sally Allison! You're already a part of her story. You were there, with her, all along! To pull off her drowning, to keep this lovely enclave. It was you, all you!"

Fenton stood, staring at him, shocked at the intrusion.

Brent Davis entered behind him, his cellphone held front and center, recording the encounter. "And we want to interview you! We want to know it all! Don't do anything that would keep that from happening! We want to know the Rutherford Fenton story!"

"Such drama, such color!" Jerry enthused. "Although, I'm sorry to tell you, you did not kill Pepper Porter. She died of natural causes. Heart simply gave out."

"What are you talking about? I sent up the tea that morning—the poisoned tea! Took it from the waiter and left it there myself. Called out her name to wake her up."

"Ah, but she didn't answer, did she? It's a very poignant scene in my book. She had already died in her sleep, never got up to drink the tea nor to eat the breakfast that had arrived. So you haven't done all the bad things you've felt guilty of."

As he spoke, Brent suddenly said, "What's that?" and wheeled around to look out through the back window.

As he did, Addie appeared from the kitchen. She moved stealthily to come up behind Fenton—then thwapped him on the side of the head with a rolling pin. A big, heavy rolling pin.

The minute his grip slackened, Sally slipped downwards, out of his lethal embrace.

Fenton groaned and fell to his knees but wasn't knocked out. "Who's got rope?" I asked, and I kicked the knife across the floor and pushed Fenton down onto his stomach. Then I sat on him.

There was a brief moment of stillness before Sally charged at me, hair flying, eyes blazing. "What are you doing?" she asked. "Get off him! He would never do any of those things! I know him; you don't!"

She flung herself at me and we tumbled sideways. I lay there in shock, as Sally held my hands to the floor.

"And he's right. I haven't been grateful enough. Ford, get out of here. Go home. We'll talk tomorrow."

"Sally!" I said, "Sally! He kidnapped Philip! He shot Philip in his basement. Philip's there now, bleeding out!"

Sally stared down at me as Fenton shook his head and started to clamber to his feet.

"Sally!" I shouted. "I know it's crazy, but he *is* like that! Don't let him go!"

Addie, Brent, and Jerry started moving toward the exits, blocking every door.

Outside, sirens grew steadily louder.

"It's the ambulance, coming to help Philip! He's shot, Sally, but he's not dead!"

"You shot Philip?" Sally got up and stood, trying to comprehend the terrible truth.

Rutherford Fenton stood shakily, choosing his most likely escape path.

"You shot Philip?" Sally asked. Fenton looked at her and said nothing. "You lousy fuck!"

Sally grabbed the rolling pin from Addie and lunged at him with gusto. Fenton, seeing the fury in her eyes and still reeling from his last go-round with the kitchen tool fell to his knees and held up his hands.

"You," she said, nodding at Addie. "There's thick rope in the back bedroom there. Under the bed on the window side. Go. Hurry!"

Addie took off down the back hall.

"Brent, call the police," I said, but he was already dialing.

I picked up my own phone, keeping the shovel at easy reach, and dialed Marta.

"Avalon?"

"Marta. Have the police arrived?"

"Yes. And the ambulance."

"Okay. Tell them to send some officers up to the lodge. We've got Fenton up here. He tried to kill Sally."

"Holy shit!" she said.

Addie emerged from the back hall, carrying a thick rope. Whistle followed her, released from the bedroom. Sally walked curtly around Fenton, jerked one hand behind him, and encircled it firmly with the rope, then the next.

Whistle circled Fenton, growling.

Marta, meanwhile, had handed her phone off to Investigator Spaulding. "Avalon," he said, "are you inside?"

"Yes," I said, watching Sally walk around to the front of Fenton, who was on his knees on the floor.

She grabbed him by his coiffed hair and pulled his face up to look at her. "Is it true?" she asked. "Did you shoot Philip?"

"Is the suspect still at large?" Spaulding asked. "Is there danger to anyone inside?"

"Yes," Fenton mumbled to Sally.

Without a beat, she kicked him hard in his man-parts and shoved him backwards, where he lay moaning on the floor. Whistle joined the action, yipping and biting at Fenton's ankles.

"Where is Philip?" she asked wildly, turning to me.

"Down at Fenton's," I said.

Sally turned and ran through the porch out into the night.

"The suspect is secured," I told the detective. "But get up here quickly, please."

Minutes later, we heard boots climb the outside steps, and four officers entered the room. As they did, I couldn't help myself. I went over to Fenton.

"But why?" I asked. "Why did you kill Joseph?"

"Joseph?" he asked, and looked at me with what I can only describe as crazy eyes. "What does Joseph have to do with anything? I didn't killed Joseph."

"Where is the suspect?" asked one officer.

All of us pointed in unison.

They surrounded Fenton, admittedly a bit surprised to find him already tied up. They sat him up, untied him and cuffed him.

"No one leave," said a female investigator to the rest of us. "We're going to need statements from all of you."

We nodded our assent.

"I need to use the restroom," I said, and headed for the one I'd used when I'd stayed over.

Inside, I closed the door and dialed Marta once again. "Have you given any statements yet?" I asked.

"No," she said. "What do we say?"

What did we say? That a ghost sent us over?

"We tell them we were on our way to my place when I thought I heard moaning," I said. "Everything else, we tell the truth. We'd been at your place, listening to our EVP session, decided to go to my place because the film crew was coming over, and, passing Fenton's house, I thought I heard moaning. I didn't know who it was, thought maybe Fenton was hurt, the front door was open, and I went in. The trick to a good cover story is to make as much of it the truth as possible."

"You mean, the trick to telling a good lie," Marta said.

"I suppose," I said, feeling only a bit bad. "I'll tell Investigator Spaulding the truth later. I will."

"Okay," she said. "We can add that we were already wary of Fenton."

"Say what you feel comfortable with. You can add how I was freaked out because I knew Philip had been shot."

She agreed. We hung up and I went back outside to the great room.

Two of the patrolmen were already seated at a table, notebooks open, tape recorder on, starting to take Brent's statement.

I went to stand with Brent, Jerry and Addie.

As I did, Jerry leaned over to me, eyes aglow. He said, "Best. Meeting. Ever."

I smiled at him, and realized there was somewhere else I needed to be.

"Officers, I'm not leaving," I said. "I'm just going down to talk to Investigator Spaulding."

I left without waiting for permission. Once in the yard, I stopped, bent over, and breathed heavily. Then I headed down toward Sally. And Philip.

As I ran, I tried to make sense of Fenton's last remark. If he hadn't killed Joseph, who had?

Damn.

I crossed the bridge and found the road by Fenton's house to be a light show of state police vehicles and ambulances. Many fine citizens of Tranquility had gathered across the street.

As I approached, the ambulance carrying Philip took off. Its blaring sirens were reassuring. If you're carrying a corpse, you don't need to hurry.

Inside Fenton's house, Sally was seated at the kitchen table. As I walked through toward the living room, where Marta was seated on the couch talking to another investigator, I heard the interview at the kitchen table begin.

"Name?" asked the female officer.

"Sally Chander," she replied. "Sally Allison Chander."

Primroses and Poppies
(Blood Orange Margarita)

Ingredients

1 1/2 oz of preferred white tequila
1/2 oz orange liquor 2 oz fresh blood orange juice
Juice of 1/2 fresh squeezed lime

Method

Dip rocks glass in fresh lime juice and then into a sugar and dried sage mixture.

Shake all ingredients creating a nice frothy texture and pour in rocks glass over ice.

This cocktail can be made fresh over the winter months as blood oranges are in season at this time. You can also buy already made blood orange juice in some gourmet grocery stores.

21

Crime and Punishment

I awoke to full daylight, finding myself on Sally's sofa once again, Whistle curled in the crook of my legs. She stretched as I stirred. What woke me? Phone. My new phone was going off with the four-note, pre-programmed ring. Groggily, I reached for it. 9:12 a.m.

"Nash? Mike Spaulding."

"What's up?"

"Thought you'd like to know that Philip Young is out of surgery. It went well. He's lost a lot of blood, and is still critical, but they're hoping to downgrade to serious but stable when he wakes. Can you tell Mrs. Chander?"

"Yes. Can we come over?"

"Of course. You have a little while. He's still sedated in post-op, but he should be awake in a couple of hours."

"I'll let Sally know."

"Thanks."

I moved the floral throw under which I'd slept, and sat up. Just then, Sally emerged from the back hall. Even now her hair was brushed and flowing, green silk robe over pink and blue pajamas. As if Clark Gable—or Cliff Taylor—might stop by.

"Was that the phone?" she asked.

"Philip is out of surgery, in recovery, it went well. Do you want to go over when he wakes up in a couple of hours?"

"Of course. Let's have some breakfast so we can plan on staying without worrying about food."

Whistle followed us into the kitchen. I let her out through the back door while Sally made coffee. Whistle returned shortly. I wished we could bring her to the hospital with us.

It was Sunday, and a beautiful spring day. The one we'd all been waiting for.

The perfect day for Joseph's funeral.

The service was scheduled for 3 p.m. at Hannah's church. The Battened Hatch was closed to the public today, but after the service, and the scattering of the ashes, Glenn MacTavish had invited the mourners to supper and an open bar at the pub. He'd called to ask if I would work it, which I was glad to do. I was happy to honor my predecessor.

But there was time before that.

Sally made blueberry waffles—she seemed to be telling the truth, that was her one dish—and they were, again, fluffy and wicked good. I began to awaken after our late, eventful night.

"Will your daughter and son-in-law stay with you?" I asked.

"No, my guess is they'll stay in the guest bedroom at Philip's house, ready to take care of him when he first gets home."

"Oh, of course."

After waffles, I ran home to shower and dress while she did the same. We reconnoitered half an hour later. Amazing how breakfast and a shower, coffee, and a friend—and a captured perp—could bring one back to life.

Sally had a Lexus parked in a garage behind the lodge. She asked if I'd drive, so I did.

As we entered the hospital lobby through the glass sliding doors, Glenn MacTavish was being wheeled out. He waved to us.

"I thought you were home yesterday," I said.

"They decided it would aid my recovery if I stayed one more night," he responded. "And I want to recover as quickly as possible." He nodded to Sally. "Mrs. Chander," he said.

"Are you up to attending all the events today?" I asked Glenn.

"Yes, don't worry about this. They insist on a wheelchair to get me out of the building. Hospital policy."

We looked outside to where Mrs. Rumple, from the Inn, was waiting for him in a car.

"Why are you here?" he asked us.

I didn't know how much he'd been told. "Philip was shot last night. He's just now out of surgery."

"Philip? Our Philip?"

"Yes. And they caught who did it. Rutherford Fenton. In fact, he's likely the guy who shot you."

"Fenton?" he roared. "And he shot Philip? I'm coming up with you!" He jumped to his feet.

"Mr. MacTavish—you can't!" objected the young female nurse who was pushing him. "You must sit down until you leave the hospital!"

Glenn grabbed the wheels and pushed the contraption outside the hospital doors. Then he stood up. "There!" he said.

The young woman shook her head but took the wheelchair and headed back inside.

"Go park!" Glenn instructed Mrs. Rumple. "I'll be a minute!"

Then he turned to join us, and stumbled. Both Sally and I grabbed his arms.

"We'd better take it slowly," Sally said. Glenn didn't disagree.

Investigator Spaulding met us in the hall outside Philip's room in the intensive care unit.

"Philip is just now awake," he said. "The plan is to keep him in intensive care for twelve hours, so they can monitor him more closely. But they have downgraded his condition to serious. The doctors are pleased with how well the surgery went."

We could see the nurses getting Philip settled in through the glass windows of his intensive care room.

"So it was Rutherford Fenton?" asked Glenn. "Fenton did this? And you think perhaps he attacked myself and Avalon?"

"We know he did," said Investigator Spaulding. "We had a long talk with him last night. He confessed."

"He confessed?"

"Yes, but he stuck to basic facts. Then he asked for paper to start writing his memoirs."

"What all did he confess to?" I asked.

"Attacking Sally last night. Attacking Glenn and Avalon at the inn. Setting the fire. Kidnapping Philip. Attempting to kill Pepper Porter—who, apparently, died on her own before he could. Killing Oskar Ellis, the bartender."

"And Joseph?" Glenn asked quietly.

The lines in the detective's brows deepened. "No. He claims he had nothing to do with Joseph's death."

"He told me the same thing," I said. "Do you believe him?"

"I don't know why I shouldn't," Spaulding responded. "He confessed to assault with a deadly weapon, kidnapping, murder, even. He wouldn't have anything to gain by stopping one crime short. Also, he has an alibi for the time of Joseph's death."

"Damn," said Glenn.

"Damn," said I.

Two nurses had left the room to which Philip had just been moved, and a final nurse, a woman in blue scrubs, exited the room and came to talk to us.

"He's been awake for an hour or so and was sent up here,

temporarily, from recovery. We expect to have him in a regular room by tonight. The surgeon wanted to keep a close eye on his progress during these first hours. He lost a lot of blood. The doctor will tell you the rest. Meanwhile, rest is what he needs right now."

"Can we see him?" Sally asked the last nurse who was leaving the room.

"Yes, but only two at a time," she said.

The four of us walked right in.

The hospital bed had been configured so that Philip was partially sitting up. Wires came from under his hospital gown. A heart-rate machine and a small, clipped blood pressure monitor on his finger beeped separately. A drip of some medication was taped into his left hand. His hair was a mess.

He saw us and smiled. Sally kissed him.

"Hi, Gran," he said.

There was one chair against the wall, which we forced Glenn to occupy.

I figured that even now the nurses were confabbing about how to get half of us out of the room.

Philip looked at me and said, "Boy, you don't answer your phone very often, do you?"

"He was calling my old number!" I said. "I don't have that phone anymore!"

"Someone found it in Montreal," said Spaulding. "It's what ultimately led us to you."

"Us?" I asked.

"Avalon here jumped the gun a bit. She found you in Fenton's basement."

Philip gave me a questioning look. "Someone had to," I said. "Marta helped."

"Thanks."

"How do you feel?" asked Sally.

"Like someone shot me in the gut."

"And it was Rutherford Fenton who kidnapped you. Who shot you," Investigator Spaulding asked.

"It certainly was."

"You could identify him."

"Without question."

"Did he say why he did what he did?"

Philip's voice became quieter. "It was all about Gran. He was sure someone was going to tell her secrets and 'sully her legend.' That's what he kept saying. He was the keeper of her legend. Somehow, he thought the Ghost Hunters and the new 'TV people' were out to destroy the memory of her Hollywood days, of the great star she was."

"But the Ghost Hunters were here about Pepper Porter," said Glenn.

"I know. But in his mind, they were related. You see, before she died, Pepper Porter worked with Oskar Ahlström, who was the bartender at MacTavish's at the time, but was also a writer—to pen a 'tell-all.' Since Sally and Pepper had a seemingly contentious relationship, Fenton was sure the tell-all spilled the beans on Sally's love life. Which he seemed to have very strange ideas about." Philip looked at his grandmother.

"He was misinformed," she said.

"So Pepper died—he said he killed her! But he said when he searched, the manuscript wasn't in her rooms. Turned out Oskar had it with him in the bar. So he killed Oskar and took the manuscript."

"Did anyone know about this book?" asked Spaulding.

All of us assembled shook our heads.

"It was written before computers. Typed on paper," Philip said. "I know because he had it stashed in his basement. I happened to be there with some time on my hands. So I read it."

"And?" Sally asked. "Did she sully my name?"

"No. In fact, she talked about you with rather frank admiration. She did spill the beans, though. On herself. She talked about her high standards and need for chastity and being truthful and all. How she had impossible standards and had probably caused a lot of hurt by shunning people who didn't live up to her ideals. Especially when she didn't live up to them, herself."

"She didn't?" I asked.

"No," Philip answered. "I don't know if it's up to me to tell—"

We all nodded, urging him forward. But he wasn't looking at us. He was looking at Glenn.

"Say your piece, lad," said Glenn.

"She fell in love, early on, with your father," said Philip. "They were…together…for quite a while. Even before your mother was sick. Before your mother died. After your mother died, Pepper didn't marry your father, but they were together."

"Oh," said Glenn.

"And she had a child. With your father. She went away so no one knew. When the time was right, your parents… adopted him."

We all stood, stunned into silence by the revelation.

"I'm sorry, hospital policy. You *can't* all be in here—"

All of us turned to look at the young nurse who'd obviously drawn the short straw. Then we all turned back to Philip, completely dismissing the poor man. He backed out of the room.

"So Glenn is…" started Sally.

"The son of Pepper Porter and Rusty MacTavish."

Glenn stood slowly, at a loss for words. Then he turned on his heel and left the room. He leaned against the doorframe on his way out, and a concerned technician came to check on him. MacTavish shook him off and headed, slowly but methodically, for the elevator.

"Holy shit," said Salty Sally.

A new nurse had joined the others outside Philip's room. She was obviously in charge and getting her dudgeon up to come and expel at least one of us.

I decided to spare her the confrontation.

Like Glenn, I turned and headed for the elevators, dealing with the two major revelations. Glenn was a MacTavish, after all.

And Fenton hadn't killed Joseph.

I found a quiet corner in the main lobby and waited for Sally. I still had the keys to her car.

My only experience in a hospital was going to visit Winsome when he'd overdosed several years before his death. He'd cried when he saw me, and his parents had asked me to leave.

I'd also gone to visit him in rehab, at his own request. He'd tried to kiss me as I was leaving. It was awkward. Terrible.

After that, he never tried again.

But I did love him. He was my best friend.

From my vantage point, I saw Glenn in the car with Mrs. Rumple, turning out of the parking lot and heading down toward the inn.

Sally appeared fifteen minutes later. "We wore Philip out," she said. "Hopefully now he will get some rest."

We didn't speak on the way home. It must have been crazy for her, knowing her trusted lieutenant kidnapped and shot her grandson.

Together we drove past the now empty "guard house," down the shaded lane and over the one-car bridge, into the clearing that could easily have been the set of a springtime romance or screwball comedy.

I pulled the Lexus around back, and we both went up the stairs into her kitchen.

"Shall I take Whistle?" I asked.

"If you wouldn't mind," she said. "Philip's parents will bring her to Philip's house once they're settled in."

"Just let me know."

I went to get the small dog's leash.

Then I stopped.

"Sally…" There must have been something in my voice. She stopped what she was doing.

"You haven't known me very long," I said.

"True. But it's been an eventful time."

"Yes. It has. I was going to ask you a favor."

"You mean, another favor. I did speak to your friends. They seem like stand-up folks. I'll help them. And, I must say, I think they've got quite the documentary on their hands now."

That was for sure.

"But it's not about them, is it?"

"No." It was nearly impossible to find my voice.

"In your life, you must have had many men who loved you. When you couldn't reciprocate…what did you do?"

She sat down on her brocaded sofa. "You mean like Fenton."

"Well, yeah."

"I know…I know what happened to my friend Win wasn't my fault. He made his own decisions. Addiction is a disease. I know all of that. And yet…I used him. You were right when you said women always know if men are in love with them. And I did know. But I used it. I needed him, so I used it. And I'm sorry. But now he's dead, so he can't forgive me. I can't forgive myself."

"You're right. I'm one who understands. Just between us, I knew Fenton was in love with me. And I used it. And now I have to live with the consequences."

Regret surrounded us. Sally brushed moisture from the side of her eyes with the back of her hand.

"We go forward. We do better," she said. "I'm sorry. That's all I've got."

Crime and Punishment

Ingredients

1-1/2 ounces white Tequila
1/2 ounce white creme de cocoa
1/2 ounce Milk Chocolate Liquor
1 dash of fresh cinnamon
1 dash of cayenne pepper

Method

In cocktail shaker add all ingredients with ice. Shake together creating a nice milky foam and pour into martini glass. So good it hurts.

22

At Large

I woke up before it happened, in the grey before dawn.

This time, when the old fashioned *brrrring* shattered the stillness, I knew what it was.

I walked to the telephone in the dark, trying to blink the fog from my eyes.

"Hi, Sally," I said.

There was a pause.

"Nah, it's me."

I stopped breathing.

And then, from the other end of the line, laughter.

"Winsome?"

"Get off your high horse, Nash. I knew you knew I was in love with you. Whatever I did for you, I did because I wanted to. Though it's nice to know you cared enough to feel guilty. But no need, from this end. Unless you want to."

"*Winsome?*"

"You were expecting Clark Gable?"

"On this phone, maybe."

"I can't believe it. We were friends for years. Years. And I die, and you meet Salty Sally Allison! All those years eating at Salty Sally's, and watching her films. Way to go!"

"You're not mad at me?" I asked. "That I didn't arrive in time to save you?"

"No. But if you're really feeling guilty, I suppose you could ask Sally to spank you."

I couldn't help but laugh. Win was still Win.

His next words were more measured. "I suppose you're mad at me. You have a right to be. I shouldn't have shot up before I was supposed to meet you. I didn't mean to die. It was an accident. But I am sorry. I was obviously using again. You deserve to be mad. I wish I was still around so Sally could spank me!"

"Enough already," I said, but I was smiling nonetheless.

"Please forgive me. And when you think of us, try to remember the good times…instead of the end."

"I will. I have. You were the best. Fun and funny. I loved hanging out with you. I love how you cried at old movies. I loved all of it. I miss you. I'll miss you forever."

"Not forever," he said. "You'll be here, by and by. Do better than I did, at fixing things with people on Earth. Like your father. I know that's why you ran."

"He was wrong."

"He was wrong."

"My father's a son-of-a-bitch," I said.

"He is indeed."

"I'm not ready."

"I know."

"Win, I love you."

No response.

"Winsome?"

For a moment, I cradled the heavy receiver against my chest. Then I softly set it down.

When I was awakened by morning sun spilling across my bed, I lay there wondering if the phone had rung during the night. Had I had gotten up?

To this moment, I have no idea.

I wore a little black dress to the funeral as it could go from church to pub.

Saint Barnabas Episcopal Church was filled. It seemed the whole town was present. I stood with a line of fellow mourners against the back wall.

Joseph's family was in a front pew. Glenn was in a pew behind. He didn't look comfortable, but he was upright. Sophie, Joseph's sometimes girlfriend and improv partner, and friends were in the next pew. I was glad she'd claimed it. Marta sat with her father. She appeared stoic, while the Reverend Layton looked ill-at-ease. I wondered if he'd ever been to a service at Saint Barnabas before. He didn't seem like the type to start—or belong to—an ecumenical council.

Saint Barnabas was modern, light, and airy. Behind the lectern was a wall of windows that framed the far hills.

Sally hadn't come, as she hadn't known Joseph, but basically everyone else I'd met in town was present. I glanced past the open door.

Standing in the back, on the other side of the aisle was Investigator Spaulding, in a dark suit and tie. He saw me look and gave a small nod.

It occurred to me that he was working.

Of course he was. It was likely Joseph's killer was in this room, right now.

That certainly gave the sanctuary more of an electric feel.

The service was uplifting. It was obvious that Hannah had spent time with Joseph's family as well as his local friends. She told about him growing up as the son of a mayor and successful lawyer in Ohio, complete with funny stories from when he was a kid. She'd also gotten some good tales from college and law school. She told again how he'd taken the bar exam, but had left home to find a different life before getting the results.

She told how he'd landed in Tranquility, and the town had been better off for it. I hoped his family found some comfort in hearing about this part of his journey. Hannah told how he'd supported and encouraged many people. She didn't mention names, but apparently Joseph's quiet ability to be there when people most needed help fueled many stories.

As she spoke, I wondered if I would be staying in Tranquility. If perhaps one day there would be a service like this about me landing in Tranquility. Joseph's parallels with my own life were striking. Would my family be called one day to come to my service in a town where they knew no one? Would they think I'd failed in life, eschewing the grand path for which I was destined? From the sound of it, Joseph lived a life full of meaning. Not what his family had wished for, perhaps, but a life of meaning nonetheless.

At the conclusion of the service, Hannah extended the family's invitation for everyone to come over to the Inn to say a final good-bye as Joseph's ashes were scattered, and Glenn's invitation to raise a glass to Joseph in the pub.

While the others milled respectfully, I jumped on my bike and headed over.

My plan was to do my set-up in the bar so I could join the others for Joseph's farewell out on the lake.

I bypassed the street door, hurrying through the lobby to the Battened Hatch. I didn't turn on the lights, as I didn't want anyone to think we were open.

I got to work cleaning, put out Joseph's spill mats, made sure the ice was filled, checked the well bottles and the mixers. It occurred to me, should I truly decide to stay, that after today the bar would really be mine. I could design my own drink menu, order my own bottles, make my own mixers.

Apparently, I'd forgotten to relock the lobby door.

I looked up, ready to shoo off a tourist. Instead, I stopped dead in my tracks. A large man, seen only in relief—dim light from the hallway outlining his large frame and long hair.

"We're closed," I said. "We're closed today for a wake."

"I heard."

The deep voice had a familiar tone. The large, muscled person took a heavy step toward me. I could tell it wasn't Michael Michel, which was something of a relief.

I took a step backward, anyway.

Who was it? How stupid had I been not to lock the door?

I glanced behind me to see if anyone was in the kitchen but saw no one through the small porthole.

Damn.

"What do you want?" I asked, trying to remain calm. "Like I said, we're not open."

As I spoke, the kitchen door behind me swung open, and Marta cruised through.

"Hi," she said to me, then glanced over. "Hey, Flying Crow."

I expelled breath I didn't know I'd been holding. It was Flying Crow. Lesley.

"Hey," he said.

"So you heard he died? Joseph died just after you left." Marta said sadly, grabbing a cloth to polish up the bar.

"I heard. Tragic. Can't believe it. I went out of town for work starting the next morning, but since then I've spoken to the police about it. Apparently, they knew I was here that night."

"So are you on the suspect list?" I asked, then realized the question might have been a little straightforward.

"Not that I know of. And I wasn't much help with naming any names."

The three of us stood in a strange obtuse triangle. "I didn't know you were working here," he said to me. "Kind of unexpected."

"Yeah, for me, too."

"So. Could I dramatically overpay you for some scotch before everyone else gets here? I liked Joe a lot. He was a mensch."

"All right. But stop with the cross-cultural talk. You're confusing me."

"You've never met a Jewish Mohawk i.t. guy before?"

"You're the first."

On Monday night, Flying Crow had been sitting at the end of the bar, where the fatal limes had been cut. I hadn't seen him leave that afternoon. He'd simply been gone, and Glenn, in full tartan, had been in his place.

Flying Crow went and sat on that same barstool—his spot, apparently—and I poured him a Glennlivet 15 Year French Oak Reserve. He gave me a $20. "Forget it. There's an open bar today. Although I won't be pouring this later."

"Nah, you keep it," he said. "A tip. For taking over."

Maybe after Joseph was at rest, his ashes scattered, that would seem a happier prospect.

"I didn't see anything, you know," Lesley said. "I was sitting here since shortly after the bar opened. If anyone had come along with poisoned limes, I would have seen it. And there wasn't anybody. So it must have happened before opening."

"Yeah, that makes sense," I said. "But before the bar was open, both the lobby door and the street door would have been locked."

"Small town. Anyone who's been around knows you can come

through the Breezy kitchen, which has an outside door."

"It's true," said Marta. "What should I be doing? Garnishes?"

"Sure," I said. We went together to the fridge to grab the lemon, oranges and limes. We both smelled all the fruit.

"Okay," I said quietly. "There's a conversation we still need to have."

"There is," she said. "But not now."

"Okay. But answer me this. Pepper wasn't the first? You've seen other things…that most people don't see?"

"I have," she said.

"Am I the first person you've told?"

"No," she said. "But last time, it didn't go very well."

She grabbed a knife and started to cut. As she did, I noticed her hair was parted and brushed in a new way. Her black dress fit her nicely, accentuating her curves. She'd gone out of her way for Joseph. She wore a navy-blue jacket that covered the tattoos on her arms.

We prepped while Lesley finished his drink. I'd opened the door to the smoker's porch, and soon heard the crowd begin to arrive.

"I think we're in good shape," I said. "Let's go."

"I'd sure feel better if we knew who killed him," Marta said.

"You and everyone else," said Lesley.

The three of us walked together through the small dark hall into the lobby. I locked the door behind us.

Folks from the funeral headed out the back door to the inn's lakefront. Others chose to go through the Breezy to the deck overlooking the water.

Marta and I continued on together, through the open double doors, out onto the back lawn.

It was a classic April Sunday afternoon. Buds were opening in pastels of pinks, blues and purples. Forsythia still arrested the eye with blazes of yellow gold. I remembered the sense of peace I'd felt those first nights staying at MacTavish's, looking over the rippling waters burrowed safe into the surrounding hills. The shimmering lake still offered a sense of calm, and I made a silent agreement to take whatever peace was offered.

We continued down to the beach, where the inn's rowboats sat in a line, kayaks on either side of the six larger boats. The plan was to row out and scatter Joseph's ashes, kind of like they do on surfboards in Hawaii.

Joseph's family gathered around the center boat. A brother—and what seemed to be a niece and nephew—were talking to his parents.

"I wish Philip was here," Marta said. I knew she would like to row out. Philip would undoubtedly have done so, and invited her into his boat. Together we stood toward the front of the gathering.

Glenn had been helped into the boat next to the family, and was joined by two other employees of the inn. Glenn also saw Sophie, Joseph's last girlfriend, and motioned her and a friend to join them.

Knots of mourners started claiming other vessels. Suzanne from The Spice Trade was being assisted into one by Bronze medal Jillian and a woman who looked like another skater-turned-coach. "Thank you, Callie," Suzanne said to this other woman, who gave her a steadying hand. "Say, you two know the mayor's daughter, Polly. Perhaps Polly would like to come in our boat?"

Jillian shot a look at Callie. "You know we can't, Suzanne," said Callie.

"What? Why not? Doesn't Polly spend time with you when she's skating?"

Young Polly was up on the deck with the mayor's party, which included both her parents as well as other prominent businessfolk.

"Oh, for pity's sake!" said Jillian. She sounded put out. "How long have we been friends now?"

"Years," said Suzanne.

"Yes, years," said Jillian, quietly. "You have to know that Callie and I are a couple! Polly comes over so she has somewhere she can be herself! Where there are people who understand her. Her parents aren't thrilled about that. So we all pretend it's about skating. But that isn't enough that they would consider letting her be in our boat! It's probably part of the reason Arthur disliked Joseph so much. Joseph introduced Polly to us, trying to show her it gets better."

"What?" Suzanne asked. "What?"

Instead of sitting down, she stumbled backwards, then caught herself, turned, and clambered back out of the boat.

Tranquility! This town! I had to love it. I took a moment and looked around. A week ago, I hadn't known any of these people. I hadn't known this town existed.

A week ago, Joseph was alive.

Think, Avalon, think. You've been collecting stories all week. Who had motive?

Suzanne headed back up the rise towards the lobby, visibly upset. This had not been an easy week for her. As she neared the doors to the inn, she saw Reverend Layton, Marta's father. He stood, rather ill-at-ease, with several of his congregants. If not for Joseph's prominence in the town, this was not a funeral he would have attended.

Suzanne saw the reverend, and headed toward him as a port in the storm. Was she going to inform him of her discovery about Gillian and Callie here and now?

The fact there was a group assembled around the good minister undoubtedly gave Suzanne pause. After all, Gillian had been her good friend, apparently, for years. Instead, Suzanne put her arms around her pastor and gave him a hug. She was weeping. I saw him give a roll of the eyes to the folks around him. I understood he couldn't be seen going around hugging women in public, but really? Have a little respect for a person's feelings. Then he did, for a moment. He gave Suzanne a "there, there," kind of hug and whispered something in her ear. He even offered her his handkerchief. She took it, looked rather apologetically at the others in the crowd, and let herself be led off by another of the men, who locked eyes with Pastor Layton as he led Suzanne away. They disappeared into the lobby.

The Reverend Layton immediately turned back to the other parishioners, who were also vying for his attention.

That was it. I made a solemn vow that Whistle and I would take a midnight walk right past the rectory.

"Avalon!" I turned to find Brent Davis behind me. "I don't think you've met my wife, Susan."

"Hello," I said. Susan was an attractive, woman with a fit figure and salt-and-pepper hair.

Addie and Avantika were behind them as they angled for one of the remaining boats. Jerry was up the hill, his ever-present cellphone pressed to his ear. He gave them a "one sec" signal.

"Quite a night last night," said Brent, having claimed a silver craft by taking its oars in hand.

"You can say that again," I replied.

"It seems we have a hell of a documentary after all."

"You have no idea," I replied, then I took a step closer and said more quietly, "Later you might want to talk to Glenn. There may have been...even more developments in Pepper's story."

"Yeah?"

I nodded.

Brent and company invited Marta into their boat, and she gladly accepted the invitation.

When all the lake-worthy crafts had been claimed, Joseph's father stood up in his boat. "Here it is, Joseph, the results of your Bar Exam."

He tore open the envelope and took out its contents. His eyes teared up and he said, "Passed with high marks."

He put the paper back into the decades-old envelope, and carefully tore it into pieces. Then he sat down. One of his nephews launched the craft. Boat after boat took off after him.

I slowly walked up the hill.

"Nice service."

"Yes, I thought so," I answered, turning to find Inspector Mike Spaulding had come up behind me. "Are you here working?"

"Joseph's killer is still at large."

"And you're thinking the person is here?"

"Likely."

I shuddered, even though I'd expected the answer.

"Can you and I talk?" he asked. "Before the wake gets rolling."

"Why? Am I back on the suspect list?"

"Not my version," he said. "It's helpful to be able to extricate Joseph's death from the other attacks, now that Rutherford Fenton is off the street. But it also gives us a larger pool of suspects."

"I guess," I said. "I've been collecting… information all week. Yes, there are people in town who didn't like Joseph's politics or his religion or his sexual orientation, but he was such a stand-up guy, I've had a hard time putting together a motive for murder. Perhaps that's because I wish I had known him. I think we would have understood each other."

Investigator Spaulding added, "I haven't yet put together motive and opportunity myself."

The two of us stood, looking out over the fair citizens of Tranquility.

I had to admit—if we were looking solely for opportunity, the person with the most obvious access was Marta. She was there all night, she knew where everything was—including the fruit. No one would have thought it was strange to see her behind the bar.

But she had no motive. None at all. And I remembered how upset she'd been when she couldn't find Joseph and people were asking for drinks. Of everything I knew about her, had come to know about her character, nothing pointed to her being able to pull off a murder and hide the fact she'd done it. She wanted to work in the bar. When I took over, she'd been afraid she might lose her job. And she'd been genuine friends with Joseph. She'd gone to him for help with Polly.

Flying Crow said he'd been sitting there all night. To be unobserved, it would have had to be someone who'd planted the deadly lime before the bar opened.

I remembered the Chamber of Commerce folks had come in after their meeting. What time had their meeting started? Had they all been at the inn since before opening? Although Lesley pointed out that many local folks knew you could get to the Battened Hatch through the Breezy kitchen.

"Might we assume that the person who did it was there, in the bar, to make sure it happened?" I asked.

"Well, you can never assume anything. But often the murderer wants to be certain the deed gets done."

Never assume, Avalon. Never assume.

Okay, assumption number one was that the intended victim was Joseph. But, as we'd originally thought, if the perp didn't realize the strength of the nicotine, hadn't realized simply handling it could kill, he or she could have targeted anyone who routinely ordered a drink with lime.

Arthur, the mayor, ordered a drink with lime. That's how I'd found the remaining poisoned fruit.

What if Joseph had wanted to murder the mayor and it was Joseph who didn't realize how poisonous the limes actually were?

That seemed like a huge reach.

Michael Michel had ordered a drink with lime. Would someone want to kill Michael?

Yet, if you meant to kill someone who ordered a drink, poisoning limes was just so non-specific. Anyone could have ordered a drink that required a lime garnish. Many people had—in fact, so many people had that more garnish was required.

"Holy shit," I said, and Investigator Spaulding turned to look at me. "I think I know who did it."

Now I had his full attention. "Here's the problem," I said. "I don't have proof. And it's been a week. I don't know if the proof we need even still exists."

"What kind of proof? I can get a warrant to search home or office."

"I have another idea," I said. "It's risky but it might work. But we'd have to do it now, before the ashes are scattered and everyone comes back in."

"Why don't we start with you telling me both your suspect and your plan, and let's see if there's anything to it."

At Large

Ingredients

3 wedges of lime
1 oz of fresh or frozen raspberries (frozen work better, they become juicy when they thaw)
2.5 oz Stoli Raspberry Vodka
.75 oz Triple Sec
Splash of cranberry juice
Club soda
Ice
Shaker
Strainer
Pint glass

Method

Fill pint glass with ice. Squeeze two lime wedges over the ice, add the raspberries, pour in the 2.5 oz of raspberry vodka and .75 oz of triple sec, and add a tiny splash of cranberry juice. Pour into shaker and shake until raspberries are broken up. Fill the now empty pint glass with fresh ice and strain the shaken mixture into the glass. Top glass up with club soda and garnish with a lime.

23

Final Gambit

Investigator Spaulding agreed it was worth a try. Thus it became a race against time.

I unlocked the door to the pub for him before he went to find our man in the crowd.

Then I ran back to the hallway off the lobby. I saw the detective and our man enter the pub. The man was objecting but accompanied him anyway.

I gave them a couple of minutes, then tore through the open atrium, headed for the tavern door. I barely skirted a large circular lobby chair. In doing so, I bumped into Suzanne, who had been pulling herself together, and had chosen to stand just moments before I ploughed through.

"Oh," I said. "I'm sorry."

"Me, too, I didn't see…"

I tried to wave her off. "It's okay. I've got to get to the pub. Investigator Spaulding is making an arrest. Right now. He's got the guy who killed Joseph."

I started off again, but she put a hand on my sleeve. "Stop. What?"

"Suzanne, I have to go. We've got him. Reverend Layton. He hated Marta working here. He hated the things Joseph stood for and was 'filling her mind' with. I've got to get in there!"

I yanked away from her and ran for the door marked That Ship Has Sailed.

Inside, lights were only on over the bar and the back bar. Mike Spaulding and Tim Layton were effectively spot-lit as they talked. It was turning into an argument.

"We know," the detective said, "we know."

"This is such crap! You don't know anything! You can't prove anything!"

As Reverend Layton said this, two things happened simultaneously. Investigator Spaulding took out his set of handcuffs, and the lobby door swung open behind me.

It swung closed, and the four of us in the room stood for an instant in frozen tableau.

Suzanne had followed me in. "You monster!" she yelled.

We all stood, uncertain to whom she was speaking. "You monster!" And she flew across the room like a harridan from hell, arms raised, ready to attack.

It became clear she was going for Spaulding.

I flung myself after her.

"Don't you touch that man. Don't you touch him! You don't know what he's been through. He's the best... good man... in this town!"

Tim Layton looked at her. "Suzy," he said, "this doesn't concern you. Get out of here. Get out of here now."

"It does concern me," she said. "You're arresting the wrong man. Let him go. Don't touch him!"

"I'm afraid...," Spaulding said.

"No," Suzanne said, her black and silver scarf flashing in the semi-darkness. "It was me. It was me. It was me." She dropped into a chair, her head in her hands. Sobs soon wracked her frame.

"What are you saying?" asked the pastor. He looked stunned. "You killed Joseph?"

"I didn't mean to!" she said.

"Suzanne," Investigator Spaulding said, but his voice was softer now, nearly gentle. "Whatever you're going to tell us, you have the right to remain silent. Anything you say can and will be used against you in a court of law."

"Oh, shut up," she said. "I can't live like this anymore. I didn't mean to kill Joseph!"

"Then who did you mean to kill?" I asked quietly, sitting beside her.

She looked at Tim Layton. The two of them locked eyes. Then she looked away. "Marta," she said. "I meant to kill Marta."

"*What?*" said Pastor Layton.

"I saw how she worried you! I saw how miserable she made you! I tried to send her away. I offered to send her to art school, but she wouldn't go. And you said… you said you couldn't date anyone until Marta was seen to. You need someone to care for you, Tim, so desperately. To cook and clean and talk to after long days…." Tears started again. "But I never meant to hurt Joseph. I never meant to…"

There was a whoop from outside. Joseph's ashes, and the results of his Bar Exam, were apparently scattered.

Investigator Spaulding said to Suzanne, "It must have been hard to live, knowing you'd killed someone by mistake. Come on now. Let's get out of here before everyone comes in. Let's go down to the station, and get this sorted out."

She took a minute, and then stood up. "All right," she said. "All right."

Reverend Layton stuttered, "I'm going to get Myron Otte, an attorney who's outside, Suzanne. Don't talk to anyone until your lawyer gets there."

She nodded, though she didn't seem to hear.

"Send Mr. Otte over," said Mike. "You've got some time, though.

It will take a while for her to be processed before anyone takes her statement."

Mike cuffed her, as gently as possible, and nodded to the street door. I walked before them, to let them out.

"Did you get it?" I asked.

"Yes, it's recorded," he said. "Did you record it, also?"

"I did. But if you've got it, I'd like to delete mine."

"Let me just make sure it's all good," he said. And, more quietly, "I guess you were right."

"I'm sorry I was," I said. "But usually Marta would be the one cutting more garnishes. Thinking of Marta as the intended victim… Suzanne was the only one who made sense."

He nodded, and the two of them headed to the station.

I turned around. Reverend Layton still stood by the bar. He looked dumbfounded.

I hit the switch for the room lights.

"Suzanne wanted to kill Marta," he said, barely able to speak. "My Marta."

"It seems that way."

"The detective said he suspected that, but I didn't believe him." He stood for a moment, considering. Then he raised his head. "So, this is where she works?" The minister looked around the bar, and I realized he was seeing it for the first time. "It isn't dark."

"No, it isn't. It's a nice place."

"A nice place," he repeated.

It occurred to me in that moment, how I was one of a very small handful of people to see the great Reverend Layton at a loss for words.

He looked at me, as if asking what should happen next.

"You said you were going to get your lawyer friend and send him to the station," I said.

"Yes. Myron, yes."

Layton walked rather slowly toward the lobby door. He turned around to inspect the premises one more time. Then he looked at me. "Watch out for her when she's here, won't you?" he asked.

"I will."

And he was gone.

The kitchen door swung open. "Hey, can we start setting up the buffet?" asked one of the sous chefs.

"Absolutely," I said.

"Great!" he said, and he disappeared, shouting the news to his cohorts.

As he did, the door opened again, and Marta walked through. "It's done. Folks are headed over."

"Okay," I said. Then, much to her surprise, I gave her a hug. "Your father loves you."

"What?" she said.

"I'll explain later." As I propped open the door to the lobby, I saw Tim Layton and Myron the lawyer walking quickly past. I made the decision not to blab what had just happened. This afternoon would just be a celebration of Joseph. We'd get to the law and order part later.

Behind the bar, I stooped to the lower shelf and brought out Joseph's spill mat. "Wish I'd known you," I said to him. "I'll take care of your bar as best I can."

He seemed the kind of man who, if given the choice, would have chosen to die if it had saved Marta's life. Was I making that up, or was he somehow letting me know he was okay with how things had turned out?

"I'll do my best," I said, "though I might only be here for a little while."

Folks started milling in from the lobby as the first of the steam trays came through from the kitchen.

Glenn took his regular seat at the bar. Without asking, I poured him his whiskey. "To Joseph," I said.

"To Joseph."

And the party started.

FINAL GAMBIT

Ingredients

1-1/2 oz. Vanilla Vodka
1/2 oz Creme de Cacao
1/2 oz. Godiva White Chocolate liquor
1-1/2 oz. Frozen Hot Chocolate Mix powder
1/2 & 1/2 (optional)

Method

Put into shaker. Mix thoroughly. Strain into glass.

Descend into bliss.

24

Postlude

The next morning, I was on my back patio beneath the wisteria having coffee when Whistle began to bark.

"It's only us," said Brent, as he and Addie and Jerry came across the bridge and up the rise. "We've brought pastries."

"Isn't it early for you?" I asked Jerry.

"We had to stop by Rutherford Fenton's," he said nonchalantly.

"But isn't the house a crime scene? How did you get in?" I asked.

"Well, he's confessed, so there's no trial," said Jerry.

"Unless he goes for insanity," said Brent, clearly not quite on the same page.

"It's just that yesterday, as soon as Glenn mentioned that Pepper Porter wrote a tell-all, and it was just lying in Fenton's basement—"

"Covered in Philip's blood," I added.

"A few pages had a little blood on them," Jerry said. "I only borrowed it. I borrowed it and copied it and put it back. All the blood is back."

"You removed evidence and put it back?"

"Darling, he confessed. There won't be a trial. And it might take months to get official permission to read that thing."

"So did you?" I asked.

"Read it?" asked Jerry. "Oh, you betcha. I also made good use of my hotel's copy machine."

"And?"

"And I've told my publishers to stop the presses. With the new information, we've got a bestseller on our hands."

"How about the documentary?" I asked Brent, as I went inside to get a plate for the luscious pastries from the Cardamom. I returned momentarily, leaving only the screen door to entice the summer breeze.

"When you put together the new info on Pepper with an interview from Salty Sally—who was never married to Cliff, and never dead—"

"And whom I had the presence of mind to video on my phone when she was being held hostage by Fenton, who spilled the whole crazy story," added Jerry, choosing a cherry turnover.

"You took video?"

"Which I would have had to hand over, *was there to be a trial*," he said, again glaring at Brent.

"In any case, we've got a slam-dunk of a film," Brent admitted. "I'm thinking of calling it 'Salt-Pepper Catch-Up.'"

"Working title," said Addie, "Working title."

"You heard about Suzanne?" I asked.

"Yes," said Brent. "Last night, early enough to make it today's front page."

I chose a blueberry Danish. We were all silent for a minute.

"There's more good news," Addie ventured.

"Always up for that," I said.

"Avantika has been persuaded to run for mayor, to oppose Arthur."

"She was backing Joseph's campaign, wasn't she?"

"The biggest donor. She owns a good deal more property in this town than most people know, and she helped craft Joseph's platform. It makes perfect sense for her to run."

"Wow," I said, and raised my mug. "To Avantika."

They joined the toast. "Avantika."

"What time does the pub open today?" asked Brent. "Are we holding you up?"

"I know that Joseph had the bar open seven days a week," I said, "but I think I'm going to take Mondays off. After all, it was only a week ago today I stepped into the Battened Hatch for the first time. Only a week ago I discovered this quiet little town."

"Boring berg," said Brent.

"Sleepy village," added Jerry.

"Where nothing ever happens," said Addie.

"Yeah," said, stretching and looking up at the enormous, uninterrupted sky. "I might hang around for a while."

Tranquility Sunshine

Ingredients

1 oz. vodka
½ oz. peach or raspberry schnapps
3 oz. Sprite
Orange Juice fill

Method

Add ingredients in order listed.
Add ice, stir, and enjoy.

Acknowledgements

This book was started shortly after our family experienced a catastrophic house fire. There is so much to rebuilding after such an event, I discovered the one thing that kept me sane was writing. My husband, Robert Scott, suggested I write "something fun," and the Bartender's Guide was born. Thank you, Bob.

I am happy to give special thanks to those who supported me and this book in very practical ways during that time: Pam Smith, Barb Sherer, Judy Girod, Susan Webber, and the Doubleclicks. Note to Pam: Brent Davis may or may not owe you thanks until the end of time.

To my first readers who made the story better: Barb Sherer, Lisa Cullen, Mary Ann O'Roark, Sharrata Hunt, and Karen Lee. Thanks, too, my fellow artists from Creators Haven who always made helpful suggestions. Also to my favorite input group, including Josephine Buck, Sarah Lane, Liz Parkinson, Lorrie Sniderman, Marcy Talbot, Cari Keith and John Keith, who came up with the series title. Thanks, John!

To the fabulous female bartenders of Lake Placid, New York, who are as creative and fun as someone can be. Kudos first to Jamielynn Brydalski with whom I first bonded over a strawberry rhubarb concoction at the Dancing Bear and who has been a great help every step of this journey—while she was picking up national awards for mixology. Thanks also to Kalen Griffen from MacKenzie's Restaurant and Great Room Bar on the other end of Main Street who does crazy good things with local spirits.

To contacts inside the State Police who explained how they work with local law enforcement and why their uniforms fit so well.

Thanks to my son Jonathan Scott, who decided we should train to be bartenders together, and my daughter Linnéa Scott, who always believes.

Last but surely not least, profound gratitude to my father, William Webber, who loved being part of the process and listening to new chapters as they emerged, always making astute observations. I couldn't have finished it without you. Miss you forever.

Sharon Linnéa has been a storyteller for as long as she can remember. She is a bestselling novelist, award-winning biographer, and TIPS certified bartender.

Watch for Avalon's next adventure...

THE BARTENDER'S GUIDE
TO MURDER

Book Two

Death by Gravity

Twenty Years Ago

Seven-year-old Davy Edison awoke alone in the dark. He had a moment of frightened confusion before he was able to orient himself.

He was in a tent that he and his older sister, Misty, had concocted out of sheets and chairs downstairs in the television room.

Davy loved it when their parents went out and Misty babysat. They always thought of fun trouble to get into—like building a fort out of blankets, eating barbecue wings, and watching shows of which their parents didn't approve.

However, the television was now off and the sleeping bag next to him was empty. Misty must have gone up to bed.

Davy briefly considered going back to sleep, but he had to pee, and his real bed was more comfortable, anyway. He used the downstairs bathroom and walked through silent halls to the staircase in the bedroom wing. To his right at the first landing, the door to the staircase that led to his parents' floor was closed, which meant they'd come home.

He padded down the long hall towards his room.

When he passed Misty's room, he was surprised to find the door slightly ajar. He pushed against it silently and opened it a few inches to see if she was still awake.

Her bed hadn't been slept in. One of the French doors to her balcony was open.

"Mist?" he whispered, as he stepped into the room.

The sheer curtain by the outside deck fluttered and he stopped.

He could see shapes outside. More than one.

This threw him enough that he didn't hear the person who stepped up behind him until the man grabbed him firmly with one hand and planted his other hand over Davy's.

Davy heard him kick the hall door closed behind them.

"What the hell are you doing here?" asked an angry whisper.

Davy did the first thing he thought of: he chomped down on the top of the hand over his mouth.

"Where's my sister?" he hissed.

"You are in so much trouble, you little freak. You've got two choices. You shut up, now, right now, and you stay silent, *silent*, till morning, or your sister and your parents all die. We have your sister already. I can shoot your parents before they even wake up!"

Davy was thinking fast. He'd heard about kids who were kidnapped and their siblings keeping quiet way too long because they were scared. That wasn't him. He had to pretend to go along.

He nodded his head. When the man took his hand away a few millimeters, he said, "Okay. Okay! I'll be quiet. Just don't hurt her! Put me down. Let me go to my room!"

"Fat chance, idiot kid," said the voice. It sounded rusty, like it had to bounce over lots of nails to get from the voice box to the air.

"Put me down," he said, with a bravado he didn't feel.

The man put him down, but awkwardly, so he landed on the dude's shoe and lost his balance.

The kidnapper was suddenly furious. His other hand grabbed something, and suddenly there was steel against the boy's throat.

"No!" Davy cried.

"First you, then her," came the raspy reply.

And everything went black.

Davy woke up in Misty's bed while it was still dark outside. Her balcony door was closed. She was gone.

He knew he had to sound the alarm as soon as possible, no matter what the kidnapper had threatened, but his arms were bound behind him and he had duct tape over his mouth.

It hurt to have his arms pulled back that way. His shoulders were burning, but there was nothing he could do. The tape over his mouth was sticky and it smelled like oil. He couldn't move his lips or open his mouth or swallow his saliva properly.

Worst was that he couldn't get anyone's attention. He couldn't save Misty.

Warm tears traced his cheeks and moistened Misty's pillow.

By morning, when his parents finally found him, she was long gone.

1

Torturing the Newbies

It was the first Saturday night in June. Tranquility, New York, is far enough north that the warm evening breezes over the lake still felt new and intoxicating. Why folks needed further intoxication I do not know, but the Battened Hatch was hopping. Everyone was in high spirits.

Shortly after 8 p.m., Brent Davis and his wife, Susan, took seats at the beautifully carved wooden bar.

"Hey, Avalon," Brent said. He was of British heritage and wore a long-sleeved button-down shirt, sleeves rolled up, the quintessential newspaper editor. His beard was trimmed and comfortably salt-and-pepper, his glasses wire-rimmed. "Throw me a Stella and a white wine for the wife."

I smiled at Susan. "Chardonnay?" I asked.

"Perfect." She nodded.

"When did you get back from LA?" I queried Brent as I poured. "How's the film shaping up?"

"Got home a few hours ago," he responded, a spark behind his eyes. He was producing a documentary on the town's golden-era movie stars, Pepper Porter and Sally Allison, which had some unexpected new plot twists, due to a recent murder investigation. It now looked to be a humdinger, as Pepper might have said. "It'll be a challenge to finish it in time for the Tranquility Film Festival in August."

"Can't wait to see it!" I responded truthfully. Sally Allison was one of my favorite movie stars of all time. Not to mention, my current landlord.

"Thanks for your help," Brent added, lifting his glass.

"Hope there are no upcoming giant news stories to split your attention."

Brent was also the editor-in-chief of the local newspaper.

"It's Tranquility. I think we're safe," he said.

The ding of new drink orders came to the bar from the POS on the restaurant floor. I exchanged an eyeroll with Marta, my teal-haired bartender-in-waiting, as the paper continued to scroll. Our new waiter, Davros, shrugged at us from the mid-floor machine.

Olympic medalist Brian Eddings was holding court tonight, and the liquor was flowing. Brian wasn't the only Olympian who frequented the Battened Hatch. Gillian Petrakov, a former bronze medalist in figure skating, sat at the bar, her blonde hair in a bun, fitted pink sweater set embracing her still-taut figure, next to her partner, Callie (non-skater, brown hair, ran a nonprofit).

"Brian is torturing the Newbies again." Gillian smiled.

Tranquility is one of two places in the United States where athletes can train for winter sports year-round. Brian lived locally. I met him when he turned up here at the Scottish tavern shortly after I'd moved to town. You knew when he was in the room—as did everyone in town, apparently—and they started arriving in groups to join his instant party.

"The Newbies?" I asked.

"Bobsledding is a unique sport," Gillian said. "Take figure skating—you have to train for decades. But bobsledders—all you have to be is strong, fast, and able to jump. Every year, Olympic scouts head for colleges to entice track stars and even shot-putters to come and try out for Olympic bobsled team."

"Really?" I asked. "Does it ever work out?"

Davros' drink orders had come mostly from the Olympic hopefuls. Beer. Beer. Beer.

"Yep, there have been times when a college kid shows up in June and has competed in the next Winter Olympics!"

As she said that, a tall man walked into the bar from the door to MacTavish's Seaside Cottage, the hotel that housed us. It was a sprawling, hundred-year-old establishment that was not seaside (though lakeside) and had no cottages. There was, however, a MacTavish.

The newcomer was European-American, maybe six feet, short brown hair, trim, and wearing a gray polo tucked into gray slacks. His eyes scanned the place and he smiled, as if entertaining memories from his past. I turned, ready to ask if he wanted to be seated, when he saw the group at the back of the room. His smile vanished. He turned on his heel and walked out.

Alrighty, then. I turned my attention back to Gillian. "So how does Brian torture them?"

"He's not their coach, obviously. He competed in luge. But he can't resist so many freaked-out, naïve athletes. They've been living like monks in Olympic housing for the past three weeks. As soon as they're allowed out, he brings them here and buys them beer. They— and their coaches—won't be happy tomorrow morning!"

"So why do they keep letting him do it?"

"Good question." Gillian sipped her drink. "The truth is monks don't make very good bobsledders, but the coaches can't be seen to be condoning a night at the bar. And—whew—the kids gotta get this energy out somehow! Brian's like a father figure . . . but father figures aren't always the best influences!"

"Tell me about it."

A huge whoop went up. I looked up—to find the previously full tables suddenly emptied of athletes and their adult beverages.

"What the . . . ?"

The door to the smoker's porch was open. Another group cry went up, followed by a loud splash.

Marta followed me to the open door. And there, on the smoker's porch, Brian Eddings had built himself a luge. He'd put two square tables together with another four-top on it. He'd added a sturdy wooden chair with arms on top of that table. He'd appropriated all my tablecloth clips to attach a long tablecloth to the wooden chair, again to the lower table, and then to the front of the lower level to jerry-rig a mini-luge run. Seriously. One prospective Olympian stood on the top table, holding the chair solid while two others held the cloth taut lower down. Two prospective bobsledders had already careened down the tablecloth and off into the lake. Another was climbing the rickety contraption even now, holding a bussing tray to ride on his journey.

"Baron McNulty for the win!" crowed the young man, throwing himself onto the slanted tablecloth, sliding off the porch and into the lake.

"Dear God, Brian, what are you doing?" I asked. "MacTavish's insurance does not cover reckless porch slides!"

"Aw, lassie," he said, in an affected voice purposely reminiscent of Glenn, the owner of MacTavish's.

The next young man at the top of the climb pushed off, and hurled down into the lake.

"Back inside! Everyone!" I instructed. "Free buffalo wings. On the house."

That did it. A different kind of whoop and the portion of young men who had little interest in killing themselves jumping off metal chairs headed back in.

Marta and I dismantled the furniture sculpture and stood for a moment. I have no doubt she was joining me to silently pay respects to my predecessor who had died on this very porch.

The rest of the night slid past quickly, as busy pub nights do. At midnight, a minibus pulled up to return Olympic hopefuls to their apartments at the training facility. Shortly thereafter, a trio of young women left, helping their friend walk between them. They'd each had one drink, and I wondered if their affected friend had an intolerance or allergy. Or if she'd simply downed all three drinks herself.

Brian Eddings stayed to help Manuela, the bus-person, clear, as his group's tables were in shambles. Brian's face and chin were square, with an indent in the bulb of his nose, as if someone has pressed a fingerprint to it. His hair was blond and close-cropped, although Olympic photos of him showed it longer and unruly. His eyes were alert, brimming with intelligence and mischief. Living in Tranquility, you heard pretty quickly that life after being an Olympian—medalist or not—was rough going for many athletes. I appreciated that Brian was willing to be a bit wild but truly thoughtful at the same time.

I closed out the POS and came back as Manuela and Brian finished separating the now-cleaned tables.

"Thanks, Manuela," I said.

"Good night," she replied and headed out.

"Sorry if we made more work," said Brian, eyes flashing. "But it's a rip."

"A rip?"

"Rip-roaring time!"

He was so pleased as he said it, I couldn't help but laugh. At least no one had broken their neck on his jerry-rigged luge. As we worked together, I noticed that he wasn't inebriated in the least. He said he didn't drink, and he stuck to it.

"Good night," he said. As he passed, he crushed a bill into my hand. "For the extra trouble," he said. "And the wings."

I'd comped the wings, figuring they'd be cheaper for MacTavish's than the bad publicity of a future Olympian breaking his neck luging off the smoker's porch.

"Night," I replied, following, turning out the lights. As I locked the door behind him, I glanced at the tip. It was a one-hundred-dollar bill.

That was, allegedly, the last time anyone saw Brian Eddings alive.

Torturing the Newbies

Ingredients

Sour mix
Seltzer
limes

Method

Add 2 ounces of sour mix to a glass with ice.
Top with seltzer.
Add lime for garnish.
Sip all night and be proud of yourself in the morning.